Praise for Ed McBain & the 87t… …t

"Raw and realistic...The b… …are better." —*Detroit Free Press*

"Ed McBain's 87th Precinct s… …als being written in the United St…

"The best crime writer in the bu… … —*Houston Post*

"Ed McBain is a national treasure." —*Mystery News*

"It's hard to think of anyone better at what he does. In fact, it's impossible."—Robert B. Parker

"I never read Ed McBain without the awful thought that I still have a lot to learn. And when you think you're catching up, he gets better."
—Tony Hillerman

"McBain is the unquestioned king...light years ahead of anyone else in the field." —*San Diego Union-Tribune*

"McBain tells great stories." —Elmore Leonard

"Pure prose poetry...It is such writers as McBain who bring the great American urban mythology to life." —*The London Times*

"The McBain stamp: sharp dialogue and crisp plotting."
—*Miami Herald*

"You'll be engrossed by McBain's fast, lean prose." —*Chicago Tribune*

"McBain redefines the American police novel...he can stop you dead in your tracks with a line of dialogue." —*Cleveland Plain Dealer*

"The wit, the pacing, his relish for the drama of human diversity [are] what you remember about McBain novels." —*Philadelphia Inquirer*

"McBain is a top pro, at the top of his game." —*Los Angeles Daily News*

LONG TIME NO SEE

LONG TIME NO SEE

AN 87TH PRECINCT NOVEL

ED McBAIN

THOMAS & MERCER

The characters and events portrayed in this book are fictitious. Any similarity to real persons, living or dead, is coincidental and not intended by the author.

Printed in the United States of America.

Published by Thomas & Mercer
P.O. Box 400818
Las Vegas, NV 89140

ISBN-13: 9781477805565
ISBN-10: 1477805567

This is for Ronnie and Lucille King

The city in these pages is imaginary.
The people, the places are all fictitious.
Only the police routine is based on
established investigatory technique.

1

He thought of the city as a galaxy. A cluster of planets revolving around a brilliant sun. Asteroids and comets streaming through the blackness of space. Behind his eyes, bursts of color sometimes exploded, tracer bullets flashed jaggedly and vanished, skyrockets soared against the nighttime of his sightlessness.

He was blind, but he knew this city.

It sometimes got bitter cold in November, this city. Far as he was concerned, that was the worst month here. Never *could* keep himself warm in November. Even the dog got to shivering in November. The dog was a black Labrador, trained as a guide dog. The dog's name was Stanley. He had to laugh when he thought of that dog, a black man with a black dog. Just this morning somebody put a coin in the cup, a quarter by the sound of it, and then asked, "What's the dog's name, man?" Knew right off it was a black man talking. He could tell what a person was, what color or what nationality, just by hearing the voice.

"Dog's called Stanley," he said.

"Hang in there, Stanley-brother," the man said, and walked off.

Stanley-brother. Dog was black, he automatically got to be a brother. Stanley must've looked at the dude like he was crazy. Good old dog, he'd be lost without him. "Right, Stanley?" he said, and patted him on the head. Dog said nothing, hardly ever said a word, old Stanley. Lucky to have that dog. Got home from the war, eyes shot to hell, people on the block chipped in to buy him the dog. Wasn't a German shepherd, but trained just the same way, took him wherever he wanted to go in this city. *Loved* this city. Used to love it when he could see, and *still* loved it. On the subway tonight, coming uptown, man offered him a seat. Italian from the sound of him. "Hey, buddy, you wanna sit?" Touched his elbow. Must've known some blind people, didn't just reach up and scare hell out of him. Gently touched the elbow, that was all. "Hey buddy, you wanna sit?" Something in the way he said it—he must've known blind people, had to be the case. Wasn't nothing in his voice made it sound like he was talking to an old lady or a cripple. Just man to man, you want the seat you can have it. He'd taken the seat. Would've refused it otherwise, but the man wasn't taking pity, the man was just making things a little easier for him. That was acceptable.

You get to be blind…

You're twenty years old and you get to be blind, people all of a sudden think of you as an old man. Got home from the war ten years ago, eyes gone, wearing the shades, Mama and Chrissie crying like anything, *Come on, come on,* he'd said, *it ain't nothin, it ain't nothin.* Shit, it ain't nothin. It's I'm *blind* is what it is.

But then you begin learning how to see again. How to use that old Stanley-dog to take you around where you want to go. How to read Braille and how to write it with a guide slate.

Things like tying your own shoelaces, you already know how to do—most people don't even *look* when they're lacing their shoes, so ain't nothing wrong with being blind when it comes to tying laces. And rattling a few coins in a cup's an easy job. Get yourself a hand-lettered sign to hang around your neck, and you're in business for yourself. Free enterprise, HERE BUT FOR THE GRACE OF GOD GO THEE. Chrissie lettered the sign for him. Made it on a piece of cardboard, threaded string through a hole in each corner. The sign, the tin cup, Stanley the black Lab, and he was well on his way to making a fortune. He would forever be grateful to the war. Otherwise, how could he have got started in his own business?

That was ten years ago.

Full disability pension. Tin cup. Rattle, rattle the coins in it, listen for the sound of more coins. Add them up at the end of the day. Take them home to Isabel and add them up together. Sit at the kitchen table, spread the coins on the oilcloth cover, her hands and his hands feeling the coins, separating them, feeling, feeling. He'd met Isabel in a bar on The Stem six years ago. He was a pretty good beggar by then, shuffling along behind old Stanley, listening to the hum of the city around him, picking out sounds in the air, entertaining himself with the sounds as he moved slowly along the sidewalk, jingling the coins in the cup, sign around his neck—a new one lettered by a man who ran a shop on South Twelfth—right hand holding onto Stanley's harness. He'd had a good day, he stopped in the bar for a drink, this must've been about four in the afternoon. Woman sitting next to him. The scent of perfume and whiskey. Jukebox going at the back of the bar.

"What'll it be, Jimmy?" the bartender asked.

"Bourbon and water."

"Right."

"My daddy used to drink bourbon and water," the woman said.

White woman by her voice. Southerner.

“That right?”

“Yes. Bourbon and branch water’s a big thing down home. I’m from Tennessee.”

“Yeah,” he said.

“Here you go, Jimmy.”

The sound of the glass being placed on the bar top. His hand moved forward exploringly, found the glass, “Cheers,” he said, and drank.

“Cheers,” the woman said. “My name’s Isabel Cartwright.”

“I’m Jimmy Harris.”

“Nice to know you.”

“Are you white?” he asked.

“Don’t you know?”

“I’m blind,” he said.

She laughed softly. “So am I,” she said.

Married her six months later. Blind as bats, both of them. Took an apartment on Seventh near Mason, didn’t want to be living in Diamondback uptown, not because he had himself a white wife now, but only because Diamondback was bad news for blacks *or* whites. Named by the blacks themselves, supposed to be sarcastic and comical, was just about as funny as a rattler itself, and every bit as deadly. Her father came up from Tennessee for the wedding. They’d been living together six months by then, wouldn’t have mattered if the old man yelled and hollered, they’d have told him to go back home and drown in his bourbon and branch water. Nice old man, though, said he knew his daughter would be well looked after. Marrying a man who couldn’t see his own hand in front of his own black face, but sure, he’d look after her.

Well, he had.

They danced together sometimes.

Put on the radio, danced to it. He used to be some dancer before the war. Secret music, he heard secret music all the time. Same as the lights that flashed. Used to think being blind meant darkness all the time. Wasn't so. Lights flashing. Electrical impulses from the brain, memory images, whatever. Lots of action in his head all the time. Couldn't see nothing in front of his eyes, but saw plenty behind them. Touched her face. Beautiful face. Blonde hair, she said. Old Jimmy Harris got himself a honky chick, loved her to death. Rattled that old cup for her, rattled her bones in bed, too.

He was, by his calculation, two blocks from the building he lived in on Seventh Street. He had taken the subway uptown to Fourth, and was now crossing Hannon Square, where the statue of the World War I general on a horse dominated a small grassy patch overhung with chestnut trees. Weren't no horses in *his* damn war. Punji sticks and vill sweeps, surround the village, go right through it—that had been *his* war. Leave your eyes on the floor of a jungle. *Nice work, Jimmy. You got him.* His M-16 was still on automatic, he'd sprayed the bushes on the right side of the trail, where the sudden machine-gun fire had started. There was stillness now. The sergeant's voice. *Nice work, Jimmy. You got him.*

He waited.

He was wearing a fiberglass flak jacket over his cotton jungle shirt and field pants, leather-soled, canvas-topped jungle boots with holes for water drainage, black nylon socks, a helmet liner, and a steel pot with a camouflage cover over it. Hanging from his belt suspender straps was a first aid kit containing gauze, salt tablets, and foot powder; an ammo pouch containing magazines for his automatic rifle; a Claymore pouch containing six M-26 fragmentation grenades and two smoke grenades; a bayonet, a protective mask, and two canteens of water. He crouched in the underbrush, waiting, listening. He could hear their RTO radioing back to Bravo for help.

The grenade came from somewhere far over on the right. One of the men in Alpha yelled a warning too late. He turned to see the grenade flickering through the dappled jungle heat like a rare tropical bird. He was about to throw himself away from it, flat into the bushes behind him, when it exploded some four feet above his head. Lucky it didn't blow his whole head off. Opened his forehead, made scrambled eggs of his eyes. Doctor at the base hospital told him he was lucky he was alive. That was after Bravo came to the rescue. Hadn't seen a thing since that day. December the fourteenth. Eleven days before Christmas, ten years ago. Blind since then.

The chestnut trees in Hannon Square were leafless now in November. He could hear the wind keening through their naked branches. He was approaching the statue—there were things a blind person could sense, objects that bounced back echoes or warmth, movements that caused changes in the air pressure to be felt on the face. Somewhere up on Culver Avenue, he heard a bus grinding into gear. There was the smell of snow in the air. He hoped it would not snow. Snow made it difficult to—

Stanley suddenly stopped.

He jerked at the harness. The dog would not move.

"What is it?" he asked.

The dog was growling.

"Stanley?" he said.

Silence except for the dog still growling.

"Who's there?" he said.

He smelled something he identified at once. From when they'd operated on him back at the base hospital. Smelled it carried on the November wind. Chloroform. He could feel the dog's tenseness vibrating up through the leather harness in his hand.

And then suddenly the dog began to whimper. The scent of the chloroform was overpowering. He turned his head away from it, and felt the weight of the dog tugging on the harness. Stanley was falling to the sidewalk. He tried to keep the dog on his feet. Struggled. He bent over to his right, leaning into the wind. The dog was on the sidewalk now. Above, he heard the crackle of the swaying limbs of the chestnut tree. He was suddenly lost. He did not want to let go of the harness because he felt, irrationally, that if he did so he would be truly blind; the dog was his eyes. But he knew that Stanley was unconscious, knew the dog had been chloroformed. His hand opened. He let go of the harness as though he were letting go of a lifeline. He backed away from the dog. The November wind roared against his ears. He could hear no footfalls.

"Where are you?" he said.

Silence. The wind.

"Who are you? What do you want?"

He was seized suddenly from behind. He felt his chin caught in the crook of someone's elbow, felt his head being jerked back, his jaw raised. And then pain. A searing line of fire across his throat. The collar of his shirt was suddenly wet. Warm. The widespread fingers of his left hand pushed spasmodically against the air. He coughed, choked, gasped for breath. In a moment he fell to the pavement beside the dog. Blood gushed from his slit throat, ran in bright red rivulets to the base of the statue, and around the base, and then slanted across the pavement to disappear into the barberry bushes.

The woman who found the body at ten minutes to 8:00 that Thursday night was a Puerto Rican lady who spoke no English. She looked down at the man and the dog and thought they both were dead, and then realized the dog was breathing. At first she thought to forget the entire matter; it did not pay to involve oneself in another's business, especially when there was a man on the sidewalk with the insides of his neck showing. She realized then that the dog was a seeing-eye dog, and she felt at once enormous pity for the dead man. Shaking her head, clucking her tongue, she went to the phone booth across the street, inserted a coin into the slot, and dialed 911. She knew how to dial 911 because all the advertisements for the number were in both English and in Spanish, and in this part of the city it was a good idea to know how to dial the police in an emergency. The man who answered the telephone understood Spanish. He, too, was of Hispanic background, his family having come from Mayagüez during the great influx following World War II. He was twelve years old then. He now spoke English without a trace of accent; if anything, it was his Spanish that was somewhat faulty. He was able to gather from the woman's excited babble that she had found a dead blind man near the statue in Hannon Square. When he asked her what her name was, the woman hung up.

He understood that completely; this was the city.

A radio motor patrol car was angle-parked into the curb when Detectives Carella and Meyer arrived at the scene. Behind that was a black sedan that looked like a hearse. Carella guessed it belonged to Homicide.

"Well, well," Monoghan said, "look who's here."

"Well, well," Monroe said.

The two Homicide detectives stood with their hands in their pockets, one on either side of the man who lay crookedly on the pavement. They were dressed almost identically, each wearing black overcoat and gray fedora, blue woolen muffler. Both of them were sturdily built, with wide shoulders and beefy chests and thighs, craggy faces and eyes that were used to seeing dead men, blind or otherwise. Monoghan and Monroe looked exactly like hit men for the mob.

"We been here ten minutes already," Monoghan said at once.

"Twelve," Monroe said, checking his watch.

"We're a little shorthanded tonight," Carella said.

"We radioed for a meat wagon already," Monoghan said.

"And the ME is on his way."

"Lab boys, too."

"You can thank us," Monroe said.

"Thank you," Carella said, and looked down at the body.

"Guy's dead as a doornail," Monoghan said.

"Somebody opened his throat nice," Monroe said.

"Look at them tubes in there."

"Makes you want to puke."

In the city for which these men worked, the appearance of Homicide cops at the scene of a murder was mandatory, even though the subsequent investigation was handled by the precinct detectives catching the squeal. In rare instances, and presumably because they were specialists serving in a supervisory and advisory capacity, the Homicide detectives would come up with an idea or a piece of information that helped expedite the solution to a case. More often than not, they simply got underfoot. Monoghan and Monroe had already confused the issue by calling for an ambulance *before* the ME was on the scene. This was a cold night. Nobody liked dancing a jig when the temperature was hovering near the freezing point. And the hospital team would not be able to move the body till the ME checked it out.

"I hate stabbings," Monoghan said.

"This ain't a stabbing," Monroe said.

"No, then what is it? A poisoning? Man's laying there with his throat cut open—what is it, a hanging?"

"This is an incised wound," Monroe said. "There's a difference. A stabbing—" His right hands suddenly appeared from the pocket of his coat, the fist clutching an imaginary dagger. "A stabbing is when you *urh, urh, urh*," he said, pushing his fist at the air. "That's a stabbing. An incised wound is when you *zzzt*," he said, and smoothly drew the imaginary dagger across the same empty air.

"To me," Monoghan said, "a man gets cut with a knife, that's a stabbing."

"To me also," Monroe said.

"Then what are you—"

"I'm talking about what the autopsy's going to say. The autopsy'll say this is an incised wound."

"Yeah, but I'm talking about what I'll tell my wife at breakfast tomorrow morning. Can I tell her we found a man who was *incised* to death?" Monoghan said, and burst out laughing.

Monroe started laughing, too. Vapor plumed from their mouths onto the brittle air. Their hilarity rang in the small square where the dead man lay on his back near the statue. In the distance, Carella could hear the impatient *eee-wah*, *eee-wah*, *eee-wah* of an ambulance siren. The dead man's dark glasses had fallen from his head and lay shattered on the pavement beside him. Carella looked into the open scarred sockets where his eyes should have been. He turned away. The black Labrador lay on its side some four feet from the dead man. Meyer was crouched near the dog. Blood from the dead man's open throat had run across the sidewalk and into the black hair tufted on the dog's massive chest. The dog was still breathing. Meyer wondered what to do about the dog. He'd never had a case where there was an unconscious dog.

"What do we do about the dog?" he asked Carella.

"I was just wondering the same thing."

"It's a seeing-eye dog," Monoghan said. "Maybe he saw who done it. Maybe you can ask him who done it."

Monroe burst out laughing again. Monoghan, as originator of the witticism, modestly restrained himself a moment longer, and then joined his partner. Together they bellowed to the night.

The dog was still unconscious when the ambulance arrived. There were four RMP cars at the scene now, dome lights rotating. Barricades were going up all around the square. It was a cold night, but people were beginning to gather nonetheless and patrolmen were already urging them to go about their business—"Nothing here to see, folks, let's keep it moving." The intern got out of the ambulance, looked around immediately for somebody with a police shield pinned to his coat, and went to where Carella and Meyer were standing with the two Homicide dicks. He looked down at the body.

"All right to move him?" he asked.

"Not yet," Carella said. "The ME hasn't seen him yet."

"Then why'd you call us?" the intern asked.

"You can wait a few minutes," Monoghan said. "It won't kill you."

The intern looked at him.

"Yeah," Monoghan said, and nodded.

"You in charge here?" the intern asked.

"I'm the one ordered the ambulance."

"You should have waited," the intern said flatly, and turned on his heel and walked back to where the ambulance was parked at the curb. The attendant had already opened the rear door. The intern told him to close it.

The assistant medical examiner arrived ten minutes later. By that time the intern had threatened to leave four times. Carella mollified him each time. Each time the intern said, "There are people dying in this city." The ME was a man named Michael Horton. He was wearing a suit and tie, dark overcoat, no hat, black leather gloves. He took off the glove on his right hand before he shook hands with Carella. Then he knelt to examine the body. The man from the Photo Unit moved off and began taking pictures of the dog.

"Cute, very cute," Horton said. "Severed the trachea, carotids, and jugular. There's your cause of death right there. Not another mark on the man. Look at his hands. No defense cuts, nothing. Cute. Must've been a big blade. Just one slash, very deep, nobody did this with a penknife, I can tell you. Oh yes, very cute. No hesitation marks, clean-cut edges to the wound, help me roll him over." Carella knelt. Together they rolled the man over. Horton looked at his back. "Nothing here, clean as a whistle," he said. He pulled on the collar of the dead man's coat, studied the back of his neck. "Slash runs almost through to the spine. Okay, on his back again," he said, and he and Carella rolled the corpse over again. "I want his hands bagged, there may be scrapings under the nails. You won't need him fingerprinted here at the scene, will you?"

"We don't know who he is yet," Carella said.

"I'll wait around till you go through his pockets," Horton said. "Pending autopsy, you can say your cause of death is the incised throat wound."

"What'd I tell you?" Monroe said.

"What?" Horton said.

"Nothing," Monoghan said, and scowled at Monroe.

"What about the dog?" Carella said.

"What dog?"

"Over there. You want to look at the dog, too?"

"I don't look at dogs," Horton said.

"I thought—"

"I'm not a veterinarian, I don't look at dogs."

"Well, who does?" Carella asked.

"I don't know," Horton said. "I have never in my years with the Medical Examiner's Office had to examine a dead dog."

"The dog's still alive," Carella said.

"Then why do you want me to look at him?"

"To see what's wrong with him."

"How would I know what's wrong with him? I'm not a veterinarian."

"The dog's unconscious there," Carella said. "I thought you'd take a look at him, tell us what—"

"No, that's not my function," Horton said. "I'm finished here, give me what I have to sign. I'll wait while you check for identification."

"I don't know if the Photo Unit's done with him yet," Carella said.

"Well, find out, will you?" Horton said.

The intern walked over from the ambulance. He was blowing on his hands. "All right to take him now?" he asked.

"Everybody slow down, okay?" Carella said.

"I've been waiting here—"

"I don't *give* a damn," Carella said. "This is a homicide, let's just *cool* it, okay?"

"There are people dying in this city," the intern said.

Carella didn't answer him. He walked over to where the police photographer was snapping pictures of the unconscious dog. "You finished with the dead man?" he asked.

"Only my Polaroids," the photographer said.

"Well, take whatever else you need," Carella said. "Everybody's getting itchy."

"I haven't fingerprinted him yet, either."

"The ME wants his hands bagged."

A lab technician was already chalking an outline of the body on the pavement. The photographer waited till he was finished, and then began taking the additional pictures he needed. Flash bulbs exploded. The assistant ME blinked. At the ambulance, the attendant had opened the rear door again, in expectation. Meyer took Carella aside. They had been about to leave for a stakeout in a warehouse when the squeal came. Both men were wearing mackinaws and woolen watch caps.

"What do we do with the dog?" Meyer asked.

"I don't know," Carella said.

"Can't just leave him here, can we?"

"No."

"So what do we do?"

"Call a vet, I guess. I don't know." Carella paused. "Have you got a dog?"

"No. Have you?"

"Because I was wondering—maybe we ought to get a vet here right away. The dog may have been poisoned or something."

"Yeah," Meyer said, and nodded. "Let me call in, see if we can't get Murchison to send somebody."

"Maybe there's somebody downtown…you know the unit that has those dogs who sniff out dope?"

"Yeah?"

"They must have a vet who takes care of those dogs, don't you think?"

"Maybe. Let me call in, see what I can do."

"Yeah, go ahead. I think Photo's done with the body, I want to toss him."

Meyer walked toward the closest RMP car, exchanged a few words with the patrolman, and then climbed into the car and reached for the hand mike. Carella walked to where the photographer was putting a fresh roll of film into his camera.

"Okay to go through his pockets?"

"He's all yours," the photographer said.

In the dead man's coat pockets, Carella found only a book of matches and a subway token. In the right-hand trouser pocket, he found another subway token, a key chain with two keys on it, and $12.04 in quarters, dimes, nickels, and pennies. In the left-hand pocket, he found a wallet with $17 in it, all singles, and a Lucite-enclosed card from the Guiding Eye School at 821 South Perry. The typewritten text on one side of the card read:

THIS WILL IDENTIFY JAMES R. HARRIS OF 3414 SOUTH SEVENTH STREET, ISOLA AND HIS GUIDE DOG STANLEY, BLACK LABRADOR RETRIEVER.

The card was signed by the director of training, a man named Israel Schwartz, and the seal of the school was in the lower right-hand corner of the card. On the reverse side of the card there was a picture of Harris and the dog in harness, and the printed text:

ISSUED FOR THE CONVENIENCE OF TRANSPORTATION COMPANIES GRANTING USE OF THEIR FACILITIES TO GUIDE DOGS ACCOMPANIED BY THEIR OWNERS. NONTRANSFERABLE.

The 3400 block was just off Mason Avenue. James Harris had been less than two blocks from home when he'd been killed. Pinned to the inside of the leather wallet was a medallion that looked Catholic to Carella. On Harris's left wrist, there was a Braille wristwatch. On the third finger of his left hand, there was a wedding band. On his right hand, he wore a high school graduation ring. Emory High. A school in Diamondback. That was all.

The technician walked over. He squatted beside Carella and began putting the dead man's belongings into brown paper bags, sealing them, tagging them.

"What do you suppose this is?" Carella asked, and showed him the medallion.

"I'm not religious," the technician said.

"It's a saint, though, don't you think?"

"Even if I *was* religious," the technician said, "there are no saints in my religion."

"Get what you need?" Horton asked.

"Yes," Carella said.

"I want his hands bagged," Horton said to the technician.

"Okay," the technician said.

"I'll have a man at the morgue first thing tomorrow," Carella said.

Horton nodded. "Good night," he said, and walked off.

Carella went over to where the photographer was taking pictures of the terrain surrounding the square. "I'll need somebody from Photo to print him in the morning," he said. "I'll have a man there to back up the prints and deliver them to the ID Section."

"What time?" the photographer asked.

"Make it eight o'clock."

"Crack of dawn."

"What can I do?" Carella said, and gestured helplessly toward where the lab technician was already slipping a plastic bag over the dead man's right hand.

Meyer came over from the RMP car. "Get a make?" he asked.

"His name's James Harris," Carella said, "lives on South Seventh. What about the dog?"

"Murchison's sending a vet right away."

"Good. You want to stay here while I check out this address?"

"Have you made the sketch yet?"

"Not yet."

The intern approached just as Meyer was asking about the sketch. "Listen," he said, "if you think we're going to hang around while you make a goddamn drawing of the—"

"It'll just take a few minutes," Meyer said.

"Next time call when you're *ready* for us," the intern said. "And about that dog—"

"What about the dog?"

"Cop there said we'd have to take the dog, too. I'm not carrying any dog in the ambulance. That's—"

"Who said you had to take him?"

"The big cop over there. The one in the black coat."

"Monoghan?"

"I don't know his name."

"You don't have to take the dog," Meyer said. "But I can't let you move the body till I've got a sketch of the scene, okay? It'll only take a minute, I promise."

Carella knew it would take more like a half hour. "Meyer," he said, "I'll be back."

2

There was no light in the small entrance foyer.

Carella took a small penlight from his coat pocket and flashed it over the mailboxes. The nameplate for apartment 3C read J. HARRIS. He snapped off the light and tried the inner lobby door. It was unlocked. Inside, there was a hanging bulb on the first-floor landing, casting a yellowish glow onto the linoleum-covered steps. He started up the steps. The tenement smells were familiar to him. He had grown accustomed to them after years of working out of the 87th.

He took the stairs two at a time, not because he was in any hurry, but only because he always climbed stairs two at a time. He had started doing that when he was twelve and beginning to get lanky and long-legged. His mother used to call him a long drink of water. He'd stopped growing when he was seventeen, just short of six feet tall. He was broad-shouldered and narrow-waisted now, with the muscular leanness and effortless grace of an athlete. His hair was brown, his eyes were brown, too; they slanted downward to give his face a peculiarly Oriental look.

The tenements in the precinct territory were always either too hot or too cold. This one was suffocatingly hot with the contained steam heat of the day. He took off the woolen watch cap as he climbed the steps, stuffed it into a pocket of the mackinaw, and then unbuttoned the short coat. Behind closed doors he could hear television voices. Somewhere in the building someone flushed a toilet. He came onto the third-floor landing. There were three apartments there. Apartment 3C was at the end of the hall, farthest from the stairwell. He knocked on the door.

"Jimmy?" a woman's voice said.

"No, ma'am, police officer."

"Police, did you say?"

"Yes, ma'am."

He waited. The door opened a crack, held by a night chain. The apartment beyond was dark, he could not see the woman's face.

"Hold up your badge," she said.

He had the tin ready in his hand, they always asked to see it. It was pinned to the flap of a small leather case that also contained his Lucite-enclosed ID card. He showed it to her, and waited for recognition.

"Are you holding it up?" she asked.

"Yes," he said, and frowned, puzzled.

Her hand appeared in the narrow open wedge of the door. "Let me touch it," she said, and he realized belatedly that she was blind. He held out the shield, watched as her fingers explored the blue enamel, the gold ridges set in a sunburst pattern around the city's seal.

"What's your name?" she said.

"Detective Carella," he said.

"I guess it's all right," she said, and pulled her hand back. But she did not remove the night chain. "What do you want?" she asked.

"Does James Harris live here?"

"What is it?" she asked at once.

"Mrs. Harris..." he said, and hesitated. He hated this moment more than anything in police work. There was no kind way to do it, nothing that would soften it, nothing. "Your husband is dead," he said.

There was silence in the open wedge of the door, silence in the darkness beyond.

"What...what...?"

"May I come in?" he asked.

"Yes," she said. "Yes, please..."

He heard the night chain being removed. The door opened wide. In the light spilling from the landing, he saw that she was a white woman, blonde, slender, wearing a long belted blue robe and oversized dark glasses that covered her eyes and a goodly portion of her face as well. The apartment behind her was dark. He hesitated before entering, and she sensed this, and understood the cause at once. "I'll put on a light," she said, and turned and moved surely to the wall, and then along it, her left hand scarcely grazing it. She found the light switch, snapped it on. An overhead ceiling fixture illuminated the room. He stepped inside and closed the door behind him.

They were standing in a kitchen. This did not surprise him; the front doors to many of the precinct's apartments opened into kitchens. Some of those kitchens were spotlessly clean, others were filthy. This one was neither. Had he not known the occupants of the apartment were blind, he would have guessed they were only careless housekeepers. She was facing him now, head tilted in the characteristic position of the blind, chin bent, waiting.

"Mrs. Harris," he said, "your husband was murdered."

"Murdered?" She began shaking her head. "No," she said, "you must be...No, there's some mistake."

"I wish there were, Mrs. Harris."

"But why would...no," she said. "No, he's blind, you see."

He understood her reasoning completely. The thought was inconceivable. You did not slay blind men or little children. You did not strangle bluebirds or pull the wings off butterflies. Except that people did. Someone *had*. Her husband was lying dead on the sidewalk this very moment. Someone had slit his throat. Carella said again, very slowly this time, "He's dead, Mrs. Harris. He was murdered."

"Where is he?"

"He'll be taken to Buena Vista Hospital in just a little while."

"Where is he now?"

"In Hannon Square."

"How was he killed?" she asked.

She had the mildest of Southern accents, and her voice was pitched so low that he had trouble hearing her. But she spoke directly and she said what was on her mind, and she was asking now for information he had deliberately withheld.

"He was stabbed," Carella said.

She was silent for what seemed a long time. On the street outside, automobile tires squealed against asphalt, an engine roared, the tires squealed again as a corner was turned. The sound of the engine receded and was gone.

"Sit down, please," she said, and gestured unfailingly toward the kitchen table. He pulled out a chair and sat. She came across the room; her hand found the top of the chair opposite him. She sat immediately.

"We can talk another time, if you like," Carella said.

"Isn't it better to talk now?"

"If you want to, it might be helpful, yes."

"What do you want to know?" she asked.

"When did you see him last, Mrs. Harris?"

"This morning. We left the house together at ten o'clock."

"Where were you going?"

"I have a job downtown. Jimmy was going to Hall Avenue. He usually works Hall, between the Circle and Montgomery." She paused. "He's a beggar," she said.

"Where do you work, Mrs. Harris?"

"I work for a direct-mail company. I insert catalogues into envelopes."

"What kind of catalogues?"

"Advertisements for what the company is selling. We send them out twice a month. There's another girl who types up the mailing list, and I fill the envelopes. We sell souvenir items like ashtrays, salt and pepper shakers, coasters, swizzle sticks…things like that."

"What's the name of the company?"

"Prestige Novelty. On Dutchman's Row. In the garment center."

"And you and your husband both left the house together at ten this morning?"

"Yes. We try to avoid the subway rush hours. Jimmy's got the dog, and so we—" She stopped abruptly. "Where's Stanley?"

"He's being taken care of, Mrs. Harris."

"Is he all right?"

"I don't know. He may have been drugged, he may have been…" Carella let the sentence trail.

"What were you about to say? Poisoned?"

"Yes, ma'am."

"Stanley won't accept food from strangers. Jimmy's the one who feeds him. That's how he was trained. He won't even take food from *me* if I offer it. It has to be Jimmy who feeds him."

"We'll know in a little while," Carella said. "A vet was on the way when I left. Mrs. Harris, was this the usual routine with you and your husband? Did you always leave the house together at ten A.M.?"

"Mondays to Fridays."

"What time did you get back?"

"I generally get home at about three, three-thirty. Jimmy waits through the end of the day—people going home from work, he makes a lot of money between five and six o'clock. Then he waits another half hour, stops for a drink in a bar, just to make sure he'll miss the rush hour. He takes the subway uptown around six-thirty, a quarter to seven. He's usually home by..." She hesitated. She had suddenly realized that she was talking in the present tense about a man who was dead. The realization was painful. Watching her face, Carella saw tears beginning to run down her cheeks from the lower edges of the oversized glasses. He waited.

"I'm sorry," she said.

"If you'd rather..."

"No, no," she said, and shook her head. "He...he was usually home by seven-thirty the latest," she said, and rose abruptly and walked directly and unfalteringly to the countertop alongside the sink. Her hands found the box of Kleenex there, she pulled a tissue loose and blew her nose. "I usually had supper ready by seven-thirty. Or else we'd go out for a bite. Jimmy loved Chink's, we'd go out for Chink's a lot. With the dog, we could go anywhere we wanted to," she said, and began weeping again.

"Is there just the one dog?"

"Yes." The tissue was pressed to her mouth, she mumbled the single word into it. She pulled a second tissue from the box, blew her nose again. "Guide dogs are expensive," she said. "I didn't need one, only time I was without Jimmy was when I was at work, or coming back home from work. I've got the cane, I...I..." She began sobbing now, deep racking sobs that started in her chest and made it difficult for her to breathe.

He waited. She sobbed into the tissue. Behind her, through the kitchen window, he could see a light snow beginning to fall. He wondered if they were through at the scene. Snow would make it more difficult for the lab people. Silently, the snow fell. She could not have known it was snowing. She could neither see it nor hear it. She kept sobbing into the same rumpled tissue, and then at last she drew back her shoulders and raised her head, and said, "What else do you want to know?"

"Mrs. Harris, is there anyone you can think of who might have done something like this?"

"No."

"Did your husband have any enemies?"

"No. He was blind," she said, and again he followed her reasoning completely. Blind men did not have enemies. Blind men were objects of pity or sympathy, but never of hate.

"You haven't received any threatening telephone calls or letters in recent—"

"No."

"Mrs. Harris, this was a mixed marriage..."

"Mixed?"

"I mean..."

"Oh, you mean I'm white."

"Yes. Were there any of your neighbors or...someone where you worked...anyone...who might have strongly resented the marriage?"

"No."

"Tell me about your husband."

"What do you want to know?"

"How old was he?"

"Thirty. He was just thirty in August."

"Was he blind from birth?"

"No. He was wounded in the war."

"When?"

"Ten years ago. It would have been ten years this December. December the fourteenth."

"How long have you been married?"

"Fivc ycars."

"What was your maiden name?"

"Isabel Cartwright."

"Mrs. Harris…" he said, and hesitated. "Was your husband involved with another woman?"

"No."

"Are you involved with another man?"

"No."

"How did your relatives feel about the marriage?"

"My father loved Jimmy. He died two years ago. Jimmy was there at his bedside in Tennessee."

"And your mother?"

"I never knew my mother. She died in childbirth."

"Were you born blind?"

"Yes."

"Do you have any brothers or sisters?"

"No."

"How about your husband?"

"He has one sister. Chrissie. Christine. Are you writing this down?"

"Yes, I am. Does that bother you? I can stop if—"

"No, I don't mind."

"Are *his* parents alive?"

"His mother is. Sophie Harris. She still lives in Diamondback."

"Do you get along well with her?"

"Yes."

"Mrs. Harris, can you think of anything that's happened in recent weeks, anything that might have caused *anyone* to bear a grudge or—"

"No."

"*However* impossible it may seem?"

"I can't think of anything."

"All right, then," he said, "thank you very much," and closed his notebook.

Ordinarily, he'd have asked the wife of a murder victim to accompany him to the morgue for identification purposes. He hesitated now, wondering what to do. Isabel Harris could no doubt explore her husband's face with her hands and identify him as positively as could a sighted person. But identifying a corpse was a trying experience for anyone, and he could only imagine how emotionally unsettling it would be for someone who had to *touch* the body. He thought he might call Jimmy's mother instead, ask her to meet him at the morgue in the morning. Sophie Harris in Diamondback. He'd written her name in his book, he'd give her a call later tonight. But then he wondered whether he wasn't denying Isabel Harris a right that was exclusively hers—and denying it only because she was blind. He decided to play it straight. He had learned over the years that playing it straight was the best way—and maybe the only way.

"Mrs. Harris," he said, "when a murder victim is married, it's usually the husband or wife who identifies the body." He hesitated. "I don't know whether you want to do that or not."

"I'll do it, yes," she said. "Did you mean now?"

"The morning will be fine."

"What time?"

"I'll pick you up at ten."

"Ten o'clock, yes," she said, and nodded.

He walked to the door, turned toward her again. Behind her, the snow was still falling silently.

"Mrs. Harris?" he said.

"Yes?"

"Will you be all right? Is there anything I can do?"

"I'll be fine," she said.

When the knock sounded on the door, she was already in bed.

She lifted the cover on her watch and felt for the raised Braille dots. The time was twenty minutes to 12:00. She thought immediately that it was the detective coming back; he had probably sensed that she was lying. He had heard something in her voice or seen something flicker on her face. She had lied to him deliberately, had given him a flat "no" answer to the question he'd asked. And now he was back, of course; now he would want to know why she had lied. It made no difference any more. Jimmy was dead, she might just as well have told him the truth from the beginning. She would tell him now.

She was wearing a long flannel nightgown, she always wore a gown in the winter months, slept naked the minute it got to be spring; Jimmy said he liked to find her boobs without going through a yard of dry goods. She got out of bed now, her feet touching the cold wooden floor. They turned off the heat at 11:00, and by midnight it was fiercely cold in the apartment. She put on a robe and walked toward the bedroom doorway, avoiding the chair on the right, her hand outstretched; she did not need her cane in the apartment. She went through the doorway into the parlor, the sill between the rooms squeaking, past the piano Jimmy loved to play, played by ear, said he was the Art Tatum of his time, fat chance. It was funny the way she'd cried. She had stopped loving him a year ago—but her tears had been genuine enough.

She was in the kitchen now. She stopped just inside the door. Whoever was out there was still knocking. The knocking stopped the moment she spoke.

"Who is it?" she said.

"Mrs. Harris?"

"Yes?"

"Police department," the voice said.

"Detective Carella?"

"No, ma'am."

"Who is it, then?"

"Sergeant Romney. Would you open the door, please? We think we've found your husband's murderer."

"Just a minute," she said, and took off the night chain.

He came into the apartment and closed the door behind him. She heard the door whispering into the jamb, and then she heard the lock being turned, the tumblers falling. Movement. Floorboards creaking. He was standing just in front of her now.

"Where is it?"

She did not understand him.

"Where did he put it?"

"Put what? Who…who are you?"

"Tell me where it is," he said, "and you won't get hurt."

"I don't know what you…I don't…"

She was about to scream. Trembling, she backed away from him and collided with the wall behind her. She heard the sound of metal scraping against metal, sensed the sudden motion he took toward her, and then felt the tip of something pointed and sharp in the hollow of her throat.

"Don't even breathe," he said. "Where is it?"

"I don't know what you mean."

"Do you want me to kill you?"

"No, please, but I don't know what—"

"Then where is it?" he said.

"Please, I—"

"Where?" he said, and slapped her suddenly and viciously, knocking the sunglasses from her face. "Where?" he said, and slapped her again. "Where?" he said. "*Where*?"

3

"You can't explain to anyone about seasons," Meyer said. "You take your average man who lives in Florida or California, he doesn't know from seasons. He thinks the weather's *supposed* to be the same—day in, day out."

He did not look much like a sidewalk philosopher, though he was indeed on the sidewalk, walking briskly beside Carella, philosophizing as they approached the Harris apartment. Instead, he looked like what he was: a working cop. Tall, burly, with china-blue eyes in a face that appeared rounder than it was, perhaps because he was totally bald and had been that way since before his thirtieth birthday.

The baldness was a result of his monumental patience. He had been born the son of a Jewish tailor in a predominantly Gentile neighborhood. Old Max Meyer had a good sense of humor. He named his son Meyer. Meyer Meyer, it came out. Very comical. "Meyer Meyer, Jew on fire," the neighborhood kids called him. Tried to prove the chant one day by tying him to a post and setting a fire at his sneakered feet. Meyer patiently prayed for rain. Meyer patiently prayed for someone to come piss on the flames. It rained at last, but not before he'd decided irrevocably that the world was full of comedians. Eventually, he learned to live with his name and the taunts, jibes, wisecracks, and tittering comments it more often than not provoked. Patience. But something had to give. His hair began falling out. By thirty his pate was as clean as a honeydew melon. And now there were other problems. Now there was a television cop with a baldpate. If one more guy in the department called him…

Patient, he thought. Patience.

The flurries had stopped by midnight. Now, at 10:00 on Friday morning, there was only a light dusting of snow on the pavements, and the sky overhead was clear and bright. Both men were hatless, both were wearing heavy overcoats. Their hands were in their pockets, the collars of their coats were raised. As Meyer spoke, his breath feathered from his mouth and was carried away over his right shoulder.

"Sarah and I were in Switzerland once," he said, "this was late September a few years ago. People were getting ready for the winter. They were cutting down this tall grass, they were using scythes. And then they were spreading the grass to dry, so the cows would have that to eat in the winter. And they were stacking wood, and bringing the cows down from the mountains to put in the barns—it was a whole preparation scene going on there. They knew it would start snowing soon, they knew they had to be ready for winter. Seasons," he said, and nodded. "Without seasons there's a kind of sameness that's unnatural. That's what I think."

"Well," Carella said.

"What do you think, Steve?"

"I don't know," Carella said. He was thinking he was cold. He was thinking this was very goddamn cold for November. He was thinking back to the year before when the city became conditioned to expect only two different kinds of weather all winter long. You either woke up to a raging blizzard, or you woke up to clear skies with the temperature just above zero. That was the choice. He was not looking forward to the same choice this year. He was thinking he wouldn't *mind* living in Florida or California. He was wondering if any of the cities down there in Florida could use an experienced cop. Track down a couple of redneck bank robbers, something like that. Sit in the shade of a palm tree, sip a long frosty drink. The thought made him shiver.

The Harris building seemed more welcoming in broad daylight than it had the night before. There was grime on its facade, to be sure—this wouldn't be the city without grime—but the red brick showed through nonetheless, and the building looked somehow cozy in the bright sunlight. That was something people forgot about this city. Even Carella usually thought of it as a place tinted in various shades of black and white. Soot-covered tenements reaching into gray sky above, black asphalt streets, gray sidewalks and curbs, a monochromatic metropolis, ominous in its gloom. But the absolute opposite was true.

There was color in the buildings—red brick beside yellow, brownstone beside wood painted orange or blue, swirled marble, orange cinder block, pink stucco. There was color in the billboard posters—overlapping and blending and clashing so that a wall of them advertising attractions varying from a rock concert to a massage parlor achieved the dimension of an abstract painting. There was color in the traffic and the traffic lights—reds, yellows, and greens flashing on rain-slick pavements reflecting the metallic glow of Detroit's fancy, every color in the spectrum massed here in these crowded streets to create a moving mosaic. There was color in the debris—this city had more garbage than any other in the United States, and more often than not it went uncollected because of yet another garbage strike. It lay in plastic bags against the walls of apartment buildings, the greens, beiges, and pale yellows of modern technology enclosing the waste product of a city of eight million—or torn open by rats to spill in putrefying hues upon the sidewalks. There was color, too—God help the subway rider—in the graffiti that was spray-can-painted onto the sides of the shining new mass transit cars. Latin curlicues advertising this or that *macho* male, redundant, but then, so was spraying your name fourteen times on as many subway cars. And lastly, there was color in the people. No simple blacks or whites here. No. There were as many different complexions as there were citizens.

Both men were silent as they climbed the steps to the entrance lobby. One of them was thinking about seasons, and the other was thinking about colors. Both were thinking about the city. They climbed the steps to the third floor and knocked on the door to apartment 3C. Carella looked at his watch, and knocked again.

"Did you tell her ten o'clock?" Meyer asked.

"Yes." Carella knocked again. "Mrs. Harris?" he called. No answer. He knocked again, and put his ear to the door. He could hear nothing inside the apartment. He looked at Meyer.

"What do you think?" Meyer said.

"Let's get the super," Carella said.

They went downstairs again, found the super's apartment where most of them were, on the ground-floor landing at the end of the stairwell hall. He was a black man named Henry Reynolds, said he'd been superintendent here for six years, knew the Harrises well. Apparently, he did not yet know that Jimmy Harris had been slain last night. He talked incessantly as they climbed the steps again to the third floor, but he did not mention what he would most certainly have considered a tragedy had he known of it, nor did he ask why the police wanted access to the apartment. Neither Meyer nor Carella considered this strange. Often, in this city, the citizens did not ask questions. They knew cops only too well, and it was usually simpler to go along and not make waves. Reynolds knocked on the door to apartment 3C, listened for a moment with his head cocked toward the door, shrugged, and then unlocked the door with a passkey.

Isabel Cartwright Harris lay on the floor near the refrigerator.

Her throat had been slit, her head was twisted at an awkward angle in a pool of her own blood. The refrigerator door was open. Crisping trays and meat trays had been pulled from it, their contents dumped onto the floor. There were open canisters and boxes strewn everywhere. Underfoot, the floor was a gummy mess of blood and flour, sugar and cornflakes, ground coffee and crumpled biscuits, lettuce leaves and broken eggs. Drawers had been overturned, forks, knives, and spoons piled haphazardly in a junk-heap jumble, paper napkins, spaghetti tongs, a corkscrew, a cheese grater, place mats, candles all thrown on the floor together with the drawers that had contained them.

"Jesus," Reynolds said.

The body was removed by 12:00 noon. The laboratory boys were finished with the place by two, and that was when they turned it over to Meyer and Carella. The rest of the apartment was in a state of disorder as violent as what they had found in the kitchen. Cushions had been removed from the sofa and slashed open, the stuffing pulled out and thrown onto the floor. The sofa and all the upholstered chairs in the room had been overturned, their bottoms and backs slashed open. There was only one lamp in the living room, but it was resting on its side, and the shade had been removed and thrown to another corner of the room.

In the bedroom, the bed had been stripped, the mattress slashed, the stuffing pulled from it. Dresser drawers had been pulled out and overturned, slips and panties, bras and sweaters, gloves and handkerchiefs, socks and undershorts, T-shirts and dress shirts scattered all over the floor. Clothing had been pulled from hangers in the closet, hurled into the room to land on the dresser and the floor. The closet itself had been thoroughly ransacked—shoe boxes opened and searched, the inner soles of shoes slashed; the contents of a tackle box spilled onto the floor; the oilcloth covering on the closet shelf ripped free of the thumbtacks holding it down. It seemed evident, if not obvious, that someone had been looking for something. Moreover, the frenzy of the search seemed to indicate he'd been certain he would find it here.

Carella and Meyer had no such definite goal in mind, no specific *thing* they were looking for. They were hoping only for the faintest clue to what had happened. Two people had been brutally murdered, possibly within hours of each other. The first murder could have been chalked off as a street killing; there were plenty of those in this fair city, and street killings did not need motivation. But the second murder made everything seem suddenly methodical rather than senseless. A man and his wife killed within the same twenty-four-hour period, in the identical manner, demanded reasonable explanation. The detectives were asking why. They were looking for anything that might tell them why.

They were hampered in that both the victims were blind. They found none of the address books they might have found in the apartment of a sighted victim, no calendar jottings, no shopping lists or notes. Whatever correspondence they found had been punched out in Braille. They collected this for translation downtown, but it told them nothing immediately. There was an old standard typewriter in the apartment; it had already been dusted for prints by the lab technicians, and neither Carella nor Meyer could see what other information might be garnered from it. They found a bank passbook for the local branch of First Federal on Yates Avenue. The Harrises had $212 in their joint account. They found a photograph album covered with dust. It had obviously not been opened in years. It contained pictures of Jimmy Harris as a boy and a young man. Most of the people in the album were black. Even the pictures of Jimmy in uniform were mostly posed with black soldiers. Toward the end of the album was an eight-by-ten glossy photograph.

There were five men in the obviously posed picture. Two of them were white, three of them black. The picture had been taken in front of a tentlike structure with a wooden-frame lower half and a screened upper half. All of the men were smiling. One of them, crouching in the first row, had his hand on a crudely lettered sign. The sign read:

Alpha Fire Team
2nd Squad

Among some documents scattered on the bedroom floor, they found the dog's papers. He was a full-blooded Labrador retriever and his name was Stanley. He and his master had been trained at the Guiding Eye School on South Perry. The other documents on the floor were a marriage certificate—the two witnesses who'd signed it were named Angela Coombes and Richard Gerard—a certificate of honorable discharge from the United States Army and an insurance policy with American Heritage, Inc. The insured as James Harris. The primary beneficiary was Isabel Harris. In the event of her death, the contingent beneficiary was Mrs. Sophie Harris, mother of the insured. The face amount of the policy was $25,000.

That was all they found.

The phone on Carella's desk was ringing when he and Meyer got back to the squadroom at twenty minutes past 4:00. He pushed through the gate in the slatted wooden railing and snatched the receiver from its cradle.

"87th Squad, Carella," he said.

"This is Maloney, Canine Unit."

"Yes, Maloney."

"What are we supposed to do with this dog?"

"What dog?"

"This black Labrador somebody sent us."

"Is he okay?"

"He's fine, but what's his purpose, can you tell me?"

"He belonged to a homicide victim," Carella said.

"That's very interesting," Maloney said, "but what's that got to do with Canine?"

"Nothing. We didn't know what to do about him last night—"

"So you sent him here."

"No, no. The desk sergeant called for a vet."

"Yeah, *our* vet. So now we got ourselves a dog we don't know what to do with."

"Why don't you train him?"

"You know how much it costs to train one of these dogs? Also, how do we know he has any aptitude?"

"Well," Carella said, and sighed.

"So what do you want me to do with him?"

"I'll get back to you on it."

"When? He ain't out of here by Monday morning, I'm calling the shelter."

"What are you worried about? You haven't got a mad dog on your hands there. He's a seeing-eye dog, he looked perfectly healthy to me."

"Yeah, that ain't it, Carella. He's got more fuckin' tags and crap hanging from his collar than all the dogs in this city put together. That ain't it. It's what are we supposed to *do* with him? This ain't a zoo here, this is an arm of the police force and we got work to do, same as you. You want this fuckin' dog in *your* office? You want him up there fuckin' up *your* operation?"

"No, but—"

"Well, we don't want him *here* either fuckin' up ours. So what I'm telling you is we don't hear from you first thing Monday morning about what disposition is to be taken with this dog here, then he goes to the shelter and may God have mercy on his soul."

"Got you, Maloney."

"Yeah," Maloney said, and hung up.

The squadroom on any given Friday looked much as it did on any other day of the week, weekends, and holidays included. A bit shabby, a bit run-down at the heels, tired from overwork and overuse, but comfortable and familiar and really the only game in town when you got right down to it. To those who knew it, there were no other squadrooms anywhere else in the world. Plunk Carella down in Peoria or Perth, in Amsterdam or Amherst, and he wouldn't know what to do with himself. Transfer him, in fact, to any one of the new and shining precincts in this very city, and he would have felt suddenly transported to Mars. He could not imagine being a cop anyplace else. Being a cop meant being a cop in the Eight-Seven. It was that simple. As far as Carella was concerned, this was where it was at. All other precincts and all other cops had to be measured against this precinct and these cops. Territorial imperative. Pride of place. *This* was it.

This was a room on the second floor of the building, separated from the corridor by a slatted wooden railing with a swinging gate. In that corridor, there were two doors with frosted-glass panels, one of them marked CLERICAL, the other marked MEN'S

LAVATORY. If a lady had to pee, she was invited downstairs to the first floor of the building, where a door on the wall opposite the muster desk was marked WOMEN'S LAVATORY. There was once a Southern cop in the station house, up there to extradite a man on an armed robbery warrant. He saw the doors marked LAVATORY and knew this was where you were supposed to wash your hands, but he wondered aloud where the commodes were. In this precinct, a toilet was a lavatory.

In all of America, a toilet was something other than what it was supposed to be. It was a bathroom or a powder room or a restroom, but it was never a toilet. Americans did not like the word "toilet." It denoted waste product. Americans, the most wasteful humans on the face of the earth, did not like to discuss waste products or bodily functions. Your average polite American abroad would rather wet his pants than ask where the toilet was. In the Eight-Seven, only criminals asked where the toilet was. "Hey, where's the terlet?" they said. Get a clutch of muggers up there, a snatch of hookers, a stealth of burglars, they all wanted to know where the toilet was. Criminals had to go to the toilet on the average of three, four times a minute. That's because criminals had weak bladders. But they knew what to call a toilet, all right.

There were only two criminals in the squadroom at that moment, which was a bit below par for a Friday afternoon. One of those criminals was in the detention cage across the room. He was pacing the cage, but he was not muttering about his rights. This was strange. Most criminals muttered about their rights. That was a sure way of telling a criminal from your ordinary citizen accused of a crime. Your criminal always muttered about his rights. "I know my rights," he said, and then invariably said, "Hey, where's the terlet?" The second criminal in the squadroom was being interrogated by Detective Cotton Hawes at one of the desks just inside the row of filing cabinets on the divider side of the room. Looking at Hawes and looking at the man he was interrogating, it was difficult to tell who was the good guy and who was the bad.

Hawes was six feet two inches tall and weighed 190 pounds. He had blue eyes and a square jaw and a cleft chin. His hair was red, except for a streak over his left temple where he had once been knifed and the hair had curiously grown in white after the wound healed. He had a straight unbroken nose and a good mouth with a wide lower lip. He looked somehow fierce, like a prophet who'd been struck by lightning and survived. The man sitting opposite him was almost as tall as Hawes, somewhat heavier and strikingly handsome. Black hair and dark-brown eyes as soulful as a poet's. A Barrymore profile and a Valentino widow's peak—both before *our* time, Gertie, but not before the gentleman's. He was sixty-five years old if he was a day, and he had been caught burglarizing an apartment that afternoon. Caught right on the premises, burglar's tools on the floor at his feet. Working on a wall safe when the doorman walked in with a passkey and a cop. There was nothing he could say. He listened quietly to Hawes's questions, and answered them in a low, exhausted voice. This was his third fall. The rap was Burglary Two—he'd been caught inside a dwelling, during the day, and he'd been unarmed. But they'd throw the key away nonetheless. He was not too happy a burglar on that Friday afternoon as dusk seeped into the squadroom.

Meyer turned on the overhead lights. Hawes looked up as if a mortar had exploded over his head. His prisoner kept staring at his own hands folded in his lap. But at a desk just inside the windows facing the street, Detective Richard Genero also looked up. Genero was typing a report. He hated typing reports. That was because he did not know how to spell. He especially did not know how to spell "perpetrator," a word essential to advancement in the police department. Genero invariably spelled it "perpatrator," which was exactly how he pronounced it. He also pronounced toilet "terlet." That was because Genero came from Calm's Point, a part of the city that spoke American the way the people in Liverpool spoke English. Genero was a relatively new detective. He had achieved this lofty rung on the ladder of police succession by shooting himself accidentally in the foot. Or at least that had been the opening gun, so to speak, in a series of events that brought him to the attention of the department brass and earned for him the coveted gold shield. He was not much liked in the squadroom. He was adored, however, by his mother.

He signaled to Carella now, and Carella walked over to his desk.

"P-e-r," Carella said.

"Yeah, I know," Genero said, and indicated the word on his report. He had spelled it correctly. This meant that he would ask for promotion to lieutenant next week. "Steve," he said, "there was a call for you while you were out. Captain Grossman from the lab. Something about nail scrapings."

"Okay, I'll get right back to him."

Genero looked up at the wall clock. "He said if it was after five, you'd have to call him Monday."

"Did he find anything?"

"I don't know."

"Who's that in the cage?"

"That's my prisoner."

"What'd he do?"

"He was fornicating in the park."

"Is that a crime?"

"Public Lewdness," Genero said, naming the appropriate section of the State's Criminal Law. "PL 245, a Class B misdemeanor. 'In a public place, intentionally exposing the private or intimate parts of one's body in a lewd manner or committing any other lewd act.' Caught him cold."

Carella looked at the cage. "Where's the woman?" he asked.

"She escaped," Genero said. "I've got her panties, though."

"Good," Carella said. "Good evidence. Very good, Genero."

"I thought so," Genero said proudly. "He can go to jail for three months, you know."

"That'll teach him," Carella said, and went back to his desk. The offender in the cage looked to be about twenty years old. He'd probably been picked up by one of the hookers cruising Grover Park, figured he'd spend a pleasant half hour on a bright November afternoon, thinking his only risk would be frostbite, but not counting on the ever-alert protectors of the Law, as represented by Richard Genero. The offender in the cage looked as if he was more worried by what his mother would say than by the possible jail sentence he was facing. Carella sighed, opened his book of personal telephone listings, and dialed the police laboratory. Grossman answered the phone on the sixth ring. He sounded out of breath.

"Police lab, Grossman," he said.

"Sam, this is Steve."

"I was down the hall, let me get the folder," Grossman said. "Hold on."

Carella waited. He visualized Grossman in the glass-walled silence of the Headquarters building downtown. Grossman was tall and angular, a man who'd have looked more at home on a New England farm than in the sterile orderliness of the lab. He wore glasses, his eyes a guileless blue behind them. There was a gentility to his manner, a quiet warmth reminiscent of a long-lost era, even though his speech rapped out scientific facts with staccato authority. He had just been promoted to captain last month.

Carella had gone all the way downtown to police headquarters to buy him lunch in celebration.

"Hello, Steve?"

"Yeah."

"Here it is. James Randolph Harris, five feet ten inches tall, weight a hundred and—"

"Where'd you get this, Sam?"

"Identification sent it over. I thought you'd requested it."

"No."

"Maybe somebody here did."

"Has he got a record?"

"No, no, this is Army stuff. It's ten years old, Steve, the picture may have changed."

"It's changed in one respect for sure, Sam. He wasn't blind then."

"Do you want me to read the rest of this? I'm sure they'll be sending a copy to you. They know it's your case, don't they?"

"They should know, yes. I had a man at the morgue this morning when Photo was taking prints. Wait a minute, here it is on my desk."

"So you don't need me to fill you in."

"No, just tell me about the nail scrapings."

"Your man was a gardener."

"How come?"

"Soil under his fingernails."

"Dirt?"

"Soil. Big difference, Steve. Dirt is what you and I have under *our* fingernails, right?"

"Right," Carella said, and smiled.

"And all refined people like us," Grossman said.

"Yes, to be sure."

"But soil is what James Harris had under his fingernails. Combination of one-third topsoil, one-third sand, and one-third humus. Good rich potting soil."

"Where do you garden in this city?" Carella said.

"On the windowsill," Grossman said.

"Mm," Carella said.

"Help you any?"

"I don't know. Sam, his wife's been killed, too, did you know that?"

"No, I didn't."

"Your boys were there this afternoon. I'd appreciate it if you got back to me with anything they found."

"I'll have Davies call you in the morning."

"I'd appreciate it."

"Will you be in the office?"

"Tomorrow's supposed to be my day off," Carella said. "Have him try me at home."

"Okay. That it?"

"That's it, Sam. Thank you."

Carella hung up, started to open the manila envelope from the IS, looked up at the clock, and instead opened his personal telephone directory again. It was now ten minutes to 5:00, but he dialed the number anyway.

"Fort Jefferson," a man's voice said.

"Extension 6149, please."

"Hold," the man said.

Carella waited. In a moment another man's voice came onto the line.

"CID."

"Detective Carella, 87th Precinct. I need some information, please."

"Captain McCormick is on another line, can you wait, or shall I have him call you back?"

"I'll wait," Carella said.

While he waited he opened the manila envelope from the IS. It was addressed to Det. Steven Carella, 87th Squad. Close, but no cigar. As Grossman had reported on the telephone, Harris did not have a criminal record; his fingerprints were on file solely because he'd once served in the United States Army. If he'd ever been fingerprinted for a civil service job, the IS would have come up with a similar make. The sheet told Carella very little. It gave a description of Harris, a date of birth, and prints for the fingers and thumbs of both hands. He was putting the sheet back into the envelope when McCormick came onto the line.

"Captain McCormick."

"Captain, this is Detective Carella of the 87th Squad here in Isola. I wonder if you can help me."

"Well..." McCormick said, and Carella knew he was looking at the clock.

"I realize it's late," he said.

"Well..." McCormick said.

"But we're investigating a pair of homicides here, and I'd appreciate any help you can give me."

"What is it you need?" McCormick asked.

"One of the victims served with the Army. I'd like his service record."

"You'd have to put the request in writing," McCormick said.

"This is a homicide, Captain, we like to move a little faster than—"

"Is the murder directly related to the victim's service in the Army?"

"I don't know. I'm looking for someplace to hang my hat."

"Mm," McCormick said. "In any case, we don't have the records for anyone who isn't currently assigned to Fort Jefferson."

"I realize that. You'd have to call St. Louis."

"And it'll take them anywhere from twenty-four to seventy-two hours to make the search."

"Would it help if I called them directly?"

"I doubt it," McCormick said.

"Well, *would* you call them for me?"

"It's almost five."

"Not in St. Louis," Carella said.

"Give me the man's name."

"James Randolph Harris."

"When was he in the Army?"

"Ten years ago."

"I'll make the call. Do you want the entire Field 201-File?"

"Please. And would you tell them it's a homicide and ask them to expedite it?"

"Yes, I'll do that."

"And would you ask them to send the file directly to me?"

"They'll start quoting the Freedom of Information Act."

"That wouldn't be in conflict with the act."

"They like to go through channels. My guess is I'll have the file on Monday, if I put enough pressure on them. My further guess is you'll have to come all the way out to Calm's Point to get it. Unless I can find some sergeant who's heading into the city."

"Please do your best."

"I'll try."

"Thanks," Carella said, and hung up.

It was a few minutes past 5:00 on the wall clock. At the other end of the room, Genero began typing again. Hawes rose abruptly from his desk, said to his prisoner, "Okay, pal, let's go," and led him across the squadroom to the fingerprinting table. Behind the lieutenant's closed door, a telephone rang. It rang again, and then was silent. Carella reached into the bottom drawer of his desk where he kept the telephone directories for all five sections of the city. He opened the one for Isola, turned to the P's, and ran his finger down the page till he came to a listing for Prestige Novelty. He dialed the number at once.

"Prestige Novelty," a woman's voice said.

"This is Detective Carella of the 87th Squad," he said. "I'd like to speak to the owner of the company, please."

"I think Mr. Preston may be gone for the day," the woman said.

"Would you check, please?"

"Yes, sir." There was a click on the line. He waited. While he waited he speculated that half his time as a working cop was spent on the telephone; the other half was spent typing up reports in triplicate. He was thinking of taking up cigar smoking.

"Hello?" the woman said.

"Yes, I'm here."

"I'm sorry, sir, Mr. Preston *has* gone already."

"Can you give me his home number, please?"

"I'm sorry, sir, we're not permitted to give out—"

"This is a homicide investigation," Carella said.

"Sir, I'm sorry, I still can't take it upon myself—"

"Let me speak to whoever's in charge there right now," Carella said.

"Well, there's only me and Miss Houlihan. I was just getting ready to leave, in fact, when—"

"Let me talk to Miss Houlihan," Carella said.

"Yes, sir, but she won't give you his number, either," the woman said. There was another click. Carella waited. His father smoked cigars. His father had smoked cigars for as long as he could—

"Miss Houlihan," a voice said. A nasal, no-nonsense voice. "Can I help you?"

"This is Detective Carella of the—"

"Yes, Mr. Carella. I understand you want Mr. Preston's home number."

"That's right."

"We are not permitted—"

"Miss Houlihan, what is your position with Prestige Novelty?"

"I'm the bookkeeper."

"Miss Houlihan, we're investigating a pair of murders here."

"Yes, I understand. But—"

"One of the victims worked for Prestige Novelty."

"Yes, that would be Isabel Harris."

"That's right."

"We know."

"I need Mr. Preston's telephone number."

"I understand that," Miss Houlihan said. "But you see, Mr. Carella, we're not permitted to give out the private telephone numbers of company personnel."

"Miss Houlihan, if I have to go all the way downtown to get a warrant forcing you to divulge a telephone number—"

"We were just about to close for the weekend when you called," Miss Houlihan said.

"What does that mean?"

"It means that if you went for your warrant, there'd be no one here till Monday, anyway. And by that time you could just as easily call Mr. Preston at *this* number."

"This can't wait till Monday."

"I'm sorry, but I can't help you."

"Miss Houlihan, are you familiar with Section 195.10 of the Penal Law?"

"No, I'm not"

"It's titled *Refusing to Aid a Peace Officer.* I'm a peace officer, Miss Houlihan, and you're refusing to aid me." He was telling only the partial truth. The Class B misdemeanor was defined this way: "Upon command by a peace officer identifiable or identified to one as such, unreasonably failing or refusing to aid such peace officer in effecting an arrest or in preventing the commission by another person of any offense."

Miss Houlihan was silent for an inordinately long time.

"Why don't you just look it up in the phone book?" she said at last.

"Where does he live?"

"Riverhead."

"What's his first name?"

"Frank."

"Thank you," Carella said, and hung up. He pulled the Riverhead directory out of his drawer, opened it to the P's, and ran his finger down the forty or so Prestons listed. There was a Frank Preston on South Edgeheath Road. Carella looked up at the clock and dialed the number.

The number rang five times before a woman picked it up.

"Hello?" she said.

"Hello, may I please speak to Mr. Preston?"

"Who's this, please?"

"Detective Carella of the 87th Squad."

"Who?"

"Detective Carella of the—"

"Is this the police?"

"Yes," Carella said.

"He's not home yet."

"Who am I speaking to, please?" Carella asked.

"His wife."

"Mrs. Preston, what time do you expect him?"

"He's usually home by six on Fridays. Is this about the blind girl?"

"Yes."

"What a shame."

"Yes. Mrs. Preston, would you tell your husband I'll try to reach him again later tonight?"

"I'll tell him."

"Thank you," Carella said, and put the receiver back onto the cradle.

Meyer was on the telephone at his own desk, talking to Sophie Harris, Jimmy's mother. "We'll be up there in about half an hour, does that sound all right?" he said, and nodded. "We'll see you then." He hung up, turned in the swivel chair. "You feel up to it?" he asked Carella.

"Yes, sure," Carella said.

"She was bawling like a baby on the phone. Just got back from identifying both bodies. What'd you get from the Army?"

"Not much. I just placed a call to the man Isabel worked for, Frank Preston's his name. I'll try him again later, see what he can tell us. They're both kind of blanks so far, aren't they?"

"Jimmy and Isabel, do you mean?"

"Yeah. We don't really know who they *were*, do we?"

"Not yet," Meyer said. "Let's go talk to Mama."

4

The tempo of the city was changing.

From the dreary four/four of the workaday week, it was moving into a swifter beat, a quarter note played with the speed of an eighth, a sixteenth flashing by like a thirty-second—this was Friday night and the weekend was ahead. On the island of Isola, uptown and down, the citizens poured out of subway kiosks, heading for hot baths and fresh threads. In Riverhead, Calm's Point, and Majesta, the public transportation system was mostly aboveground, the elevated structures winding above the city streets with all the grace of poor planning, steel supporting pillars embedded in concrete that was wedded to cobblestones that went back to the turn of the century. The elevated tracks and elevated platforms created a landscape of eternal shade below. The graffiti-sprayed subway cars came up out of their underground tunnels and clattered along the tracks toward distant destinations; to someone who lived at the other end of Riverhead, the farthest station stop in Calm's Point was a two-hour-and-ten-minute ride away. You could get to Paris on the Concorde in just a little while longer. Here in Diamondback, the tracks were underground, and the only ugliness to be seen was in the tenements that lined the avenues and streets.

Diamondback was black, and black is beautiful—but Diamondback wasn't. The blacks coming up out of those subway kiosks worked in a variety of jobs during the day, most of them menial. Many of the women cleaned house for other women, soaping fine china and polishing heavy sterling, dusting furniture bought abroad in French and English antique shops, hanging custom-designed dresses in closets where sables and minks nuzzled side by side, rinsing out crystal champagne glasses, and putting into the garbage outside the kitchen door empty magnum bottles with labels they could not pronounce. Some of the men worked in the kitchens of restaurants, washing dishes or sweeping floors, fetching or carrying while in the dining rooms out front the patrons ordered pâté de foie gras or filet mignon *a la béarnaise*. Some of the men were responsible for keeping the garment industry going, pushing racks of clothes from dress house to dress house in the teeming area below Kerry Cross, weaving in and out of traffic with the skill of toreadors dodging bulls. The cabs they avoided and eluded as they pushed their wheeled wardrobes were largely driven by black men like themselves, who carried wealthy passengers to luxurious apartment buildings on terraces overlooking the River Dix, where black women worked washing fine china and polishing heavy sterling, the cycle repeating itself ad infinitum.

The building in which Sophie Harris lived was a far cry from the river-view apartments on the city's South Side, an even farther cry from the cloistered private homes in Smoke Rise, hugging the city's other shore. There was no doorman here; there was not even a door. Someone had removed it from its hinges, leaving only the gaping jamb, beyond which was an entrance alcove. The alcove was a five-by-eight cubicle with a row of mailboxes on its left. They found a nameplate for Sophie Harris, pressed the bell under her name, and went to the inner-lobby door, which was still there though badly scarred with names in hearts. They did not expect an answering buzz, and got none. In Diamondback, the locks on most lobby doors had been broken when there were still Indians running in the forests, and the landlords hadn't bothered to replace them. Instead, the tenants fortified their own apartment doors with enough locks to keep out an army of thieves. A man who got to be forty and still wasn't his own best doctor was a man who needed a doctor. And a man who lived in Diamondback for more than forty minutes without becoming an expert locksmith was a man who needed his apartment burglarized.

The stink of piss hit them the moment they opened the inner-lobby door. Carella backed away from it as if struck in the face with a slops bucket. Meyer said, "Phhh," and hurried toward the stairs. A radio blared from behind a door on the first-floor landing, the disc jockey's rapid-fire spiel riding in over the rock-and-roll beat as he extolled the merits of a skin cream. On the second floor a scrawny calico cat was sitting in the hallway. She looked at the detectives warily, as though she were a burglary suspect. There were cooking smells and all the smells of living in the building, combining to render the nostrils numb. They knocked on the door to Sophie Harris's apartment.

A woman said, "Who is it?"

"Detective Meyer," Meyer said. "We spoke on the phone just a little while ago."

They heard the locks being undone. First the deadbolt, then the Fox lock, its heavy buttress bar thudding to the floor as she lowered it. The door opened.

"Come in," she said.

As they stepped into the apartment, Carella wondered what the majority of black people in the United States of America felt when they were watching black people portrayed on television. Did they think, *Golly, that's me*? If they lived in a Diamondback apartment—where the first thing you saw upon entering was the exposed and rat-gnawed electrical wiring over the sink—did they think what they saw on television was an accurate portrayal of their own human condition? Or did those blacks cavorting on the small screen symbolize for them the hope of America? Could their own problems be one day reduced to the mindless sitcom chatter that flowed into their own living rooms, where overhead leaking pipes bloated the ceiling and would continue to do so till the plaster caved in, despite repeated phone calls to the landlord (who was white) and to the Department of Health (which didn't give a damn)?

Sophie Harris was a woman in her late forties. She might have been a beauty when she was younger—her complexion was a warm chocolate brown, her eyes an amber the color of the cat's, she was still slender and tall—but the burden of living in the non-television black world had stooped her shoulders and grayed her hair, lined her face and reduced the timbre of her voice to a hoarse whisper further weighted by the tragedy of the recent murders. She apologized at once for the appearance of the apartment—it seemed spotlessly clean to both Carella and Meyer—and then offered the detectives something to drink. Whiskey? Tea? There might be a little wine in the refrigerator—anything? The detectives declined. Outside the living room window, where they sat beneath the bloated and threatening ceiling, the neon sign of the bar across the street flickered against the curtainless night. There was the sound of an ambulance siren someplace—in this city, there was always the sound of sirens.

"Mrs. Harris," Carella said, "there are some questions we'd like to ask about your son and daughter-in—"

"Yes, certainly," she said. "I'll try to assist you as best I can."

She was adopting the kind of formal speech many blacks used with whites, especially when the whites were in a position of authority. It was phony and fake, it denied the ethnicity that the phony and fake television sitcom shows simulated so well. To television-watchers, the sitcom shows were real. Never mind this shitty apartment in Diamondback. Whatever they saw on the *tube* was the reality. The *real* Depression family was the one on television, forget your own father who struggled along on five bucks a week in 1932. The television doctors were real, the television cops were real, everything on television was real except science fiction, and even that was more real than the moon shots.

So here they sat. Two real cops and a real black woman. One of the cops was Italian, but he didn't wear a dirty raincoat, and he didn't fumble for words and he didn't pretend he was dumb. The other cop was bald, but he didn't suck lollipops and he didn't shave his pate clean and he didn't dress like the mayor. The black woman wasn't married to a man who owned a string of dry-cleaning stores, and she wasn't dressed as if she were going to bingo. She was embarrassed by the presence of the two men because they were white—even though her own daughter-in-law had been white. And she was intimidated by them because they were cops. All three sat there in real and uncomfortable proximity because someone real had murdered two other people. Otherwise, they might never have met each other in their entire lives. That was something television missed—the purely accidental nature of life itself. In televisionland, everything had a reason, everyone had a motive. Only cops knew that even Sherlock Holmes was total bullshit, and that all too often a knife in the back was put there senselessly. They were here to learn whether there'd indeed been a motive; they would not have been surprised to learn there hadn't been the shred of one.

"Mrs. Harris," Carella said, "did your son and daughter-in-law have many friends?"

"Some, I believe." Still the phony speech. Carella guessed she would use the word "quite" within the next several sentences. "Quite" was a sure indication that someone was using language he or she did not ordinarily use.

"Would you know their names?"

"I did not know any of their friends personally."

"Did they ever talk bitterly about any of them?"

"No, I never heard them say anything nasty about anyone."

"Would you know if they'd argued recently with—"

"I believe they got along quite well with everyone."

"What we're trying to find out is whether anyone—"

"Yes, I know. But you see…They were blind."

Again the blindness. Again the blindness as a reason for denying the fact that they'd both been murdered. They were blind; therefore, they could not have been brutally slain. But they had been.

"Mrs. Harris," Carella said, "please try to think beyond their blindness. I know it's difficult to believe anyone would harm two helpless—"

"But someone did," Mrs. Harris said.

"Yes. That's exactly my—"

"Yes," she said.

"*Who*, Mrs. Harris? Can you think of anyone at all who might have wanted to harm them?"

"No one."

"Were there any problems either of them were having? Did Jimmy or your daughter-in-law ever come to you for advice of a personal nature?"

"No, never."

"Were they happy together, would you say?"

"They seemed very happy."

"Did Jimmy have another woman?"

"No."

"You're sure?"

"I would have heard about it."

"How about Isabel?"

"She was devoted to him."

"Did they visit you often?"

"They came at least once a month. And on holidays, Christmas, Thanksgiving—they were supposed to come here next week. I already ordered the turkey," she said. "Ten pounds. There was going to be six of us—Jimmy and his wife, my daughter Chrissie and her boyfriend, and a man's been coming around to see me."

Her speech had suddenly changed. Talk of the Thanksgiving holiday next week, of the homey preparations for it, had jerked her back into her own familiar speech pattern. These two white detectives might not be able to understand or to share her blackness, but at least they understood Thanksgiving. White or black, in America everyone understood turkey drumsticks and pumpkin pie, sweet potatoes and a word of grace.

"When they came to visit—"

"Yes," she said, and nodded. She was thinking they would not come to visit ever again. The knowledge was plain on her face; it turned her amber eyes to ashes.

"Did anyone in the neighborhood comment about the nature of their marriage?"

"What do you mean?"

"That she was white,"

"No. Not to me, anyway. I guess there were some figured Jimmy had no cause marryin' a white girl. But they wouldn't dare say nothing to me about it."

"How did *you* feel about it, Mrs. Harris?"

"I loved that girl with all my heart."

"Did you know you're the contingent beneficiary of your son's insurance policy?"

"After Isabel, yes," she said. "The second beneficiary." She shook her head. "Bless their hearts," she said.

"Twenty-five thousand dollars," Carella said, and watched her.

"Bless their hearts," she said again.

"Mrs. Harris," Carella said, "this man you say you've been seeing…May I ask you his name?"

"Charles Clarke."

"How long have you known him?"

"About six months."

"How serious is your relationship?"

"Well…He's asked me to marry him."

"Have you accepted?"

"No. Not yet."

"Do you think you *might* marry him?"

"I might."

"Have you told him this?"

"I told him maybe after Chrissie was out of the house. She's about to get married herself next year, the weddin's set for June, that's when her boyfriend'll be graduating high school."

"How old is she?" Carella asked.

"Chrissie's seventeen."

"And you told Mr. Clarke you might marry him in June?"

"After Chrissie's out of the house, yes."

"What'd he think about that?"

"Well, he's in a hurry, same as any man."

"What sort of work does he do?"

"He's a fight manager."

"Who does he manage?"

"Fighter named Black Jackson. You ever heard of him?"

"No, I'm sorry."

"He fights at St. Joe's all the time. St. Joseph's Arena."

"Mrs. Harris," Carella said, "I hope this won't offend you." He hesitated. "Did you and Mr. Clarke ever discuss money?"

"Sometimes."

"Did *he* know that you were the contingent beneficiary of a twenty-five-thousand-dollar insurance policy?"

"Yes."

"You told him?"

"Jimmy did. He was talking about if anything should happen to him and Isabel, I'd be well taken care of. He had all to do to take care of hisself, but he was always worryin' about me." She looked directly into Carella's eyes. "If you're thinkin' Charlie had anything to do with killing my boy and his wife, you're dreaming, mister."

"We'd like to talk to him, anyway," Carella said.

"You can talk to him if you like, he lives right around the comer on Holman, 623 Holman. But it wasn't Charlie who killed them. You ask me..."

"Yes, Mrs. Harris?"

"It must've been somebody crazy," she said. "It *had* to be somebody crazy."

Well, maybe it *had* been somebody crazy.

The city was full of bedbugs, true enough, and whereas they usually surfaced during the hot summer months, there was no law that said a lunatic couldn't come out of the woodwork in the middle of November and kill two helpless blind people. The trouble with the crazies of the world, however, was exactly that: They were crazy. And with crazy people, you couldn't go looking for reasons, you couldn't start thinking about motives. With crazies, you just went along on the theory that maybe you'd stumble over a solution somehow, maybe the guy would go berserk in a crowded restaurant and you'd arrest him and he'd confess to having killed sixty-four blind people in the past month, all in different cities. One of them in London. There were a lot of crazies on television cop shows, the network reasoning being that the home viewer felt more content watching a show where a *nut* was doing all the killing, instead of a nice sane person with a motive, just like you or me. Crazies made very soothing killers. They were not much fun to track down, however, since there was no place to start and no place to go. All you could do was hope, and hope is the thing with feathers.

So they went to see Charlie Clarke, who at least had a *possible* reason for wanting Jimmy and Isabel Harris out of the way. In the land of the blind, and so on. And in the absence of any solid suspects, you grabbed for the nearest floating straw, hoping it would take on the dimensions of a lifeboat or a log.

The building on Holman was similar to the one in which Sophie lived. Lettered in white paint on successive risers of the front stoop were the warnings NO LOITERING and NO STOOP BALL. They went into the outer lobby, where a row of broken mailboxes was on the wall to their left. There was a nameplate for Charles C. Clarke in the box for apartment 22. The upper half of the inner-lobby door was a piece of frosted glass that had a crack running diagonally across it from the lower left-hand corner to the upper right. The door was unlocked. The ground-floor landing stank of piss and wine. There were no lights. Carella turned on his flash, and together they climbed the steps.

"What do you suppose the C is for?" Meyer asked.

"What C?"

"Charles C. Clark," Meyer said.

"Oh. Clarence?"

"My guess is Cyril."

"No, either Clarence or Clyde."

"Cyril," Meyer said.

The lightbulb on the second-floor landing had not been smashed or pilfered. Carella snapped out his flash. The metal numerals on Clarke's door were painted the same brown color as the door itself. There were three visible keyways on the door; Charlie Clarke was no fool. There was also a metal bell twist just below the numbers. Carella took it between his thumb and forefinger, and gave it a twirl. The sound from within the apartment was sharp and jangling. He tried it again. He looked at Meyer, and was about to try it another time when a door at the end of the hall opened. A small boy looked out into the hallway. He was perhaps eight years old. He had brown skin and brown eyes, and he was letting his hair grow into an Afro. He was wearing bedroom slippers and a plaid bathrobe belted at the waist.

"Hi," he said.

"Hi," Carella said.

"You looking for Mr. Clarke?"

"Yes," Carella said. "Do you know where he is?"

"At the gym. He's got a prizefighter, did you know that?"

"Name of Black Jackson," Carella said.

"You *did* know, huh?"

"Yep."

"What's his middle name?" Meyer asked.

"Black Jackson's? He ain't *got* no middle name," the boy said. "Black *Jackson*, that's his name," he said, and raised his fists in a boxer's classic pose. "I got the flu," he said. "I'm s'posed to be in bed."

"You better get back there, then," Meyer said. "Where's the gym?"

"Up on Holman."

"What's Mr. Clarke's middle name?"

"Don't know," the boy said, and grinned and closed the door.

They started down the steps again. On the first-floor landing, Carella turned on his flashlight again. A huge black woman wearing a green cardigan sweater over a flowered housedress was standing at the foot of the steps as they came down to the ground floor. Her hands were on her hips.

"What's the heat, Officers?" she asked. They had not identified themselves, but she knew fuzz when she saw it.

"No heat," Carella said.

"Who you lookin for, then?"

"None of your business, lady," Meyer said. "Go back in your apartment, okay?"

"I'm the super in this building, I want to know what you two men are doing here."

"We're from Housing and Development," Meyer said, "checking on whether there're lightbulbs on every landing. Go put in some lightbulbs or we'll be back with a warrant."

"You ain't from no Housing and Development," the woman said. Meyer and Carella were already in the outer lobby. They did not know whether or not Charlie Clarke had done anything, but they did not want a telephone call warning him that the police were on the way. Behind them, they heard the super saying, "Housing and Development, sheeeee-it."

Charlie Clarke was a dapper little man wearing a yellow turtleneck shirt and a tan cardigan sweater over it. Dark-brown trousers. Brown patent leather shoes. Cigar holder clamped in one corner of his mouth, dead cigar in it. They found him on the second floor of the gym on Holman and Seventy-eighth, elbows on the ring canvas, watching a pair of black fighters sparring. One of the fighters was huge and flatfooted. The other was smaller but more agile. He kept dancing around the bigger fighter, hitting him with right jabs. All around the gym other fighters were skipping rope and pounding the big bags. In one corner a small pale man who looked like a welterweight kept a punching bag going with monotonously precise rhythm. Carella and Meyer walked over to the ring. Clarke had been described to them downstairs. The description proved to be entirely accurate, right down to the dead cigar in his mouth.

"Mr. Clarke?" Carella asked.

"Yeah, shh," he said. "What the fuck you *waitin'* on, man?" he shouted to the rink. The smaller, more agile fighter stopped dancing around the larger one, and dropped his hands in exasperation. The back of his sweatshirt was lettered with the name BLACK JACKSON. "You *never* gonna knock the man out, you keep jabbin' all the time," Clarke said. "You had plenty opportunity for the left hand, now what were you waitin' on, man, would you tell me?"

"I was waitin' on an opening," Jackson said.

"Man, there was openings like a hooker's Saturday night," Clarke said.

"Ain't no sense throwin' the left till there's an opening," Jackson said.

"You want to be the heavyweight champ of the world, or you want to be a dance star?" Clarke asked. "All I see you doin' is dancin' and jabbin', dancin' and jabbin'. You want to knock down a man the size of Jody there, you got to *hit* him, man. You got to knock his fuckin' *head* off, not go dancin' with him." He turned abruptly from the ring and said, "What is it, Officers?"

"What you want us to do now?" Jackson asked.

"Go work out on the bag a while," Clarke said over his shoulder.

"Which bag?"

"The big one."

Jackson turned and began walking toward the far side of the ring. The larger fighter followed him. Together they ducked through the ropes. A loudspeaker erupted into the sweaty rhythm of the huge echoing room. "Andrew Henderson, call your mother. Andrew Henderson, call your mother."

"So what is it?" Clarke asked.

"Jimmy and Isabel Harris," Carella said.

"You're kidding me," Clarke said. "What've *I* got to do with that?"

"Is it true you asked Sophie Harris to marry you?"

"That's right," Clarke said. "Listen, what is this, man? Is this you're lookin' for information about somebody you think *done* this thing, or is it you're tryin' to hang it on me? Cause, man, from what I read in the papers, that boy was killed at around seven-thirty last night, and I was right *here* then, man, workin' my fighter."

"Don't get excited," Meyer said.

"I ain't excited," Clarke said. "I just know some things. You don't get to be sixty years old in Diamondback without gettin' to know a few things."

"What are these things you know, Mr. Clarke?"

"I know when a black man's been killed, the cops go lookin' for *another* black man. I don't know why you're here, but I'll give you six-to-five it's cause I'm black."

"You'd lose," Carella said.

"Then enlighten me," Clarke said.

"We're here because you asked Sophie Harris to marry you, and you know she's contingent beneficiary of a twenty-five-thousand-dollar insurance policy. *That's* why we're here."

"You think I killed those two kids so I could latch onto the twenty-five, is that it?"

"What time did you get here last night?"

"Shit, man, I got half a mind—"

"If you're clean, we'll be out of here in three minutes flat. Just tell us when you got here and when you left."

"I was here at seven and I left at midnight."

"Anybody see you?"

"I was workin' with Warren and a sparring partner."

"Warren?"

"Warren Jackson. My boy."

"Who was the sparring partner? Same guy there?"

"No, a kid named Donald Rivers. I don't see him around, I don't think he's here right now."

"Anybody else?"

"Only every fighter and manager in Diamondback. Warren's got a fight Tuesday night. I been workin' his ass off. Ask anybody in the gym—pick anybody you see on the floor—ask them was I here workin' the boy last night. Seven o'clock to midnight. Had ring time from eight to nine, you can check that downstairs. Rest of the time I had him runnin' and jumpin' and punchin' the bags and the whole damn shit."

"Where'd you go when you left here?" Meyer said.

"Coffee shop up the street. I don't know the name of it, everybody from the gym rolls in there. It's right on the corner of Holman and Seventy-sixth. They know me there, you ask them was I in there last night."

"We'll ask them," Meyer said. "What's your middle name?"

"None of your fuckin' business," Clarke said.

They checked around the gymnasium and learned that at least half a dozen people had seen Clarke on the premises the night before, between the hours of 7:00 and midnight. They checked with the owner of the coffee shop up the street, and he told them Clarke and his fighter came in shortly after midnight last night, sat around talking till at least 1:00 in the morning, maybe 1:30. According to the coroner's report, Jimmy Harris had been slain sometime between 6:30 and 7:30 P.M. He had been able to pinpoint the time so narrowly because the body was discovered almost immediately after the murder; rigor mortis, in fact, had not yet set in. With Isabel Harris, the latitude was wider; the coroner guessed she'd been killed sometime between 10:00 P.M. and 1:00 A.M. In order to have killed Jimmy in Hannon Square at 6:30, and then get uptown to the gym in Diamondback by 7:00, Charlie Clarke had to have moved faster than a speeding bullet. The logistics were impossible. Nor could he have got downtown again to the Harris apartment during the time span the coroner had estimated for Isabel's murder.

This meant nothing.

In this city you could get somebody killed for $50. There was a possible $25,000 at stake here, and for a tenth of that you could hire a battalion of goons. They did not yet know whether the lab boys had lifted any good prints in the Harris apartment. In the meantime, and against that eventuality, they decided to request an I.D. run on Charles C. Clarke in the morning. It was almost 8:00 when they left Diamondback. Carella dropped Meyer at the nearest subway station, and then drove home to Riverhead.

5

The front door to the house was locked.

Night like tonight, the goddamn door *would* be locked and he'd have to stand out there in the cold fumbling for keys. He rang the doorbell, and indeed began fumbling for keys, muttering under his breath. His fingers were stiff, they rummaged awkwardly through the loose change in his right-hand pocket. He took out his key ring. There were enough skeleton keys on it to have convicted a burglar of possession of tools. The house was a huge old rambling monster near Donnegan's Bluff, purchased by the Carellas shortly after the twins were born, a house that had undoubtedly quartered a large family and an army of servants in the good old days. These were the bad new days, however. It was only Fanny who finally opened the door for him.

"Well, well, it's himself," she said.

Fanny was their housekeeper, a big woman in her late fifties, wearing a white blouse and bright-green slacks that spread wide over 140 pounds of girth, bleached red hair flaming like neon, mellow Irish brogue spilling from her lips like aged whiskey. "I thought you'd never get here, to tell the truth of it," she said.

"Fanny," he said, "I'm cold and I'm hungry."

"Don't be threatenin' me, y'bully," she said. "Theodora's in the living room. Come in, you'll catch your death."

"If you'll step out of the doorway..."

"Aye, I'll step out of the doorway," she said, and moved aside to let him in.

She had come to the Carellas years ago, as a month-long gift from Teddy's father, who'd felt his daughter needed at least that much time to recuperate after the birth of twins. In those days Fanny's hair was blue, and she wore a pince-nez and weighed ten pounds less than she did now. The prepaid month had gone by all too quickly, and Carella had regretfully informed her that he could not afford a full-time housekeeper on his meager salary. But Fanny was an indomitable broad who had never had a family of her own, and who rather liked this one. So she told Carella he could pay her whatever he might scrape up for the time being, and she would supplement her income with night jobs, she being a trained nurse and a very healthy woman to boot. Carella had flatly refused. Fanny had put her hands on her hips and said, "Are you going to throw me out into the street, is that it?" and they'd argued back and forth, and Fanny had stayed. She was still with them.

"Theodora's in the living room," she said again. "Shall I bring you a drink, or are you *still* on duty?"

"I'd like a scotch and soda, please, very strong," Carella said, and took off his coat and hung it on the hallway rack.

"You should wear a hat, this weather," Fanny said.

"I don't like hats," Carella said.

"Gentlemen wear hats," Fanny said, and went out into the kitchen, where there was a wet bar recessed into what had long ago been a dumbwaiter shaft. In the spare room, the ten-year-old twins were watching television. Carella stopped in the doorway and said, "Hi."

"Hi, Dad," April said.

"Hi," Mark said.

"No kisses?"

"Wait till she wins the money," April said.

"Who?"

"Shh, Dad, there's five thousand dollars at stake here," Mark said.

"See you later," Carella said, and started toward the living room, and then turned back and said, "Have you eaten yet?"

"Yes, Dad, shhhh," April said.

Carella went down the corridor to the living room. Teddy was sitting by the fire. She had not heard the doorbell ringing, she had not heard the conversation with Fanny or the twins, she did not now hear her husband approaching; Teddy Carella was a deaf-mute. She sat by the fire, looking into the flames, the firelight touching her midnight hair with reds and oranges and yellows, as though it had been sprinkled with sequins. He hesitated in the doorway, watching her face, the dark luminous brown eyes staring into the flames, the full mouth and finely sculpted cheekbones. As always, his heart soared. He stood watching her speechlessly, feeling as he had the very first moment he'd met her. That would never change. He could guarantee that. In a world he sometimes did not understand, he understood completely his love for Teddy. He went to her. She sensed his approach now, and turned, and her face changed in the tick of an instant from meditative privacy to shared intimacy. There was nothing hidden on that face, her eyes and her mouth declared all her tongue could not. She rose from the easy chair and went into his arms. He held her close. He stroked her hair. He gently kissed her lips.

Her hands fluttered with questions, which he answered with his own hands, using the sign language she had taught him, occasionally lapsing into speech, her eyes searching his mouth. When Fanny came into the room with his drink, she did not interrupt their animated conversation. He told her about the second victim, and Teddy's eyes clouded, and she watched as his hands and his face and his voice defined his outrage. He told her about Sophie Harris and Charles C. Clarke, whose middle name they still did not know, and Maloney from Canine, and she asked him what would happen to the dog, and he said he didn't know. They ate dinner alone in the wood-paneled dining room, and later the children came to be kissed before going off to bed. April said the lady on television had blown it. Mark said any dope could have answered the question. April, not realizing what she was saying, said, "*I* couldn't have answered it," and they all burst out laughing.

It was almost 9:30, it had been a long day. They sipped their coffee in silence, holding hands across the table. Insidiously, the case began to intrude again. Carella found himself hurrying through the last of his coffee. When he rose abruptly from the table, Teddy looked up at him in puzzlement.

"I've got to call this guy Preston," he said.

She waited, her eyes watching his mouth.

"Why don't you go upstairs, get ready for bed?"

Still she waited.

"I won't be a minute," he said, and grinned boyishly.

She nodded briefly and reached up with one hand to touch his face. He kissed the palm of her hand, and then nodded, too, and went out into the living room to dial Preston's number from the telephone there.

"Hello?" a man's voice said.

"Mr. Preston?"

"Yes?"

"This is Detective Carella, I called earlier."

"Yes, Mr. Carella."

"We're investigating the murders of Isabel and Jimmy Harris, and I'd like to ask you a few questions."

"*Now*, do you mean?"

"If it's convenient."

"Well…Yes, I suppose so."

"When I spoke to Mrs. Harris yesterday, she told me she worked for your company."

"That's right."

"In the mailroom."

"Yes."

"How long had she been working for you, Mr. Preston?"

"Two, three years."

"What were her duties?"

"She inserted our catalogues into envelopes."

"Who else worked in the mailroom with her?"

"She worked there alone. Another girl typed up the labels and put them on the envelopes. But that was in the outer office."

"What's the other girl's name?"

"Jennie D'Amato. She also answers phones and serves as receptionist."

"Would you know her address?"

"Not offhand. If you call the office on Monday, she'll give it to you."

"How many people do you employ, Mr. Preston?"

"There's just myself and three girls in the office—two without Isabel."

"What's the third girl's name?"

"Nancy Houlihan, she's my bookkeeper."

"Do you employ anyone who works outside the office?"

"Yes, at the warehouse."

"Where's the warehouse?"

"About ten blocks from the office. On the river."

"Who do you employ there?"

"Just two men to make up the orders and pack them and ship them."

"So the way the operation works…"

"It's direct mail," Preston said. "We send out the advertising matter, and when we receive orders, they're filled at the warehouse. It's a very small operation."

"These two men working at the warehouse—did they ever come up to the office?"

"On Fridays. To pick up their paychecks."

"Would they have had any contact with Isabel Harris?"

"They knew her, yes."

"What are their names?"

"Alex Carr and Tommy Runniman."

"Would you know their addresses?"

"You'll have to get those on Monday. Just call the office anytime after nine."

"Mr. Preston, how did Isabel get along with the other employees?"

"Fine."

"No problems?"

"None that I knew of."

"How did *you* get along with her?"

"Me?"

"Yes, sir."

"I hardly knew her."

"You said she'd been working there for two, three years…"

"That's right. But I rarely had any personal contact with the employees."

"How'd you happen to hire her, Mr. Preston?"

"I'd been thinking of hiring someone handicapped for a long time. The job doesn't require eyesight. It's merely inserting catalogues into envelopes."

"How much were you paying her, Mr. Preston?"

"She was being paid comparable wages."

"Comparable?"

"To the other girls."

"Not more?"

"*More*?"

"Yes, sir. I'm trying to determine whether anyone would have had a reason for bearing a grudge or—"

"No, she wasn't paid more, comparably, than the other girls."

"Sir, there's that word 'comparably' again."

"What I'm saying, Mr. Carella, is that you can't expect someone working in the mailroom to be paid the same wages as a bookkeeper or a typist, that's what I'm saying. Comparably, she was being paid what a *sighted* person doing her sort of work would be paid. Neither more nor less. The other two girls would have had no reason for enmity."

"How about the men from the warehouse?"

"I don't know what you mean."

"Mrs. Harris was an attractive woman. Did either of them ever make a play for her?"

"I have no idea."

"But they came to the office every Friday to pick up their paychecks."

"That's correct."

"Did you see them on those occasions?"

"Nancy made out their checks. Nancy Houlihan, my bookkeeper."

"But you told me they knew Mrs. Harris."

"Yes, I assume they did."

"Well...Did you ever see them talking to her?"

"Yes."

"But you wouldn't know whether either of them made advances—"

"No, I—"

"And were rebuffed—"

"I wouldn't know."

"Mr. Preston, I think you know what I'm looking for. I'm trying to find out whether anyone Isabel worked with would have the slightest possible reason for—"

"Yes, I know exactly what you're looking for, but I can't help you."

"Okay," Carella said. "Thank you very much, Mr. Preston. I'll call the office on Monday for those addresses."

"Fine."

"Good night, sir."

"Good night," Preston said, and hung up.

Carella sat with his hand on the telephone receiver for several moments. In the Riverhead house, just as in the squadroom, he had phone books for all five sections of the city. He lifted the Isola directory from the floor under the desk and opened it to the D's. He knew he wouldn't get the right time from Nancy Houlihan, but he was eager for more information, and he figured he might stand a chance with Jennie D'Amato. There were seventy-four D'Amatos in the Isola directory, and none of them were Jennies. He opened the Riverhead book. Twelve D'Amatos, no Jennies. In Calm's Point, there were twenty-nine D'Amatos, no Jennies, but a J on Pierce Avenue. He jotted down the number. In the Majesta book, he found another J. D'Amato, and wrote down that number as well. He did not bother looking through the Bethtown directory. It was his contention that no one but retired cops lived in Bethtown, even now that a bridge had been put in.

He dialed the Calm's Point number first, and immediately hit pay dirt.

"Hello?"

"Miss D'Amato, please."

"This is Miss D'Amato."

"Jennie D'Amato?"

"Yes?" Tentative, cautious.

"This is Detective Carella, I believe I spoke to you earlier today."

"Oh." Pause. The pause lengthened. "Yes."

"This *is* the woman who works at Prestige Novelty?"

"Yes."

"Miss D'Amato, I wonder if you can tell me a little about Isabel Harris."

"What do you want to know?"

"I'm primarily interested in how she got along with the other people in the office."

"Fine."

"No arguments or anything?"

"No. Well…"

"Yes?"

"Well, the usual."

"What do you mean by 'the usual'?"

"Well, you know how it is in an office, especially a small one. There'd be irritations every now and then, but nothing—"

"What sort of irritations?"

"Oh, I can hardly remember. Someone would answer the phone and forget to take a message. Or someone would send out for coffee and forget to ask if everybody in the office wanted anything—like that."

"You're the one who normally answers the phone, isn't that right?"

"Yes."

"But sometimes other people did, and they forgot to take messages."

"Well, that only happened once."

"Who answered the phone and forgot to take a message?"

"Isabel."

"And who got irritated?"

"Well…Nancy. Because it was her boyfriend who'd called, and Isabel just forgot to mention it."

"How long ago was this?"

"Last month sometime."

"Were there any *recent* arguments?"

"No, not really."

"What about sending out for coffee? You said—"

"That was me. I sent out for coffee one day and forgot to ask Nancy if she wanted anything, so she blew her stack. That wasn't Isabel."

"How about the two fellows who work at the warehouse?"

"Alex and Tommy, yes."

"She get along with them?"

"Oh yes. As a matter of fact, Alex was always kidding her about wanting…well, you know."

"What do you mean?"

"You know."

"Take her out, do you mean?"

"Well, more than that. You know. Go away for the weekend or something. He was just kidding. He knew she was married."

"How'd she react to these propositions?"

"Well, they weren't propositions. He'd just say, you know, 'Come on, Isabel, let's run away together.' And she'd laugh is all."

"How about Tommy? Did he joke with her, too?"

"Well, they *both* sort of joked with her. Because she was blind, you know. To make her feel good. I guess."

"Did it ever go beyond joking?"

"I don't think so."

"She never..."

"I don't think so. It was just joking, that's all. And maybe, you know, once in a while Alex'd lean over the desk and give her a kiss on the cheek, something like that."

"Tommy, too?"

"No, he never did that."

"But you don't think she was seeing either one of them outside the office?"

"Well, they once in a while walked her to the subway. They only came up on Fridays, you understand, to get their paychecks. Isabel used to leave the office about two-thirty, and they'd be there before then so they could still get to the bank with their checks. So they'd walk her to the subway sometimes."

"Alex and Tommy both?"

"Yes, both of them."

"But you don't think she was dating one of them, do you?"

"I don't know."

"What do you *think*?"

"I think she was very flirtatious for a blind person."

"In what way?"

"Well, the clothes she wore, and the way she sat...I just think she was very flirtatious."

"What sort of clothes, Miss D'Amato?"

"Very revealing clothes. We're none of us prudes at Prestige Novelty, we *couldn't* be and—"

Her voice stopped. For a moment Carella thought they'd been cut off.

"Miss D'Amato?" he said.

"Yes, I'm here."

"You were about to say?"

"Only that, in my opinion, she dressed suggestively."

"But you were saying—"

"That's what I was saying."

Carella did not press it further. Instead, he changed the subject. "Miss D'Amato," he said, "was anyone surprised when Isabel didn't show up for work this morning?"

"We all were. She never missed a day, and she was always on time. The job was important to her. When she didn't show up this morning, Mr. Preston asked me to call and find out if anything was the matter."

"Were those his words?"

"What?"

"Did he say, 'Call and find out if anything's the matter'?"

"I don't recall his exact words. He thought she might be sick or something."

"Did he say that?"

"Yes, he said Isabel had to be sick or something, otherwise she'd be there at work. So he asked me to call."

"And *did* you call?"

"Yes."

"What time was that?"

"About ten-thirty. She usually got to work by ten."

"Did anyone answer the phone?"

"No."

He and Meyer would still have been downstairs at 10:30 waiting outside the building for the ME and the lab crew to arrive. There would have been no one in the apartment but Isabel Harris—dead.

"Did you try again later?"

"Yes, I called at eleven-thirty. A man answered the phone and said he was a police officer. That's when we learned she'd been killed."

"Did the police officer identify himself?"

"Yes, but I forget his name."

That would have been one of the laboratory technicians. Handkerchief tented over the telephone receiver. He'd answered the phone because it was ringing. A ringing phone at the scene of a murder could be the killer calling.

"Did you tell Mr. Preston what happened?"

"Yes."

"What was his reaction?"

"Well, he...he was shocked, of course."

"What else?"

"Just shocked."

"You sounded—"

"No, no."

"As if there might have been something else."

"Well...He was very fond of her."

"Mr. Preston was?"

"Yes."

"So there was more than just shock?"

"He began crying."

"Crying? When you told him Isabel was dead?"

"Yes."

"Then what?"

"He asked me to please leave him alone. So I went out of his office, and in a little while he asked me to call the apartment again, to make sure there wasn't some mistake."

"*Did* you call again?"

"Yes, I did. I got the same police officer. He asked me who was calling, same as he'd done the first time, and I told him this was

Prestige Novelty where Isabel worked, and was he sure she was, you know, dead. He said, yes, she was dead. I thanked him, and then I went to tell Mr. Preston there was no mistake."

"What did he say?"

"He just nodded, that was all."

"Miss D'Amato, when you say Mr. Preston was very fond of Isabel, are you suggesting there was more between them than an employer-employee relationship?"

"I don't know what was between them."

"But something?"

"What Mr. Preston does is his own business."

"Miss D'Amato, do you have any reason to believe there was something going on between Isabel and Mr. Preston?"

"I don't know what was going on."

"But I get the feeling you *think* something was going on."

"Well, I told you, she was very flirtatious. If you didn't know she was blind…Well, she wore these big sunglasses, you know, you couldn't tell she was blind when she was just sitting there and working. And she had a big smile for everybody, especially men, and I guess if you were a man looking for something, you might think Isabel was, you know, being flirtatious and looking for something, too."

"Did Mr. Preston think she was looking for something?"

"I don't know what he thought."

"Did he joke with her the way Alex and Tommy did?"

"No. He never joked with her."

"Then what gives you the idea he might have been interested in her?"

"Look, he's a married man, I don't want to get him in trouble. Isabel's dead, nothing's going to harm her anymore. But he's still alive, and he's married."

"*Was* there some sort of relationship between them, Miss D'Amato?"

"I saw them together once."

"Where?"

"There's a cocktail lounge up the street from the office. I went there after work one day last week, and the two of them were sitting in a booth at the back of the place."

"Did Mr. Preston see you?"

"I don't think so. I went over to the other side of the room... My friend was waiting in a booth on the other side."

"Was your friend someone who knew them, too?"

"No."

"Did you mention to him—"

"Her."

"Did you mention to her that your boss was sitting there with a girl from the office?"

"Yes, I did. Because I was embarrassed, you know, and I was thinking maybe I should leave the place."

"But you didn't leave."

"No, my friend and I stayed to have a drink. They were holding hands."

"Mr. Preston and Isabel?"

"Yes. Look, I don't want to get him in trouble."

"No, no, don't worry about it," Carella said. "These are just routine questions we've got to ask, no one's about to arrest anybody for murder."

"Well, I hope not. There's no crime against...you know."

"I know that."

"Against holding a girl's hand."

"That's right."

"Or even...you know."

"That's right, Miss D'Amato, you've been very helpful, thank you for your time."

"I just don't want to get anybody in trouble," she said.

"Good night, Miss D'Amato."

"Good night," she said.

6

South Edgeheath Road was in a section of Riverhead that was still relatively untouched by urban deterioration. The street itself was rather less rural than its name suggested, but it nonetheless gave the impression of somewhat more stately living than areas as close as two miles away. Apartment buildings lined both sides of the short street, but at the northern end there was a park with a public golf course and even in November there was a sense of wide-open green space and a sky uncluttered by sharp architectural angles.

The street at 9:00 A.M. that Saturday morning seemed only half awake. Carella parked his car, and then walked toward the entrance doors of the redbrick building in which Frank Preston lived. In the lobby he passed a woman in a black coat carrying an empty cloth shopping bag in her right hand. She seemed already cold in anticipation of the weather outside, her face pinched in dire expectation. He searched out Preston's name in the lobby directory, took the elevator up to the fifth floor, went down the corridor to apartment 55, and rang the doorbell.

The woman who opened the door was in her mid-fifties, Carella guessed, brown hair cut in a stylish bob, brown eyes inquisitive behind eyeglasses too small for her face. The face itself gave an impression of angular sharpness, pointed chin and pointed nose, slender oval exaggerated by the narrow glasses and squinting eyes behind them. Carella had once worked with an English cop who told him that in England a person with a "squint" was a person who was cross-eyed. The woman standing in the doorway was not cross-eyed. She was peering out at him from behind narrow eye slits; she was squinting.

"Let me see your badge, please," she said.

He showed her the badge and the ID card. She studied both carefully, and then nodded and said, "Yes, what is it?"

"I'm Detective Carella, I called—"

"Yes, I saw that on the card. What is it, Mr. Carella?"

"I'd like to talk to Frank Preston, if he's here."

"I thought you talked to him last night."

"Are you Mrs. Preston?"

"I am."

"Mrs. Preston, there are some things I'd like to ask him in person. Is he home?"

"He's home. I'll see if he can talk to you."

"Thank you."

She closed the door. He stood in the hallway for several moments. The building was silent. These old buildings with thick walls…The door was opening again.

"Come in," Mrs. Preston said.

The apartment was shaped like an upside-down L. The door opened at the bottom of the long branch of the L, a corridor running its entire length, and then angling to the left at the far end. Carella followed Mrs. Preston down the corridor, passing a kitchen on his left, and then a living room, and then a bedroom on the right, where the short tail of the L began. At the end of this shorter corridor, there was a small room, its door open.

Preston was sitting in an easy chair watching television. He was wearing a maroon bathrobe and brown house slippers. He seemed to be in his early sixties, a massive man with a large head and enormous hands. A thin fringe of white hair clung to his head, around his ears, and the back of his skull. He was bald above that. His eyebrows were white and shaggy over piercing blue eyes. His nose would have been large in any other face, but seemed perfectly proportioned for his. He might have made a good stage actor; most stage actors had large heads and prominent features. One of the early-morning news talk shows was on. Preston rose ponderously from the chair, went immediately to the television set, and turned it off.

"You're here early," he said.

"I didn't want to miss you."

"Why didn't you call first?"

"I was in the neighborhood, I thought I'd just stop by."

"I thought we'd said everything there was to say last night on the phone."

"Few more things I wanted to ask you."

"Then go ahead and ask."

"I'd rather talk to you privately. Mrs. Preston, would you mind…"

"I'll leave you," she said, and immediately turned and walked up the corridor.

Carella closed the door behind him. Preston looked suddenly worried. He fished in the pocket of his robe, came up with a crumpled package of cigarettes, and offered one to Carella. Carella shook his head. Preston put a cigarette between his lips, fished again in the robe, found a matchbook. He struck a match, held the flaming end to his cigarette and then shook the match out and dropped it in an ashtray on the television set. There were two windows in the room. Through them Carella could see across the street and beyond to where the elevated train tracks ran above Barbara Avenue.

"Mr. Preston," Carella said. "I want to ask you about your relationship with Isabel Harris."

"My relationship?"

"Yes, sir."

"What do you mean, my *relationship*? She worked for me."

"Mr. Preston, is it true that you began crying yesterday morning when you learned she was dead?"

"Who told you that?"

"Is it true?"

"Yes."

"Is it also true that you and she met for a drink on at least one occasion?"

"Is there something wrong with that?"

"I didn't say there was anything wrong with it, Mr. Preston. I simply want to know if it's true."

"Yes, it's true."

"When was this?"

"Last week."

"You met her for a drink, is that right?"

"It wasn't the way you make it sound."

"How was it?"

"Something was bothering her. She wanted to talk about it. We went for a drink after work. Period."

"What was bothering her, Mr. Preston?"

"Well, it was something personal."

"Yes, what was it?"

"Well, really, I think that was *her* business, don't you?"

"No, I don't."

"Well, I think it was."

"What was bothering her, Mr. Preston?"

"It doesn't matter, that's not the point. I was merely trying to explain that whatever you were suggesting—"

"What was I suggesting?"

"That Isabel and I were having an affair or something."

"I didn't suggest you were having an affair, Mr. Preston."

"Well, all right. But if we *were*, I wouldn't have taken her to a place just up the street from the office. There was nothing clandestine about our meeting. I had nothing to hide. An employee came to me with a problem, and I was trying to help her."

"Don't you have a private office at Prestige Novelty?"

"Yes. What's that got to—"

"Couldn't you have talked to her there?"

"This was something that couldn't be handled in ten minutes."

"All right, tell me what happened that afternoon."

"She got there at about three, I was waiting for her in a booth at the back of the place. I saw her when she came in and went to meet her, and led her back to the booth."

"What did she say?"

"At first she didn't want to tell me what was bothering her."

"Yes, what was it?"

"Jimmy. Her husband."

"What about him?"

'Well, as I said before—"

"Mr. Preston, both of them are dead, and if whatever was bothering Isabel had anything to do with—"

"No, it didn't."

"How do you know that?"

"Well, I just…I don't think it did."

"How about letting me judge? What was it?"

"Well…She thought he had another woman."

"Ah," Carella said.

"So naturally, it…it troubled her. She was a lovely person, it…troubled her to think her husband was being unfaithful."

"Why'd she think so?"

"She just thought so."

"Intuition, huh?"

"I suppose so."

"But no real reason. She just *assumed* he was playing around, is that right?"

"Well, yes, I suppose so."

"No whispered telephone conversations, no shirts smelling of perfume…"

"No, no."

"And that's what was bothering her. That's why she came to you, and that's why you went for a drink together last week. To discuss the possibility that Jimmy Harris was playing around with another woman."

"Yes."

"What did she expect you to do about it, Mr. Preston?"

"Oh, I don't think she expected me to do anything."

"Then why did she come to you?"

"To…just to talk."

"Nobody she could talk to at the office, I guess."

"I guess not."

"None of the other girls."

"I guess not."

"Just you."

"Well…"

"Was this the first time she came to you with a problem?"

"Yes."

"First time you ever had a drink together?"

"Yes."

"You're sure about that?" Carella said.

"Yes, I'm sure."

"Because, you see," Carella said, "my information indicates otherwise." He paused. He looked into Preston's eyes. He had no information other than what Jennie D'Amato had given him: She had seen Preston and Isabel together once, last week. That's all he had. Period. He was lying, and he was gambling, and the gamble paid off.

"Well...Perhaps we had a drink together once or twice before," Preston said.

"Which was it, Mr. Preston? Once or twice?"

"Twice."

"Now you're sure about *that*, are you?"

"Yes."

Carella raised his eyebrows. That was all he had to do.

"Actually, I suppose it was several times," Preston said.

"How *many* times?"

"Half a dozen times."

"Same little bar up the street?"

"Well...no."

"Another bar?"

"Yes."

"A lot of different bars?"

"Yes."

"Anywhere *besides* a bar?"

"Mr. Carella—"

"Mr. Preston, a man and a woman have been murdered, and I'm trying to find out why. A few minutes ago you told me there was nothing between you and Isabel Harris except an employer-employee relationship. You took her out for a drink because she had a problem she wanted to discuss. Okay, fine. Now you tell me you met her away from the office on at least six occasions—"

"That's all it was."

"Six times, right, that's what you said, half a dozen times. Did you go to bed with her, Mr. Preston?"

"I don't see what—"

"Please answer the question. Did you go to bed with Isabel Harris?"

"Yes."

"Then you *were* having an affair with her."

"I didn't think of it as an affair."

"How *did* you think of it, Mr. Preston?"

"I loved her. I planned to marry her."

"Ah," Carella said, and nodded. "Did your wife know this?"

"No."

"Did Jimmy?"

"No. That's what we talked about last Wednesday. Telling them."

"Then all this stuff about Jimmy having a woman..."

"I made that up," Preston said.

"It was a lie."

"If that's what you want to call it."

"What would *you* call it, Mr. Preston?"

"A lie, I suppose."

"So the reason you met last—when was it?"

"Wednesday afternoon."

"Wednesday afternoon was to discuss how you and Isabel would tell your respective—"

"Yes."

"And what did you decide? What scheme did you hit upon?"

"It wasn't a *scheme*, Mr. Carella, I don't like the way you use the word *scheme*, we weren't *scheming* or *plotting*, we were..."

"Yes, what *were* you doing, Mr. Preston?"

"We were two people in love planning divorce and remarriage."

"After having seen each other a total of half a dozen times?"

"Well—"

"Or was it more than that?"

"Well..."

"Was it?"

"We'd been seeing each other for the past year."

"Ah."

"We loved each other."

"Yes, I understand that. Mr. Preston, where were you on Thursday night between six-thirty and seven-thirty P.M.?"

"Why do you want to know?"

"Because that's when Jimmy Harris was killed."

"I didn't kill him."

"Then tell me where you were."

"I was..."

"Yes?"

"With Isabel."

"Where?"

"At a motel on Culver."

"Did you register under your own name?"

"No."

"What name did you use?"

"I don't remember."

"Mr. Preston, remember. I suggest that you remember. I strongly suggest that you remember right this minute."

"I really *don't* remember. I used a different name each time."

"Then I think you'd better put on some clothes and tell your wife you're coming downtown with me."

"Wait a minute."

"I'm waiting."

"It was Felix something."

"Felix what?"

"Felix…something with a P."

"Take your time."

"Felix Pratt or Pitt—one of the two, I don't remember."

"Are those names you'd used before?"

"Yes."

"All right, what's the name of the motel?"

"The Golden Inn."

"On Culver, did you say?"

"Yes, near the old Hanover Hospital."

"I'm going to call and ask if you were registered there Thursday afternoon. Is that all right with you?"

"Yes."

"Where's your phone?"

"My wife…"

"You keep your wife busy while I make the call. Because if you weren't there on Thursday when Jimmy Harris was having his throat slit, you're coming with me. You understand what I'm saying?"

"I was there."

"Okay, call your wife and tell her I want to use the phone in private."

"All right."

"Go ahead, do it."

"You won't…"

"No, I won't tell her you were playing around."

"Thank you."

"Call her."

Preston went to the door and opened it. He looked out into the corridor, and then turned back to look at Carella again. Carella nodded. Preston went into the corridor and shouted, "Sylvia?"

From somewhere in the apartment she answered, "Yes, Frank?"

"Sylvia, Mr. Carella wants to use the phone...Come in here a minute, will you?"

"Yes, Frank."

"The phone's in the bedroom," Preston said. "Down the hall."

"Thank you," Carella said.

As he walked down the corridor Mrs. Preston came around the bend in the L. "It's in the bedroom," she said.

"Yes, thank you," he said, and went into the bedroom and waited until he saw Preston and his wife entering the television room at the end of the hall. He closed the door then, and went directly to where the phone was resting on a night table alongside the bed. The elevated train rattled along the tracks a block away. Through the windows at the end of the room, he saw it moving against the sky, black against the cold gray of November. There was something oddly evocative about the sight of it. A toy train somewhere? The house in Riverhead when he was a boy. His father's rich laughter.

He watched the train, and forgot for a moment that he was here to learn about murder. He kept watching it until it rumbled into the platform, and then he picked up the telephone receiver and dialed 411 for information. When the operator came on, he asked for the Golden Inn on Culver, and she gave him the number. He dialed it at once. Through the windows he could see the train moving away from the platform. A library. Something. Walking to the library with books under his arm. The elevated train overhead. Snow on the pavement.

"Golden Inn, good morning," a man's voice said.

"Good morning, this is Detective Carella, police department."

"Yes, sir."

"I'd appreciate it if you'd check your register for a couple that may have been there this past Thursday, that would have been November eighteenth."

"Sir?"

"Yes."

"I'll have to call you back on that."

"I'm not at the office."

"Well, it's...How do I know you're a policeman?"

"Call the 87th Squad, here's the number, and ask whoever's there if a Detective Carella works there. That's Frederick 7-8024. Then call me back here as soon as you've checked—the number here is Westmore 6-2275. Have you got both those numbers?"

"Yes, sir."

"Do it fast, please."

"Yes, sir, I'll do it right this minute."

"Good," Carella said, and hung up.

He waited. Another train pulled into the elevated platform. He waited. The train pulled out. He looked at his watch. On the dresser opposite the bed, there was a picture of Frank and Sylvia Preston, taken when they were much younger. There were pictures of grown children, presumably theirs. There was a wedding picture of two young people Carella assumed were also children of the Prestons. The sweep hand on the electric dresser clock wiped the dial relentlessly. Another train pulled into the station. Carella sighed. He waited. The train rumbled out again. Exasperated, he picked up the receiver and dialed the motel.

"Golden Inn, good morning."

"Good morning, this is Detective Carella again. Did you check with the squad?"

"Sir, the phone rang the minute I hung up, I haven't had a chance to—"

"What's your name?" Carella asked.

"Gary Otis."

"All right, Mr. Otis, listen to me," Carella said. "This is a homicide I'm investigating here, and I haven't got time for you to go checking all over the city to see whether I'm a bona fide cop or not. My name is—have you got a pencil?—Stephen Louis Carella, that's Stephen with a p-h, I'm a detective second/grade working out of the 87th Squad in Isola. My shield number is 714-56-32, and my commanding officer's name is Detective-Lieutenant Peter Byrnes. Have you got all that?"

"Well, I…I think so."

"Good. If it turns out I'm a fake cop, you can sue the city. In the meantime, Mr. Otis—"

"How can I sue the city?"

"Mr. Otis, you're irritating me," Carella said.

"I'm sorry, sir, but how can I sue the city? Let's say you're somebody's husband calling to find out—"

"Let's say I'm a real cop who's getting very irritated. Have you got your register there in front of you?"

"Yes, sir, but I think you can understand why I'm not at liberty to reveal the names of any of our guests."

"Mr. Otis, I can go downtown for a court order to look at your register, but that's going to make me even more irritated than I am right now. If I'm forced to do that, and I come over to the Golden Inn and find so much as a cockroach in one of the rooms, I'll call the Department of Health and have the place closed down. So you'd better make sure your establishment is spotless, you'd better make sure it's absolutely pristine if you're asking me to go all the way downtown for a court order on a Saturday morning."

"Is that a threat of some kind, Mr. Carella?"

"That is whatever you choose to consider it, Mr. Otis. What do you say?"

"There are no cockroaches in the rooms here."

"Fine. In that case, I'll see you later with the court order."

"But if you're really a cop—"

"I'm really a cop, Mr. Otis."

"And if this is really a homicide—"

"It's really a homicide. Mr. Otis, why are you a desk clerk? Why aren't you a noted Philadelphia lawyer?"

"I'm not a desk clerk. I *own* the Golden Inn."

"Ah," Carella said. "I see."

"So of course I'm eager to protect my guests."

"Of course. Mr. Otis, did you register a Mr. and Mrs. Pratt Thursday afternoon? Or a Mr. and Mrs. Pitt? Felix would have been the first name."

"Just a moment."

Carella waited.

"Yes, I have a Mr. and Mrs. Felix Pitt."

"Were you at the desk when they registered?"

"I don't recall. Oh, wait a minute. Was she the blind girl?"

"Yes," Carella said.

"Yes, I registered them. Beautiful woman, married to a much older man. I didn't realize she was blind at first. She was wearing very large sunglasses, I had no idea she was blind. Until he led her to the elevator, of course, and then I realized."

"What time did they check in?"

"The register entry doesn't indicate that."

"Would you remember?"

"Sometime in the late afternoon."

"And when did they check out?"

"At about eight o'clock, I guess it was. I'd stepped out for a bite to eat, and when I came back, they were leaving. He paid me in cash. I remember."

"Thank you, Mr. Otis," Carella said.

"I hope you understand why—"

"Yes, I understand. Thank you," Carella said, and hung up.

He sat with his hand on the receiver for quite some time. He had just confirmed that Isabel Harris and Frank Preston had indeed spent at least an afternoon and evening together in a motel on Thursday. Locked as they'd been in blind passionate embrace, so to speak, neither of the pair could have scooted uptown to Hannon Square to slit the throat of Jimmy Harris between 6:30 and 7:30 P.M. At 8:00, in fact, they had been seen leaving the establishment by none other than Gary Otis the Golden Innkeeper. Isabel Harris had probably got to her apartment just a few minutes before Carella knocked on her door. By that time her husband had been dead for at least two hours, and possibly longer.

He thought back to the question he'd asked her on the night of the murder, thought back to the specific question: "Are you involved with another man?" The terse answer: "No." Liars didn't surprise him. In the murder business, there were lots of liars. Tears didn't surprise him, either. You sometimes got tears for somebody who'd been hated for years. They came unbidden, the response as primitive as the howl of the first man who pulled a burning stick from a fire. He rose, went down the hallway, and thanked the Prestons for the use of the telephone. Preston's eyes met his questioningly. Carella nodded briefly, feeling like a conspirator.

7

The two coffins were angled into the chapel so that a passage ran between them, and those coming to pay their respects could walk past both biers simultaneously. There were white men and black men in the funeral home, chatting in whispers in the carpet-covered lobby outside, or sitting in the chapel itself on folding wooden chairs, or kneeling in prayer at the wrought-iron railings behind which the coffins rested on sawhorses draped in satin.

Sophie Harris sat on a chair in the first row, dressed entirely in black—black shoes and stockings, black dress and black veiled hat. She reminded Carella of the family women he had known as a boy, distant widowed aunts or cousins whom he had never seen wearing anything but black. He sat beside Sophie now, and she turned to look at him, and then turned away again.

"Mrs. Harris," he said, "could we step outside a moment, please?"

"I got nothing more to say to you," she said.

"Let's not argue here," he said.

She looked at the coffins.

"I'd like to talk to you," he said. "Would you please step outside?"

Reluctantly, she rose from her chair and walked silently through the open arched doorway into the lobby. Carella followed immediately behind her.

"You satisfied about Charlie?" she whispered. Her mouth was tight, her hands clenched one over the other at her waist.

"I had to talk to him," Carella said.

"Why? I told you he didn't do it."

"He was a possibility."

"You still think he's a possibility?"

"No."

"You hassled him cause he's black," Sophie said.

"No. That isn't true, Mrs. Harris. I *didn't* hassle him, I questioned him. And only because he might have killed your son and daughter-in-law."

She looked into his face.

"I want to find whoever killed them," Carella said.

She kept looking at him.

"Believe me."

"All right," she said, and nodded.

"I have nothing," he said. "Nothing at all. I need your help. I need you to remember anyone Jimmy or his wife might have argued with, or—"

"No," Sophie said, and shook her head. "No one. There was no one."

"Or even disagreed with. Sometimes a person will take offense at something, and allow—"

"No one. You didn't know Jimmy, he never said a harsh word to anyone in his life."

"Mrs. Harris, whoever killed Isabel seemed to be searching for something. Do you have any idea what it might have been?"

"No."

"Did Jimmy ever mention any hidden money or jewelry, anything like that?"

"No."

"Some people try to hide their valuables from burglars—"

"He had no valuables to hide."

"Mrs. Harris, was Jimmy involved with anyone who had a criminal record?"

"No," Sophie said, and immediately asked, "would you put that question to a white man?"

"Listen," Carella said. "Let's get off that, okay? Your son was brutally murdered, that's the worst crime there is. I want to know if he knew any criminals. That's a logical question, black *or* white, so let's cut it out." He had raised his voice, and mourners in the lobby were turning to look at him. He lowered his voice to a whisper again and said, "*Did* he know anyone with a criminal record?"

"No. Not that he ever spoke of directly."

"What do you mean? Did he speak of criminal friends *in*directly?"

"No, he never spoke of no criminal friends."

"Then what did you mean by the word 'directly'?"

"My son would never do nothing wrong in his life," Sophie said.

"Mrs. Harris, you just said he never spoke directly of any criminal friends. Now what does that mean?"

"Nothing."

"Did your son ever mention some sort of criminal activity in which he was involved?"

"He wasn't involved in no criminal activity."

"Was he *planning* some sort of criminal activity?"

“I don’t know. I honestly don’t know. He was a troubled person.”

“How? Troubled how?”

“The nightmares.”

“What nightmares?”

“From when he first got home from Fort Mercer.”

“Fort Mercer?”

“The Army hospital there. Upstate. Near the prison.”

“What kind of nightmares?”

“He’d wake up hollering. I’d go in his room, he’d be sitting up in the middle of his bed, staring into the darkness like he could see. I’d take him in my arms, he’d be covered with cold sweat. I’d say, ‘Jimmy, what is it? What is it, son?’ Nothing. No answer. He’d be shaking in my arms.”

“Did he ever mention these nightmares when he was awake?”

“No. But Isabel told me he was still having them.”

“When did she tell you that?”

“Just recently.”

“Mrs. Harris, you said you honestly didn’t know if Jimmy was planning some sort of criminal activity. Is it possible that he was?”

“I guess.”

“Did he say anything about it to you?”

“He said he was going to make them rich.”

“Who?”

“Him and Isabel.”

“Did he say how?”

“Mr. Carella, I got to tell you the truth. I think he was maybe planning something would be against the law.”

“Did he say that?”

“No.”

“Then what makes you think…?”

“Well, why else would he need his old Army buddy?”

"What do you mean?"

"He told me he'd contacted one of his buddies."

"An Army buddy?"

"I guess he meant an Army buddy."

"Who?"

"I don't remember his name."

"Did he say why he'd contacted him?"

"He said the man was going to help him and Isabel get rich."

"Did he say how?"

"No."

"Then why do you figure he was planning something against the law?"

"I don't know why. Maybe it's cause soldiers are trained to use guns."

"But your son never actually said—"

"No, he didn't."

"Well," Carella said, and shrugged. He was thinking it sounded like a movie—a pair of old Army pals getting together to knock over a bank or a Las Vegas casino. He supposed it was possible; anything was possible. But he doubted it. Still—it was possible, what the hell.

"Thank you," he said, "you've been very helpful."

But he wasn't sure she had been.

The squadroom looked rather like a cathedral that Saturday morning. Don't laugh. November sunshine slanted through the wire-mesh grilles on the long windows, and shafts of golden light touched desktops and typewriters. Dust motes sparkled in the fanning rays of the sun. The radio on Genero's desk was playing organ music. Carella expected a religious miracle, but none came.

Genero was typing.

He had bought himself a paperback pocket dictionary and was looking up words. Repeatedly, he glanced from typewriter keyboard to open dictionary. His stop-and-go typing irritated Carella; it was obscene to be typing in church. Besides, there were no more miracles in the world, and the case was getting staler than yesterday's bagels.

The organ music swelled into the squadroom. Carella felt like going to confession. He had not been to confession since he stopped going to church. That was when he was fifteen. Coincidentally, that was also when he lost his virginity on the roof of an apartment building in Riverhead, with a girl named Suzie Ryan, who was Irish. Suzie was seventeen. Woman of the world. She went to the same church Carella did. After his rooftop awakening, he figured he should go to confession and mention that he had sinned. Then he wondered if the priest would ask him who his sinful partner had been. He knew they could see your face in the dark there. The priest would know it was Stephen Louis Carella who had sinned, and then he would want to know who the willing young lady had been, and Carella would then have to implicate Suzie Ryan, who had been generous and passionate and whom he would have followed into the mouth of a cannon at that budding stage of his career. He wondered what to do. He decided not to go to confession. He also decided never to go to church again, but that had nothing to do with Suzie. He decided not to go to church because church put him to sleep. His father said, "Why don't you go to church no more?" Carella answered, "Why don't you, Pop?" His father said, "Never mind."

He realized now that if only he hadn't stopped going to church when he was fifteen, he could pray to God for a miracle or at least a clue, and all his problems would go up the chimney. Instead, the radio was playing organ music and Genero was typing in a tempo out of meter with the fat chords that floated out on the air, and Carella not only did not have a clue, he also did not have an inkling of where to go next.

He decided to call Fort Mercer.

His reasoning had nothing to do with sound deduction. It had only to do with desperation. Before talking to Sophie, he had known next to nothing about the dead man. In any homicide it was essential to learn how the victim had spent his last twenty-four hours—where he'd gone, the people he'd seen, the events that had taken place. He knew where Isabel Harris had spent at least a portion of the twenty-four hours before her death; she had spent them in bed with Frank Preston. But all he knew about Jimmy was that he'd left the house at his usual hour in the morning, and presumably walked his usual beggar's route on Hall Avenue throughout the day, and most likely stopped at a bar, as usual, before heading home after the rush hour.

Carella had neglected to ask Isabel whether Jimmy frequented the same bar each day. A mistake. Maybe a bad one. There was no Isabel to ask anymore, but there existed nonetheless the possibility that Jimmy had met someone in the bar, argued with someone, antagonized someone—who the hell knew? The bar was still a mystery, solely because of Carella's oversight. It bothered him that he had goofed. He fretted about it, but he didn't agonize over it. Instead, he examined the two pieces of information he now possessed, a pair of seemingly unrelated fragments that changed Jimmy Harris from a corpse into a living, breathing human being.

At the moment there was nothing he could do about the first piece of information. If Jimmy Harris had indeed contacted an old Army buddy with some sort of get-rich-quick scheme, possibly illegal, Carella had no way of ascertaining this without talking to the old Army buddies. Right now he knew nothing about Jimmy's Army career, except that he'd been in the 2nd Squad's Alpha Fire Team and he'd been blinded in action. If he got lucky,

Captain McCormick would get back to him before Monday with the service information he'd requested. He doubted he would get lucky. But there was one *other* thing he had learned from Sophie Harris.

Her son was having nightmares.

Carella dialed "O" for operator, and asked for the area code for Fort Mercer. The operator said she didn't have a town called Fort Mercer. Carella said it was upstate someplace near Castleview Prison. She said she didn't know where Castleview Prison was. He told her it was in Rawley. She gave him an area code, and he dialed first the number 1, and then the area code, and then the numerals 555, and then the numerals 1212. By that time he'd forgotten why he was dialing this long succession of numbers, and he'd also forgotten his shield number, his social security number, and his middle initial. Another operator said, "Information, what city?" and Carella told her he thought it was near Rawley, and said he was trying to reach Fort Mercer. The operator said, "That's in Paxton, sir," and then said, "I have several listings for Fort Mercer, which one did you wish?"

"The hospital," he said.

"I've got a General Hospital and an Evacuation Hospital."

"Let's try the General Hospital."

"Do you wish to write the number down, sir?"

"Yes, please," Carella said.

"963-7047," she said.

"Thank you," Carella said. "That's 963…"

But she'd already hung up. He sighed, dialed the number 1, and then the area code, and then the numerals 963, and then the numerals 7047. The phone rang. Across the room, Genero, whose tastes were catholic, switched the radio to a rock-and-roll station. Up in Paxton, the phone was still ringing. Carella wondered if the hospital was closed.

"Hospital," a man's voice said.

"Is this the Fort Mercer General Hospital?" Carella asked.

"Yes, sir, it is."

"This is Detective Carella, 87th Squad, Isola. I'm calling in regard to a patient you had there some ten years ago. I wonder if I could talk to someone who—"

"Who did you want to talk to, sir?"

"Whoever might have detailed knowledge of the patient."

"Well, sir…How would I know who that might be, sir?"

"Is there anyone there who goes back ten years?"

"Yes, sir, I'm sure there is. But…Sir, this is a very big facility, sir, I really wouldn't know where to connect you."

"May I speak to whoever is in command of the facility?"

"That would be General Wrigley, sir."

"Could you connect me, please?"

"Just one moment, sir."

Carella waited. A woman's voice came on the phone almost instantly.

"General Wrigley's office."

"This is Detective Carella of the 87th Squad in Isola. May I please speak to the general?"

"I'm sorry, sir, he isn't in today."

"Perhaps you can help me," Carella said.

"I'll try, sir."

"We're investigating a homicide in which the victim was once a patient at Fort Mercer. I'm trying to learn whatever I can about him."

"When was he a patient here?"

"Ten years ago."

"Mm," the woman said.

"I know that's a long time ago."

"Yes, sir, it is."

"But I'm sure your records go back that far."

"Yes, sir, they do, that's not the problem."

"What is the problem?"

"Sir, I really don't think this is something that can be handled on the telephone."

"I was trying to save myself a trip upstate. This is a homicide."

"Well, I'll put you through to Records."

"Thank you."

"Just hang on," she said. "It'll sound as if I'm hanging up, but I'm only transferring the call."

"Thank you."

Again, he waited. He decided that homicide was an intrusion. Nobody wanted intrusions in their lives, nobody wanted you calling from the big city to ask about a man who'd passed this way ten years ago. Hell with that. There was a hospital to run here, a facility. Lots of sick people here. I'll put you through to Records. Records might be interested. Records dealt with history, the distant past and the more recent. I'll put you through to Records because we here among the quick albeit sick just can't be bothered, you see, with corpses who once lived in the neighborhood.

"Records, Sergeant Hollister speaking."

"This is Detective Carella, 87th Squad, I'm looking for some information about a homicide victim."

Sergeant Hollister whistled. "Shoot," he said.

"The name is James Harris, he was in the Fort Mercer hospital ten years ago."

"Any middle name?"

"Randolph."

"This'll take some time," Hollister said. "Let me get back to you."

"The number here is Frederick 7-8024. But, Sergeant…"

"Yes, sir?"

"I'm really more interested in talking to someone who might have known him while he was there. I mean, rather than you reading to me from his records."

"Well, let me see what the records indicate, okay, sir? I'll get back to you in a little while."

"Sergeant, this is a homicide."

"Yes, sir, I understand that."

"Thank you, I'll be waiting for your call."

There was a click on the line. Carella looked up at the wall clock. The time was 10:37 A.M.

"How do you spell vehicular?" Genero asked.

"You've got the dictionary right there, just look it up," Carella said.

"How can I look it up if I don't know how to spell it?"

"Well, you know it starts with a V, don't you?"

"Yeah, but *then* what?" Genero said.

Carella looked up at the clock again.

The time was 10:38 A.M.

The call from upstate did not come till a few minutes past 11:00. By then Carella had called the IS for a routine check on Charles C. Clarke, and had finished typing his updated reports in triplicate. The IS had promised to get back to him at once. He expected he would hear from them by Monday unless he called them again later in the day. He also expected he would have to call the hospital back. In America, and maybe throughout the whole wide world for all he knew, nobody ever got anything done unless you called twice. And then followed the second call with a letter. And then called again a week after the follow-up letter. He suspected it had been this way in ancient Rome, just before the barbarian hordes broke through the northern barricades and rode their ponies into the streets. Senators picking up the skirts of their togas and running for their lives, clutching unanswered tablets to their chests. Secretaries running along behind them, chewing gum, clothes in disarray.

"87th Squad, Carella."

"This is Colonel Anderson, Fort Mercer Hospital."

"Yes, sir," Carella said.

"A Sergeant Hollister in Records called to say you were interested in a patient I treated several years back."

"Yes, sir, a man named James Harris."

"Hollister said he'd been murdered, is that true?"

"Yes, it is."

"I'm sorry to hear that," Anderson said. "What is it you want to know, Mr. Carella?"

"This will sound ridiculous."

"Try me."

"I was talking to his mother this morning, and she told me he was having nightmares."

"Yes?"

"I'd like to talk to anyone who might know something about them."

"The nightmares?"

"Yes, the nature of the nightmares."

"I'm a plastic surgeon, I didn't have anything to do with his mental rehabilitation. He'd been through three other hospitals before he reached us, you understand. Our goal was to prepare him for civilian life after the terrible trauma he'd suffered. The wound was a particularly vicious one, requiring a great deal of reconstructive surgery. But it was the psychiatric team who worked toward adjusting him realistically to his new situation. They're the ones who'd know about the nightmares."

"Who headed up the team, can you tell me that?"

"That would have been Colonel Konigsberg."

"I wonder if I could speak to him."

"He's no longer here. He was transferred to Walter Reed in Washington, you might try him there. That would be Colonel Paul—well, wait a minute, he was a colonel when he left here, he might well be a brigadier general by now."

"Colonel Anderson, where would the psychiatric records be? Would they still be there at Fort Mercer?"

"I would imagine so, yes."

"If I drove up there this afternoon, could I have a look at them?"

"That could be arranged."

Carella looked up at the wall clock. "Would two o'clock be all right?"

"Yes, fine. I'll leave word at the gate to pass you through. Could I have your full name, please?"

"Detective Stephen Carella. That's C-a-r-e-l-l-a. And it's Stephen with a p-h."

"The General Hospital is to the right of the redbrick administration building. When you come through the main gate, keep to your right and park in the oval marked for visitors. There's a receptionist just inside the entrance doors, she'll tell you how to find me. My office is on the second floor."

"I'll be there at two," Carella said.

"Yes, fine," Anderson said. "I'll see you then."

Carella hung up, looked at the clock again, and then checked the duty chart on the wall. Today was supposed to be Meyer's day off; he called him at home anyway. Sarah Meyer answered the phone, recognized his voice, and said, "Oh no."

"Is he in the middle of something?"

"We're going to a wedding."

"What time?"

"No trick questions, Steve," Sarah said. "I'll put him on."

Carella waited. When Meyer came on the line, he said at once, "No way."

"I'm driving up to Fort Mercer," Carella said.

"Where's Fort Mercer?"

"Up near Castleview."

"Have a nice drive."

"Who's getting married?"

"Irwin the Vermin."

"Your nephew?"

"My nephew. Only he grew up to be a mensch, can you imagine? Steve, I can't go with you, I'm sorry. I still have to pick up my tuxedo."

"Will you have time to make just one stop?"

Meyer sighed.

"Meyer?"

"Yeah, yeah. Where do you want me to go?"

"Sam Grossman told me there was soil under Jimmy Harris's fingernails. Check out the apartment, will you? Maybe he buried whatever the killer was looking for."

"Where do you bury something in an apartment?"

"Did you notice any window boxes?"

"I wasn't looking for any."

"Well, check out the sills, and if there aren't any boxes, you might go down to the backyard, see if anything's been buried recently."

"That's a nice job for a person on a Saturday when he has to get dressed for a wedding."

"What time is the wedding?"

"Three o'clock."

"That gives you almost four hours."

"To go digging up a backyard, and get my tuxedo, and shower and shave, and drive the whole family to Adams Boulevard. Why are you going to Fort Mercer?"

"Jimmy Harris was having nightmares."

"So am I," Meyer said, and hung up. Carella smiled and put the receiver back on its cradle.

The phone rang again almost at once. It was the IS calling back to say that Charles C. Clarke had no criminal record.

The apartment was heavy with the stillness of death.

Someone had swept up the garbage that was strewn over the kitchen floor, but the rest of the place was still a shambles. Meyer wondered who would eventually clean it up. The chalked outline of Isabel's body marked the place near the refrigerator where she'd lain crookedly in death. Sooner or later someone would wash the kitchen floor, wash away the chalked outline and the bloodstains on the linoleum. Sooner or later someone else would rent the apartment. One day the new tenant would casually mention that a murder had taken place in this kitchen: "Found the woman right here near the refrigerator, her throat was slit." "No kidding?" his visitor would say, and then they would go on to discuss the latest baseball standings.

For now, Isabel Harris was vaguely defined by her chalked outline on the floor and the dried blood on the linoleum. And in the other rooms, her torn furniture and scattered clothing. He had read someplace that blind people put clothing of different colors in different drawers, so that they would not inadvertently wear a green tie with a purple shirt, or a red blouse with an orange skirt. They identified clothing, too, by different stitches sewed into hems or shirttails, their fingers becoming eyes, touch becoming sight. He could not imagine being blind. He thought he would kill himself if suddenly he lost his eyesight.

Above the kitchen sink, there was a small window covered with frost; the apartment was cold, the super had undoubtedly turned off all the radiators the moment the police were gone—waste not, want not, and no sense making the *farshtinkener* Arabs richer than they already were. With the heel of his gloved hand Meyer rubbed at the frost, clearing a rough circle through which he saw first the brick wall of the building opposite and then the outside windowsill.

There was a flower box on the sill.

The dried and withered stalks of last summer's blooms lay like casualties across the frozen soil in the box. Meyer tried the window; more often than not, they were painted shut in city apartments. It opened easily. He took the box in off the sill, put it on the countertop, and closed the window again. From the tangle of forks, knives, and spoons on the kitchen floor, he picked up a tablespoon and began digging at the soil in the box. The crusted upper layer resisted his initial thrusts, and then suddenly gave way to softer earth. Someone had been digging here recently; the soil was loose, the spoon moved it without effort. He took off his gloves and shoved his hands deep into the soil. Nothing. He looked around for something he could dump the soil onto or into, opened the door to the cabinet under the sink, and found a nest of brown paper bags. Tearing one of these open, he spread it on the countertop and began spooning earth onto it.

In a little while the window box was empty.

There had been nothing in it but soil.

Meyer shoveled a spoonful of that soil into an evidence envelope for transmission to Grossman at the lab. Then he left the apartment and went down to the backyard.

8

The General Hospital at Fort Mercer was built just before the Spanish-American War. Carella was so informed by the WAC sergeant who was leading him to the room where the records were kept. He had no reason to doubt her word; the place *looked* turn-of-the-century, with high vaulted ceilings and thick walls, windows that rose from the floor to twice a man's height. They had taken the elevator down from Colonel Anderson's office and were walking through a ground-level corridor that resembled a colonnade running along one side of a cloister. Beyond the windows were a bloomless garden and a lawn that rolled in hillock after hillock to the River Harb below. In the distance, on a point of land jutting out from the shore, Carella could see the gray walls of Castleview State Penitentiary. He knew a lot of people in that prison, all of them convicted felons. They had been, so to speak, business associates.

The sergeant was an attractive blonde—in her early thirties, he guessed—wearing her olive-drab uniform with all the authority of a fashion model, low heels clicking rhythmically on the tiled floor of the corridor, hips swaying, blue eyes catching the flat November light and reflecting it.

"Makes you think they were *expecting* the damn war, doesn't it?" she said. "Otherwise, why would they have built *two* hospitals here? You know what they call *this* one, don't you?"

"Yes. General Hospital."

"Do you know the joke?"

"No, what joke is that?"

"Is there one for the enlisted men?"

Carella looked at her.

"The enlisted men," she said.

"Oh. *General* Hospital."

"Right, you've got it," she said, and laughed. Carella suddenly wondered if she was flirting. He decided she wasn't. But maybe she was. No, he decided she wasn't.

"Here we are," she said, and stepped swiftly to a massive wooden door on the right-hand side of the corridor, and opened it.

Carella followed her into a huge room crammed with metal filing cabinets. Again there were vaulted ceilings and tall windows streaming light. The cabinets were arranged in rows, like cemetery markers, stretching from the door to the farthest end of the room. The task of finding James Harris's medical history in this room that echoed filing cabinets suddenly seemed overwhelming. Not five minutes ago Colonel Anderson had told him the sergeant would help him locate whatever he needed. Now Carella wondered if anything less than a full platoon could manage the job. His dismay must have showed on his face.

"Don't let it scare you," she said. "It's really pretty well organized. We'll find the file in a jiffy, and then I'll help you wade through it. Do I call you Detective Carella or Mr. Carella, or what?"

"What do I call you?" he said.

"Janet."

"Steve."

"Hi."

"Hi."

They might have had trouble finding the file in the jiffy Janet had promised, if it weren't for James Harris's middle name. Over the years since the hospital was built, no fewer than forty-seven James Harrises had passed this way, the victims of no fewer than four wars; it had been a busy time for America. But only two of the wounded soldiers were named James *Randolph* Harris, and one of them was white and the other was black, so that ended the five-minute search. The folder was thicker than the search had been, if girth could be measured against minutes like apples against oranges.

Janet led Carella to another wooden door and then through it into an adjoining smaller room that seemed almost monastic—severe white walls, small windows, a simple wooden table with high-backed chairs around it. He realized all at once that many of his references today were ecclesiastical in nature: the squadroom resembling a cathedral, the corridor a cloister, and now a room he equated with a monastery cell. He all but expected a tonsured man in a brown hooded habit to come through the other door carrying a manuscript to be illuminated.

"This is my favorite place in the entire hospital," Janet said, and pulled a chair from the table, and sat.

"How shall we work this?" he asked.

"Depends on what you're looking for," she said, and crossed her legs. She had good legs. He wondered again if she was flirting. And decided she wasn't.

"I'm looking for anything that mentions the nightmares Harris was having."

"Okay," she said. "Let's split the file. You work forward from the back, I'll work toward the middle from the front. How does that sound?"

"Fine," Carella said.

"Has anyone ever told you your eyes slant downward?" Janet said.

"Yes."

"They do."

"I know."

"Mm," she said, and nodded, and smiled briefly.

"Well," he said, "let's get to work. I really appreciate your helping me this way."

"Orders is orders," she said, and smiled again.

They worked in silence, sampling the file as they might have vintage wine—tasting, discarding, tasting again, cup by cup, page by page. It was Janet who came across the first mention of the nightmares.

"Here's something," she said.

The something was a memo from a Major Ralph Lemarre to Lieutenant Colonel Paul Konigsberg regarding a dream related to the major by Pfc. James Randolph Harris.

It is shortly before Christmas.

Jimmy's mother and father are decorating a Christmas tree. Jimmy and four other boys are sitting on the living-room floor, watching. Jimmy's father tells the boys they must help him decorate the tree. The boys refuse. Jimmy's mother says they don't have to help if they're tired. Christmas ornaments begin falling from the tree, crashing to the floor, making loud noises that startle Jimmy's father. He loses his balance on the ladder and falls to the floor, landing on the shards of the broken Christmas tree ornaments and accidentally cutting himself. The carpet is green, his blood seeps into it. He bleeds to death on the carpet. Jimmy's mother is crying. She lifts her skirt to reveal a penis.

"What do you make of it?" Janet asked.

"I can't even figure out my *own* dreams," Carella said.

"Let's see what Major Lemarre thinks."

The major thought little or nothing at this point. This was the first time the dream had been related to him, and there was no indication in his memo that he believed it would become a recurring nightmare. His only comment related to information he had gleaned from previous interviews with Jimmy. The boy's father had been killed in an automobile accident when Jimmy was six, and his mother had taken on the responsibility of raising the family alone. Major Lemarre speculated that the part of the dream attributing male sex organs to a female might have had something to do with Sophie Harris becoming both mother *and* father to young Jimmy.

"Well," Janet said, and shrugged. It was clear that the interpretation of dreams left her cold.

Carella understood her position. He had grown up in a family where dreams were thought of as omens of events to come. If you dreamt that seven men were carrying eight bales of cotton up four steps, then you had best run to your local bookie and bet 784 for that day's number. If you dreamt that Aunt Clara fell off the roof, it would be a good idea to contact your neighborhood mortician or at least reserve a room at the nearest hospital. Nobody in Carella's family thought of dreams as clues to personality or behavior. It was only when he joined the police force, or more specifically when he became a detective, that he began to think of dreams in a different way. It was a police psychiatrist who told him that a recurring dream could be thought of as a dimly lighted tunnel to the past. The patient and the analyst, working together, could illuminate that tunnel, reconstruct whatever trauma was causing the persistent dream, and thereby free the patient to deal with it on a realistic level rather than a fixated one. None of which made too much sense to Carella at the time.

He was, however, the sort of man who, once presented with an idea, would not let go of it until he understood it to his satisfaction. This did not necessarily mean understanding it completely. He still didn't know exactly how Ballistics figured out the rifling twist or the number of lands and grooves on a suspect bullet, but he had a fair working knowledge of how they went about it, and that was enough. Similarly, he thought he understood the psychoanalytic process as well as a layman might. He did not subscribe to the theory that all homicides were rooted in the distant past; he would leave such speculation to California mystery writers who seemed to believe that murder was something brewed in a pot for half a century, coming to a boil only when a private detective needed a job. The last time Carella had met a private detective investigating a homicide was never.

But this morning Sophie told him that her son had recently contacted an old Army buddy. All right, that was a link to the past, a link to a man Jimmy had not seen, literally, for the past ten years. If he was going back into his past for something—and Sophie seemed to believe it was for assistance with an illegal enterprise—then perhaps Carella should go back into the past as well. Which is why he was here today. To explore that dimly lighted tunnel, to learn whether or not anyone here at the hospital had been able to unravel the nightmares that caused Jimmy to wake up sweating and trembling in the night.

The next mention of the dream came in a report dated six days after Lemarre's initial memo. The dream was identical in every respect. When Lemarre asked Jimmy what he thought of the fact that in the dream his mother had a penis, Jimmy answered, "Well, it's a dream. Anything can happen in a dream."

"Yes, but she has a penis, isn't that right?"

"That's right."

"Do you think of her as a particularly masculine person?"

"My mother? You got to be kidding."

"Then why does she have a penis?"

"It's a dream," Jimmy answered.

At their next session, two days later, Lemarre asked Jimmy if it would be all right to tape-record what they talked about. Jimmy wanted to know why, and Lemarre said it would enable him to transcribe their sessions word for word later on, and study what was said, and perhaps reach some meaningful conclusions. Jimmy gave his permission. There followed in the file at least fifty closely spaced typewritten pages dealing exclusively with Jimmy's exploration of the dream that continued to haunt him night after night. Janet lost interest after they'd waded through twenty pages of the transcript.

"Would you like some coffee?" she asked.

"I could use a cup."

"I think I know where I can find some," she said, and winked. "Did you plan on going back tonight?"

"What?" he said.

"To the city, I mean."

"I guess so, yes."

"Because with all this stuff," she said, indicating the mountain of papers on the table, "we're liable to be here all afternoon."

"You know, I think I can manage the rest of it alone, if you—"

"No, no, I'm enjoying it," she said. "Let me get the coffee, okay?"

"Sure. But seriously, if you want to go back upstairs…"

"I'm enjoying it," she said, and her eyes met his, and he knew now that she *was* flirting and he didn't know quite what to do about it.

"Well...sure," he said. "Fine."

"I'll get the coffee," she said.

"Fine."

"And then later you can decide about going back to the city."

"All right."

She nodded. She turned then and went out through the door opposite the one they'd entered. He caught a brief glimpse of the corridor outside, the windows leaping with November sunlight. She closed the door behind her, and he listened to her heels clicking into the distance. He looked at his watch. The time was 3:10 P.M. He turned back to the transcript.

Exploration upon exploration.

Is the Christmas tree a Christmas tree? Is this *really* your father? Where does he cut himself when he falls? Are you sure your mother has a penis? Over and over again, the same questions and virtually the same answers until the nightmare took on nightmare proportions for Carella himself, making him as eager to be rid of it as had been Jimmy and Lemarre.

He looked at his watch again. It was almost 3:30, he wondered where Janet had gone for the coffee. He wondered what her last name was. Colonel Anderson had said only, "The sergeant will take you downstairs and give you a hand finding what you need." Maybe the colonel had run into his sergeant in the hallway and demanded that she return upstairs to his office to resume her sergeantly duties.

Carella found it difficult to think of her as a sergeant. A sergeant was Sergeant Murchison who manned the muster desk at the Eight-Seven. A sergeant was any one of a dozen hairbags who rode in radio motor patrol cars checking on patrolmen. Janet

Whatever-Her-Name was not a sergeant, definitely not a sergeant. He really did find it extremely difficult to think of her that way. He wondered why he was thinking of her at *all*, in any way, shape or form. Then he wondered how the words "shape" and "form" had crept into his mind as regarded the sergeant, and he decided he'd been reading too many psychiatric reports and was beginning to examine with undue scrutiny his own id, ego or libido, as the case might be. He sighed and turned back to the file.

The first words he saw were "major breakthrough." These were Lemarre's words referring to a session that had occurred a month and a half before Jimmy was released from the hospital and simultaneously discharged from the Army. The major showed no appreciation of the fact that he had inadvertently used the word "major" to describe the breakthrough. Carella smiled, and wondered what Lemarre might have thought of Janet's little joke about the *General* Hospital. There was Janet again, but *where* was Janet again? She had undoubtedly gone to Colombia for the coffee. He delayed reading about the major breakthrough; once he solved the mystery of Jimmy's Christmas nightmare, he would have to climb into his car and start the long drive back to the city. He delayed, he delayed, he delayed for three minutes. When he began reading the word-for-word transcript, the time was 3:35.

LEMARRE: All right, Jimmy, let's talk about this one more time.
HARRIS: What for? I'm sick to death of talkin' about that.
LEMARRE: So am I.
HARRIS: So let's forget it, Doc.
LEMARRE: No, let's not forget it. If *we* forget it, *you* won't be able to forget it.
HARRIS: Shit.
LEMARRE: Tell me about the Christmas tree.
HARRIS: It's a Christmas tree.

LEMARRE: What kind?

HARRIS: A regular Christmas tree.

LEMARRE: And your mother and father are decorating it, is that right?

HARRIS: Right, right.

LEMARRE: And you and your friends are sitting on the floor watching them.

HARRIS: Right.

LEMARRE: How many of you?

HARRIS: Five, countin' me.

LEMARRE: Just sitting there, watching.

HARRIS: On the couch, yeah.

LEMARRE: You said on the floor.

HARRIS: What?

LEMARRE: You said you were all sitting on the floor.

HARRIS: The floor, the couch, what's the difference?

LEMARRE: Well, which was it?

HARRIS: The floor.

LEMARRE: In the living room.

HARRIS: Mm.

LEMARRE: In your living room, is that right?

HARRIS: Right, right, I told you.

LEMARRE: And how old are you in the dream?

HARRIS: I don't know. Eighteen, nineteen. Something like that.

LEMARRE: But your father died when you were six.

HARRIS: Yeah.

LEMARRE: Yet in the dream you're a teenager watching him decorate the tree.

HARRIS: Well, it's a dream, right?

LEMARRE: There was a carpet on the floor, you said.

HARRIS: A green carpet.

LEMARRE: In the living room.
HARRIS: Yeah.
LEMARRE: Is it a thick carpet?
HARRIS: Yeah.
LEMARRE: But when the Christmas ornaments fall, they break, don't they?
HARRIS: Yeah.
LEMARRE: On the thick carpet.
HARRIS: Yeah.
LEMARRE: And they make a loud noise.
HARRIS: Yeah.
LEMARRE: What kind of a noise?
HARRIS: Crashing. They're Christmas balls crashing, that's the noise.
LEMARRE: Uh-huh.
HARRIS: Drums. Like drums, you know.
LEMARRE: Is that what they sounded like? Drums?
HARRIS: Yeah. On the record player.
LEMARRE: What record player?
HARRIS: There was a…Somebody was playing the drums.
LEMARRE: Where?
HARRIS: On the record.
LEMARRE: What record?
HARRIS: There was a record playing.
LEMARRE: In the living room?
HARRIS: No, the…
LEMARRE: Yes.
HARRIS: The clubhouse. Oh, Jesus.
LEMARRE: What?
HARRIS: Oh, Jesus Christ.
LEMARRE: What is it, Jimmy?
HARRIS: He…

The door opened.

"Hi," Janet said. "I got waylaid, I'm sorry." She was carrying a cardboard container of coffee in each hand. She put them both down on the table, and then sat beside Carella and crossed her legs. "I hope you like it sweet," she said.

"I like it sweet," he said.

"Good. Did you find anything?"

"A major breakthrough."

She took the lids off the coffee containers, and then moved her chair closer. "Mind if I read with you?" she asked, her knee touched his.

"No, that's…fine," he said, and reached for one of the coffee containers and almost knocked it over. His hand was shaking when he picked it up. He sipped at the coffee, and then began reading again. He was very much aware of Janet sitting beside him, her head close to his, her knee brushing his under the table.

HARRIS: The clubhouse. Oh, Jesus.
LEMARRE: What?
HARRIS: Oh, Jesus Christ.
LEMARRE: What is it, Jimmy?
HARRIS: He…
LEMARRE: Go on.
HARRIS: It was Lloyd.
LEMARRE: Who's Lloyd?
HARRIS: The president.
LEMARRE: The president of what?
HARRIS: Our club.
LEMARRE: What club?
HARRIS: The Hawks. In Diamondback. Before I drafted.
LEMARRE: What about Lloyd?

HARRIS: He was dancing with her. In the clubhouse, down in the basement. We was sitting on the floor, the five of us. There was drums goin' on the record, lots of drums, sounded like…lots of drums.

LEMARRE: Who was he dancing with?

HARRIS: His woman. Roxanne.

LEMARRE: And you and four other boys—

HARRIS: Was sittin' on the couch watchin' them. They was dancin' fish, Lloyd turn to us, he say, "What you lookin' at, get yo asses out of here." Roxanne say, "They don't *got* to go if they tired." Lloyd say, "They got to go cause I *tell* them to go." She turn to us, she say, "You goin' let him tell you what to do? The boys say, "Hell no," they get up off the couch and grab him.

LEMARRE: Where did he want you to go?

HARRIS: Upstairs.

LEMARRE: Why?

HARRIS: 'Cause we was just sittin' there listenin' to the drums.

LEMARRE: What did Roxanne mean? About your being tired?

HARRIS: We *was* tired, man. We been rumblin' all the past month.

LEMARRE: Rumbling?

HARRIS: Gang-busting. With the enemy, man.

LEMARRE: When was this, Jimmy?

HARRIS: Just before I got drafted.

LEMARRE: How old were you?

HARRIS: Eighteen.

LEMARRE: And you belonged to a gang called the Hawks?

HARRIS: Yeah, a club.

LEMARRE: And you'd been fighting with another gang?

HARRIS: Started in December.

LEMARRE: And when did this happen in the clubhouse? Was this still December?

HARRIS: Just before Christmas.

LEMARRE: You'd been fighting with another gang all that month—

HARRIS: Heavy fighting, man.

LEMARRE: And now you were resting.

HARRIS: Yeah, and Lloyd told us to go on up.

LEMARRE: What did he mean by that?

HARRIS: I told you. Upstairs.

LEMARRE: But Roxanne said you didn't have to go if you were tired.

HARRIS: Damn straight, man. The boys told Lloyd to shove it up his ass. Then they all grabbed him, you know, pulled him away from Roxanne where they were standin' there in the middle of the floor. Record still goin', drums loud as anything. Guy banging the drums there.

LEMARRE: Who grabbed him?

HARRIS: All of them. I was just watchin' is all.

LEMARRE: Then what?

HARRIS: There's this post in the middle of the room, you know? Like, you know, a steel post holdin' up the ceiling beams. They push him up against the post. I got no idea what they fixin' to do to him, he the president, they askin' for trouble there. I tell them. Hey, cool it, this man here's the president. But they…they…

LEMARRE: Go on, Jimmy.

HARRIS: They don't listen to me, man. They just…They keep holdin' him up against the tree, and Roxanne's cryin' now, she's cryin', man.

LEMARRE:	The tree?
HARRIS:	The post, I mean. Roxanne's cryin'. They grab her. She fightin' them now, she don't want this to happen, but they do it anyway, they stick it in her, one after the other, all of them.
LEMARRE:	They raped her, is that what you're saying?
HARRIS:	I tried to stop them, but I couldn't. They carried her outside afterward, they picked her up and took her out.
LEMARRE:	Why?
HARRIS:	'Cause she bleeding. 'Cause they hurt her when they were doin' it.
LEMARRE:	Where did they carry her?
HARRIS:	The lot.
LEMARRE:	What lot?
HARRIS:	In there, man.
LEMARRE:	In where?
HARRIS:	On the corner, there. Full of weeds. They throw her there.
LEMARRE:	Then what?
HARRIS:	Ain't no…ain't no…shit, ain't no way to…
LEMARRE:	All right, Jimmy.
HARRIS:	What *I'm* cryin for? *I* didn't hurt her, *I* didn't do nothing to her.
LEMARRE:	It's all right, Jimmy. You can cry.
HARRIS:	Why God take *my* eyes, man? Was the other four hurt her. Why God punish me?
LEMARRE:	Jimmy, what happened a long time ago has nothing to do with your getting blinded.
HARRIS:	It got *everything* to do with it, man.

That was the end of the session and the end of the transcript. Dr. Lemarre's notes indicated that at this point Jimmy Harris broke down and began sobbing uncontrollably for the next half hour. The doctor finally had him taken to the ward and sedated.

At their next session Jimmy refused to discuss the incident again, or to name the members of the gang who had held Lloyd against the basement post, and later raped Roxanne. It was the doctor's opinion that the horror of the day—the irreversible set of circumstances that Jimmy had been unable to control or stop—was causing him to dream over and again of his father being killed. Lemarre couldn't quite understand why, in the nightmare, Roxanne had become Lloyd's father. He suspected that this was the reason a penis was attributed to the dream-mother: an attempt of the unconscious to explain the symbolism, a not unusual occurrence. But in addition, the unconscious mind was trying to tell Jimmy something else as well. It was saying, rather blatantly, that the symbolic death was in reality a rape. The woman in the dream had a penis under her skirt; in the actual event, there had indeed been penises under Roxanne's skirt. When Lemarre asked Jimmy what had happened to Roxanne *after* the boys carried her to the lot, Jimmy said he didn't know.

Did someone find her there?

I don't know. She just disappeared, man.

You never saw her again?

Never.

What happened to Lloyd?

We kicked him off the club and got ourselves a new president.

"So that's it, huh?" Janet said.

"I guess so."

"That explains it all, huh?"

"Mm," Carella said. He sounded very dubious.

"And now you've got what you came up here for."

"I suppose."

"Does it help you?"

"No."

"Total loss, huh?" Janet said.

"I guess."

"So why don't you take me to dinner?"

Carella looked at her.

"I'm off duty at four," she said. "You can come back to the apartment with me, and have a drink while I change. Then we can have an early dinner, and…*quien sabe*? That's Spanish," she said, and grinned. "What do you say?"

"I say I'm married."

"So am I, but my husband's in Japan at the moment. And your wife's back there in the city, which means we're here together all by our lonesomes. So what do you say?"

"I couldn't."

"You could, you could," she said, and grinned again. "Just give it a try."

"Even if I tried."

"I know a great little restaurant near the hospital, candlelight and wine, violins and gypsy music, romantic as hell. Don't you yearn for a little romance in your life? Jesus, I yearn for a little romance in mine. Let me go home and put on a red dress and then we'll—"

"Janct, I can't."

"Okay," she said.

"Janet…"

"No, that's okay, really."

"I'm sorry."

"That's okay," she said. "Come on, really, it's okay."

He thought of her on the long drive back to the city.

According to a magazine survey he'd recently read, 50 percent of all American women between the ages of thirty-five and thirty-nine were currently involved in extramarital affairs. That was a whopping huge percentage, considering the fact that back when Kinsey did his survey, the figure was only 38 percent. He did not know whether the figure applied by extension to the women of France, Germany, and Italy, belonging as they all did to the Common Market, but he suspected in his heart of Dickensian hearts that it certainly did *not* apply to the ladies of the British Empire—never, no *never.* In any event, and on any given day of the week, one out of two American women either were on their way to some gentleman's bed or else had just come from some gentleman's bed, the fellow in question not being related by marriage to the peripatetic lady. If one could reasonably assume, in the absence of any supportive slick-magazine evidence, that 50 percent of all *men* between the ages of thirty-five and thirty-nine were similarly occupied, then 50 percent of the whole damn country was fooling around with somebody who wasn't his wife or her husband or vice versa as the case might be.

The thought was staggering.

What made it even more staggering was the fact that a percentage-woman who *was* fooling around had chanced upon a percentage-man who *wasn't* fooling around. Such odds, Carella surmised, were insurmountable—so to speak. But there they'd been, Sergeant Janet Somebody and Detective Steve Carella, in a room that reminded him of a monastery cell, heads bent as if in prayer, knees touching, and damned if he hadn't behaved like a man who'd sworn vows of celibacy and near-silence. "Sorry, Janet," mumble, mumble, "really awfully sorry," mumble, finger the beads, say the vespers, drive back to the city wondering what had been missed beneath that olive-drab skirt, wondering what her lips, her breasts—

Cut it out, Carella thought.

He turned his mind instead to Lemarre's report, and found the doctor's conclusions as frustrating as had been the brief encounter with Janet. As a working cop, Carella would have felt compelled to examine more closely the criminal aspects of Jimmy's traumatic memory, but perhaps psychiatrists didn't work that way, perhaps they were only mildly curious about a bleeding rape victim dropped in an empty lot—

Did someone find her there?

I don't know. She just disappear, man.

You never saw her again?

Never.

And that had been that, except for the incidental information that Lloyd had later been replaced by a new president. The basement rape would have happened twelve years ago, when Jimmy was eighteen. Simple enough to check with Sophie Harris to learn where they were living at the time, then check with the precinct, whichever precinct it was, for whatever they had on a street gang named the Hawks, a deposed president named Lloyd, and a rape victim named Roxanne. He'd do that when he got back to the city. Yes, he'd have to do that. Maybe Lemarre had cared only about getting to the root of the nightmares—if indeed he'd done that—but Carella was interested in knowing whether the perpetrators of a Class B felony had ever been apprehended.

He kept his foot on the accelerator, maintaining a steady sixty miles an hour, the limit on the thruway. At 4:45 he was still forty miles from the city, and it was beginning to get dark.

The woman who tapped her way along the sidewalk had lived in a world of darkness from the moment she was born. She was sixty-three years old, and lived alone in a building just off

Delaware. Two dozen porn movie theaters and as many massage parlors were crowded into thc square half mile that defined her neighborhood. The flesh castles were storefront operations, sidewalk plateglass windows painted out black or bilious green, hand-lettered signs advertising complete satisfaction at ten bucks a throw, No Rip-Offs. The skin-flick houses showed movies that never made it to the posher dream palaces on the city's South Side, where ladies shopping for the afternoon stopped to rest their weary feet and simultaneously tickle their fancies with films artfully photographed and calculated to arouse.

The woman wore an accordion around her neck. She made her living playing the accordion. She did not think of herself as a beggar, and perhaps she wasn't. She was a blind musician. She played on street corners, played tunes by ear on the instrument that had belonged to her father before his death. He had died forty years ago, when she was twenty-three. She had begun taking care of herself then, and was proud of the fact that she was able to manage. She did not know that the neighborhood in which she lived had become a cesspool over the past four years.

Each morning she said hello in passing to the tailor on the corner of Delaware and Pierce, and he returned her greeting while two doors down men entered a place called Heavenly Bodies, and across the street a theater marquee advertised a movie titled *Upside Down Cake.* She knew that drunks sprawled in doorways on the route from her building to the subway, but this was the city and drunks were expected, drunks had always been there. She did most of her shopping at the big supermarket four blocks from the apartment, and did not know that it was flanked by a pair of massage parlors respectively if not respectfully called The Joint and The Body Shop. Once a hawker for one of the rub-down emporiums handed her a leaflet upon which was depicted a flash of naked young ladies and a pate of bald-headed men enjoying communal saunas and whirlpools and whatnots. The leaflet was wasted on the woman with the accordion. Her sightless world was serene; she truly saw no evil. But behind her, as she threw the leaflet away, she heard laughter dark and mysterious.

Moving along the sidewalk now, her long white cane extended and undulating as though blown by a gentle breeze, right to left, back again, touching the sidewalk, touching the air, she turned the corner onto Pierce and began walking toward her building in the middle of the block. The tailor shop was closed; it closed at 6:00 and it was now 7:30. She ran her cane along the wrought-iron railing that defined the basement area of the brownstone north of the tailor shop, here now came the open space where the steps led down to where the garbage cans were stacked, she could smell them on the cold November air, there the post on the other side of the steps, and now the front stoop of the building, and the railing on the other side, abruptly turning back in a right angle toward the brick face of the big apartment building two doors down from her own building.

She wondered how much money she had earned today. It was difficult to play once the cold weather set in. She wore woolen gloves with the fingers cut off at the knuckle joints, and though she tried to keep her fingers moving constantly, they invariably got stiff and she was forced to stop playing and put them into the pockets of her black cloth coat until they were warm again. She wore a long muffler, purple the shopgirl had told her, people were so kind. Here now the garbage cans outside 1142 Pierce, super of the building never took them in till midnight, probably sitting in his basement room drunk as a coot, remembered to take in the cans only when it was almost time to put them *out* again, stunk up the whole neighborhood.

She wouldn't mind a little nip herself just now, nothing like a little nip when there was a little nip in the air. Smiling at her own pun, she entered her building and felt along the wall for the third mailbox in the row, which was her box and which she always checked, even though the last time she'd received a letter from anyone but her niece was from the city advising her that she was being called for jury duty. The tailor had read it to her, and she had burst out laughing when he finished. She wrote back on her typewriter, telling the commissioner of jurors that she would be delighted to serve since she was as blind as justice, but that unfortunately she had to get out on the street every day to earn a living. The commissioner of jurors did not answer her letter, but neither did she report for duty, and nobody ever bothered her again.

She took the small mailbox key from her handbag now, and felt for the keyway on the box, and inserted the key—the lock had been broken and fixed again seventeen times since she lived in this building, and was now, thank God, in a state of good repair—and unlocked the box and felt inside it. Nothing. No surprises anymore. She could hardly remember the last time she'd been surprised. Well, yes, she *could* remember; it had been on her sixtieth birthday when Jerry Epstein across the hall gave her a party. Invited everybody in the building and also the tailor up the street, whose name she learned was Athanasios Parasekvopoulos, but she still referred to him as the tailor because she simply could not pronounce his name, not even in her mind. That had been a marvelous surprise, that party, with plenty of good food and whiskey—she really *did* need a little nip, she was chilled to the bone. But that was the last surprise she could remember. It was sort of sad, she guessed. She guessed there wasn't much joy in life if there weren't any surprises.

She put the mailbox key back into her purse, and the purse back into her handbag, and then she opened the lobby door and walked without needing the cane to where the inside steps began, taking the banister in her left hand, holding the cane in her right, the accordion heavy around her neck. She would be glad to take it off, pour herself a glass of whiskey, sit down to count the money. Someone had put a folded bill into the cup, she didn't know what denomination it was, she'd have to ask Jerry later tonight, if he was home. Or else ask at the tailor shop in the morning. No, he'd be closed on Sunday. Her hand glided along the banister.

She was crossing the first-floor landing when she heard the inner-lobby door opening and closing below. She listened. The stairs creaked; someone was climbing to the first floor. The banister enclosed the stairwell here, running level for the length of the landing, and then beginning to angle upward again toward the floor above. The footsteps were closer now. She reached the post where the stairs began again, felt the polished wooden ball defining the top of it. Hand on the banister, she was climbing again when someone grabbed her from behind. There was not even time to scream. The last surprise of her life was the blade that viciously sliced across her throat, opening it from ear to ear.

9

The city for which Carella worked was divided into five separate and distinct sections, but only the island of Isola was referred to as "the city." If you lived out in Calm's Point or up in Riverhead, if you lived across the bridge in Majesta or out in the middle of the river on Bethtown, whenever you went into Isola, you were "going to the city." Once you were in the city, you were either uptown, downtown, or midtown. If you were *all* the way uptown and about to cross one of the bridges into Riverhead, you would never say you were going farther uptown; you were, instead, going to Riverhead. If you were in Riverhead and heading downtown, you were going to the city. If you were in the midtown area of the city and heading for the financial area and finally the Old Port, you were still going downtown. And if you were standing in the middle of Van Buren Circle and about to head for the midtown area, you were likewise going downtown.

Crosstown was quite another matter.

For the convenience of out-of-towners, the founding fathers being considerate as well as foresighted, the city was constructed on a simple grid pattern, Hall Avenue skewering it from east to west and dividing Isola into almost equal halves. Bounding the island on the north was the River Harb, the Hamilton Bridge crossing it uptown, Castleview Prison sitting on its shoreline upstate. The Harb was long and wide and dirty, and nowhere was it wider and dirtier than where the Taslough Straits Bridge was built across it farther upstate, a contracting-cum-graft coup in the years immediately following the Second World War. The district attorney investigating the scandal was himself later indicted—but that's another story, kids. On the southern side of Isola was the River Dix, a favorite spot in the thirties for the dumping of corpses wearing cement slippers. Such activity had since been removed to Spindrift Airport out on Sand's Point, where the bodies of gangsters were all too often found moldering in the locked trunks of late-model automobiles. The streets running parallel to Hall Avenue on either side of it all joined together and turned upon themselves at the Old Port, where you could board a ferry to Bethtown or take a tunnel to Majesta or Calm's Point, or simply ride back around the island again till you got to the Devil's Break uptown and crossed over into Riverhead. It was a confusing city, but better than Tokyo. Better even than Biloxi, no offense.

The lady had been killed in the midtown area.

For simplicity's sake, and having nothing whatever to do with territorial imperative or departmental seniority, the midtown area was divided by the police into two geographical sections called Midtown East and Midtown West, which chopped the island in half across its waist rather than severing it bilaterally from the top of its skull to the tips of its toes. Once upon a time the midtown area used to be divided lengthwise rather than belly button–wise, and the police called *those* two sections Midtown

North and Midtown South. But that was when chariots were running in the cobbled streets. The city was confusing, yes, but the police department was even more confusing. The British monetary system used to be confusing, too, but all things change for the better eventually.

Things were never going to change for the better as concerned the dead woman lying at the foot of the steps leading up to the second floor. The detective who caught the squeal in Midtown East was a man named Bruno Tauber. When Tauber's grandparents first came to America, there was an umlaut over the "a." The name was spelled Täuber then. The umlaut indicated that the "äu" was to be sounded as "oy." As part of the naturalization process, the umlaut was eventually dropped, the name was spelled Tauber and pronounced to rhyme with "tower." Not even Tauber himself knew the difference. That's the way his father pronounced it. That's the way his mother and brothers pronounced it. And that's the way he pronounced it. Tauber. To rhyme with tower. Only his grandparents would have known the difference, but they were dead, and maybe they might have agreed that all things changed for the better eventually.

Tauber looked down at the dead woman. There was blood all over the landing, blood on the keys of the accordion—shit, was there ever a Saturday night that went by in this city without a fuckin' homicide?

"Where's the man called it in?" Tauber asked the patrolman at his elbow.

"Down the hall there," the patrolman said. "Guy in the gray sweater there."

"What's his name?"

"I don't know."

"Okay, thanks," Tauber said. "Don't touch nothin', you hear?"

"Why would I touch anything?" the patrolman asked.

"That's exactly what I'm sayin'," Tauber said, and walked toward the other end of the landing, where a man stood just outside the door to apartment 1A.

The man appeared to be in his late fifties, thin and balding, with gray hair spraying out from behind each ear and combed sideways across his flaking pate. He was wearing rumpled black trousers and a gray sweater over an undershirt. The sweater had burn holes in it; Tauber automatically concluded that the man was a pipe smoker. Either that, or he had tried repeatedly to set fire to himself. Black-rimmed spectacles were perched on the man's nose. Behind the glasses, his brown eyes darted nervously. As Tauber approached, the man scratched his chin. He needed a shave. Tauber figured he hadn't been out tonight. Saturday night, and he'd been home. He made a mental note.

"You the man found the body?" he asked.

"Yes, sir, I am."

"What's your name?"

"Gerald Epstein."

"Who is she, do you know her?" Tauber asked, gesturing with his head toward the body at the other end of the hall.

"She's a very good friend of mine. Her name is Hester Mathieson, she lives upstairs on the second floor."

"How'd you come across the body?"

"What do you mean?"

"How'd you happen to be out here in the hall? Were you coming home from someplace?"

"No, I was going downstairs for some milk. I ran out of milk."

"What time was this?"

"About a quarter to eight."

"How'd you happen to see her there at the other end of the hall?"

"I just saw her, that's all."

"Went over to her, did you?"

"Yes."

"Recognize her right away?"

"Yes."

"What'd you do then?"

"I went back to my apartment and called the police."

"What time was that?"

"A few minutes later. Right after I found her."

"Hear anything out here before then?"

"No."

"Nothing at all, huh? No screams, no sounds of a struggle, nothing like that."

"Nothing. I had the television on."

"You were home all night, huh?"

"Yes."

"Didn't hear anything, though."

"No."

"What'd you say her name was?"

"Hester Mathieson."

"Spell the last name for me, would you?"

"M-a-t-h-i-e-s-o-n."

"How old is she, would you know?"

"Sixty-three."

"Got any relatives that you know of?"

"She had a niece who used to come around, but she moved to Chicago."

"When was that?"

"About six months ago."

"What's her name?"

"Stephanie Welles."

"Would you know where she lives in Chicago?"

"On Warrington Avenue someplace. I'm not sure of the address. Whenever Hester got a letter from her, she'd ask me to read it out loud."

"Didn't she know how to read?"

"What do you mean?"

"Hester. The dead woman."

"She was blind," Epstein said. "Didn't you know that?"

"Blind?"

"Didn't you see the white cane?"

"No," Tauber said, "I didn't notice it. Blind, huh?

Carella had just finished dinner when the telephone rang. He was sitting in the living room, looking at the mantel clock and planning to take his wife to bed. It was only 9:00 P.M., the twins were already asleep, Fanny was watching television in the spare room, and the condition inspired by Janet up there at Fort Mercer had metamorphosed into a very real and earnest desire for Teddy, who—judging from the various provocative and insinuating postures she was striking across the room as she read a magazine—seemed to be contemplating the same sort of evening activity Carella had in mind. When the phone rang he looked immediately at the mantel clock, and then sighed and crossed the room to where the phone rested on a low table just off the entry. He lifted the receiver.

"Hello?" he said.

"Yeah, let me talk to Detective Carella, huh?" a man's voice said.

"Who's this?"

"Tauber, Midtown East."

"What is it, Tauber?"

"I got a stiff here at 1144 North Pierce, lady with her throat slit."

"What about her?"

"She's blind. We had a stop-sheet here the other day—I checked back with the squad a few minutes ago, got your name as the officer making the request, and called the Eight-Seven. Desk sergeant put me onto you at home. I hope I ain't interrupting anything."

"No, no," Carella said.

"You want to come down here, or what? I think this should be your baby, don't you? I just checked it out with one of the guys Homicide sent over. He thinks there won't be no problem transferring the case if it looks like the same thing we're dealing with here. Whyn't you come down and have a look? The ME's just about done with her, I already requested a policewoman to search her. I ain't trying to avoid work, but if this is the same killer we got here, you really should pick up on it."

"I'll leave right now," Carella said.

"We got plenty to do meanwhile," Tauber said. "That's 1144—"

"I've got it."

"See you later," Tauber said, and hung up.

They all looked the same.

The crime scenes looked the same, identical radio motor patrol cars angled into the curb, dome lights flashing, only the numbers on their sides varying from precinct to precinct. The police barricades looked the same, crosspieces painted in black-and-white diagonal stripes and sitting on sawhorses with cardboard signs tacked to them—CRIME SCENE — DO NOT ENTER. Bold black against white as pale as death, they all looked the same. The cops looked the same, too, winter or summer, spring or fall, nothing changed but the seasons in this city, and sometimes not even those. The uniformed patrolmen always seemed a bit awed by the crime of murder, urging pedestrians to move right along, nothing here to see, folks, let's keep it moving, but empathizing with them completely when it came to their curiosity, almost as if they were not part of the law-enforcement team but were instead on the civilian fringes, watching agape. It was a cold night. In this city, years ago, the patrolmen wore heavy blue overcoats in the wintertime, but now they simply wore long johns under their trousers and tunics, giving some of them a heftier look than when they were naked in their own showers. They milled about talking in whispers except when they were moving pedestrian traffic. What they whispered about was murder.

The detectives all looked the same, too. Tall men, burly for the most part; Carella often had the feeling that detectives were chosen from the uniformed force on the basis of their size and not their special ability to make reasonable deductions or even wild guesses. Most of them were hatless. Most of them smoked cigarettes endlessly. Many of them wore short car coats or zippered jackets with sweater cuffs and bottoms. If you didn't know better, you'd think the detectives at a crime scene were part of a bowling team.

The Homicide cops were immediately identifiable; they all looked and sounded like Monoghan and Monroe, the perfect prototypes, the others being slightly marred castings from the same mold. Black was the color still favored by many of the older Homicide bulls. Black for death. There had once been a famous Homicide cop named Saunders who wore black almost from head to toe. His exploits were legendary, they called him the "Black Plague." Black pants, black suit, black tie on a stark white shirt, black overcoat in the wintertime, black bowler he'd bought one time in London when he'd gone to visit his grandparents and was treated like a visiting celebrity at Scotland Yard. Black umbrella when it was raining, called it his "brolly," picked that up from Grandma sitting in her row house along Jubilee Street. Used to crack homicide cases as if they were walnuts. This was in the days when Homicide truly used to investigate a case, not like today when the precinct detective handled it. Other Homicide cops started wearing black, too. It became the mark of their elitism. You saw a plainclothes cop in black, you knew he was a Homicide dick. Even some of the garden-variety precinct detectives took to wearing black in hope they'd be mistaken for men from Homicide.

That was then, Gertie. Today, except for the old-timers, your Homicide cops were identifiable only by the proprietary air they brought to the scene of a murder, rather like comfortable burghers looking out over their vast holdings. The shields pinned to their overcoats were similar in every respect to the shields the precinct detectives wore—blue enamel set in a gold sunburst pattern—except for the single word *Homicide* stamped into the gold beneath the word *Detective.* Every detective at the crime scene had his shield pinned to his coat or his jacket. The detectives all looked the same.

The woman lying in angular disarray on the first-floor landing looked like any other homicide victim—they all looked the same. When you'd seen enough fatal wounds, they all began to lose defining characteristics except to the medical examiner. It made little difference whether the wound was inflicted by shotgun or knife, pistol or hatchet, baseball bat or ice pick, the results were the same, the results reminded a working cop day in and day out that life was fragile. But it reminded him of something else as well, and it was this that made his job so very difficult. It reminded him that life was cheap. It reminded him that death could be bought suddenly and senselessly—to Carella, it would always be senselessly. To Carella, there was never a good or valid reason for murder.

A pair of ambulance attendants lifted the body onto the stretcher. One of them started to throw a rubber sheet over it.

Carella identified himself and told them to wait a minute, he wanted to have a look at her.

"We been told to remove her from the premises," one of the attendants said.

"Right, and I'm asking you to hold a minute, okay?" Carella said.

"It's the ME says when to take a stiff or when not to take it," the attendant said. "Anyway, who are you? Are you the investigating officer here? I thought the *other* guy was the investigating officer."

Carella didn't answer him. He was stooping beside the body, looking into the dead woman's face as though trying to read the identity of the murderer there. The neck wound was gaping and raw; he turned away. Her hands had been put in plastic bags, par for the course when the weapon was a knife and the attack proximate. No dutiful ME would have neglected the possibility that the victim may have scratched out in self-defense and might be carrying under her fingernails samples of the murderer's skin or blood.

"All right, you can take her," Carella said.

"You dope it out yet?" the attendant asked sarcastically. "You figured who done it?"

Carella rose from where he'd been kneeling beside the body. He did not say a word. He looked directly into the attendant's eyes. The attendant visibly flinched, and then bent silently to cover the corpse with the rubber sheet. Silently, he and his partner picked up the stretcher and carried it down the stairs.

"You Carella?" a voice said behind him.

Carella turned. The man was a detective, his shield pinned to the pocket of his tweed overcoat. Fleshy, thickset man with blue eyes and blond hair. Smoking a cigar. Stunk up the hallway with the stench of it.

"Tauber?" Carella asked.

"Yeah," Tauber said. "You got here, huh?"

"I got here."

The men did not shake hands. Law-enforcement officers rarely shook hands with each other. Even at dances thrown by the Policemen's Benevolent Association or the Emerald Society, they did not shake hands. It was a peculiar occupational quirk, Carella thought. In days of yore, knights used to shake hands to make certain the haft of a dagger was not concealed in a closed fist, the blade hidden along the arm. Maybe cops had no daggers to hide.

"Did you see her?" Tauber asked.

"I got a look at her, yes."

"Policewoman searched her a little while ago. I've got her stuff waiting to go to the property clerk, I wanted you to see it first. You know a Homicide cop named Young?"

"No."

"He's the one told me you could take charge here if it looks like we got the same killer. I realize a slit throat's a slit throat. But if I remember your stop-sheet, both victims were blind, and nothing was stolen, am I right?"

"That's right."

"Well, the lady had twenty-two dollars and fifty cents in her handbag, and she was wearing a gold crucifix around her neck, and also a gold ring with a small diamond on her right hand. Whoever killed her didn't take the money or the jewelry, left a good accordion, too—it's over there against the wall, I already had it tagged, got to be worth a couple of hundred, don't you think? So robbery wasn't the motive here. All I'm saying is it looks like a similar m.o. to me."

"Yes, it does," Carella said.

"I'm not trying to duck out of this," Tauber said, "believe me. I got a full caseload right now, but what the hell, one more or less ain't going to break me. It's just I really think this might be yours."

"I understand that. Who found the body?"

"Guy down the hall. I only asked him a few questions, you'll want to talk to him some more if you'll be takin' this over. What do you think? Do you think you'll be takin' this over?"

"I guess so," Carella said.

"Do you want me to hang around, or what?"

"How do we work the paper on this?"

"I guess I file with Homicide, I don't know. I got Young's verbal okay, that should be enough, don't you think?"

"Maybe, I don't know."

"I'll tell you what I'll do. When I get back to the station house, I'll give Homicide a call, find out how they want us to handle the paper, okay? If you want to ring me later, I'll tell you what they suggest. What I think personally is you just handle it like it's your squeal."

"All the way downtown here?"

"On the basis of your stop-sheet," Tauber said, and shrugged. "You asked for dope on a pair of Unusual Crimes, right? Well, now you got another homicide looks related. You ask me, that's enough."

"You think the stop-sheet would cover it, huh?"

"That's my opinion."

"I just don't want to get involved in a bunch of departmental bullshit," Carella said. "That's the one thing I don't need on a homicide."

"Naw, don't worry."

"For example, what do we do with her valuables? Does the Eight-Seven's property clerk get them, or do I send them over to Midtown East?"

"I think your man gets them."

"That's what I think," Carella said.

"That's what I think, too."

"Where's the stuff?"

"There wasn't much, aside from the cash and the jewelry," Tauber said. "I got it bagged there against the wall, you want to take a look at it." He led Carella to where the woman's accordion was resting against the wall alongside a brown paper bag. The accordion was tagged, and so was the bag. Carella picked up the bag and peeked into it.

"Okay to touch this stuff?" he asked.

"It's your case," Tauber said, and shrugged.

"I mean, have the lab boys gone over it?"

"Only the stuff might've had latents. The wallet there, and the hairbrush and the address book. The book's in Braille, it ain't going to help you much."

"But it's okay to have a look at it, huh?"

"Yeah, go ahead. They dusted it already."

Carella reached into the bag and took out the address book. The book was, in actuality, a small black loose-leaf binder, some three inches in width, five inches in overall length. The pages inside were unlined, most of them punched with a series of dots. Top line, middle line, bottom line, space, and then another line. Carella assumed these constituted the name, address, and telephone number for each listing.

"I wonder how they do that," Tauber said. "Blind people."

"They probably have some kind of instrument they use," Carella said.

"Yeah, probably."

"Do you think there's anybody in the department who can translate this stuff?"

"You'll probably have to go to Languages and Codes," Tauber said.

"Here's something," Carella said. He had turned to the inside back cover of the book. Pasted to it was a message in somewhat shaky longhand:

*In case of accident or emergency,
please notify Miss Stephanie Welles,
1847 Pershing Avenue, Isola. AV 2-1474*

"Guess she figured—"

"Yeah," Carella said.

"She had to write it in longhand, otherwise—"

"Yeah."

"But it won't do you no good, anyway," Tauber said. "The address is an old one. She moved to Chicago six months ago."

"Where in Chicago?"

"Someplace on Warrington Avenue."

"Who is she?"

"The woman's niece."

"Any other relatives?"

"Not that I know of."

"She should be contacted," Carella said.

"You can check the apartment for letters soon as the lab boys are through. You might find an address."

Before World War I, Pershing Avenue used to be called Grant Avenue. Architecturally, the wide esplanade looked much as it did then. A central divider planted with forsythia bushes and maple trees, leafless now in mid-November. Huge buildings on either side of the avenue, granite cornerstones, limestone facades. Spacious entry courts with concrete flowerpots sitting atop brick pedestals. In the days before World War I, the buildings lining

Grant Avenue constituted some of the city's choicest real estate. They were now scribbled over with graffiti advertising the name of this or that street gang member. The graffiti was over-sprayed—Spider 19 giving way to Dagger 21, in turn giving way to Salazar IV, so that *nobody's* name meant a rat's ass any more.

Maybe Spider 19 felt the same way Grant in heaven must have felt when they changed the name of the avenue to Pershing. Pershing himself had narrowly missed having the name changed again to Kennedy shortly after the assassination, when even lampposts were being named after the late president. Up there in heaven, old John Joseph, for such was the general's name, most likely began muttering about *sic transit gloria mundi* and the high cost of changing street signs. But someone had the good sense to recognize that Roosevelt Street, some three blocks away from Pershing Avenue, had already had *its* name changed to Kennedy Street and another name-change of yet another thoroughfare might prove confusing to pedestrians and motorists alike. The people along Pershing Avenue were grateful. None of them knew General Pershing from a hole in the wall, and none of them would ever forget that bleak assassination day in November as long as they lived, so they didn't need street names changed, they didn't need that bullshit at all.

Carella parked his car two blocks from 1847 Pershing, the closest spot he could find, and began walking against the wind blowing through the naked chestnut trees. He had searched Hester Mathieson's apartment for any back correspondence from Stephanie Welles and had found none; he guessed there was no reason for a blind woman to have saved letters that had to be read to her aloud. He had then called the post office serving the Pershing Avenue area to ask about a forwarding address that might have been filed six months ago, and the night clerk who answered the phone told him he'd have to call back in the morning, the only people there right now were sorting mail and moving it out. He then checked the address in Hester's book against the Isola telephone directory and came up with an identical listing for Stephanie Welles. The possibility existed that she had sublet the apartment to someone she knew; Carella dialed the number. He let it ring twelve times, and then hung up.

It was 10:00 P.M. by then.

Tauber had left the scene some forty minutes earlier, promising to check Homicide in an attempt to learn how the transfer to the Eight-Seven should be handled. When Carella called him at five past the hour, Tauber said he had spoken again to Young, and the Homicide cop would be sending out written authorization to the commanding officers at both Midtown East and the Eight-Seven, so that was that. He wished Carella luck with the case. Carella wanted to get a line on Stephanie Welles *now*, tonight, before *this* one began to get cold, too. He drove to Pershing Boulevard hoping for one of two things: either the person who'd rented the apartment after her knew where Stephanie Welles was now living in Chicago, or else Stephanie had left a forwarding address with the superintendent of the building. He was less interested in notifying her of her aunt's death than he was in soliciting information from her. He did not know how much she knew about the dead woman's habits or acquaintances, but she'd been listed as the person to call in case of an emergency or an accident, and Hester Mathieson had suffered the biggest accident of them all.

He walked with his head ducked.

The wind was shrill.

He saw the graffiti-marked buildings, and tried to understand—but could not.

His grandfather had come to America from Italy because he'd been told the streets here were paved with gold. They were not, of course, and Giovanni Carella learned that almost at once, driving a horse and wagon for the milk company, the horse dropping the only golden nuggets anywhere in view. Nor were the streets as clean as those to be found in Giovanni's native Naples, or so Giovanni claimed, a premise perhaps disputable. But in those days, when Carella's grandfather first got here at the turn of the century, the European sense of tradition and of place caused immigrants like himself to look upon even their slum dwellings as something to be cared for with pride. The buildings—your own building and the building next door and the one next door to that—were *home.* Together they formed "*la vicinanza*," and you did not defile your home, you did not shit where you ate. No one would have dreamt of scribbling upon the face of a tenement, however grim the building was. No one would have marked a trolley car—the subways were in the process of being built, there *were* no subway cars to mark—because these were people who had lived with beauty centuries old, and they were not yet used to the fact that in America things existed only to be changed or destroyed.

Carella climbed the flat wide steps of the front stoop, past a pair of empty concrete urns, each scribbled over with undecipherable names. He moved across the courtyard toward the entrance doors of the building. Two young boys were playing boxball in the illuminated courtyard. They looked up at him as he went past, and then went back to their game. He entered the outer lobby of the building, and was searching the mailboxes for the super's apartment number when he came across the names. WELLES in the slot under the mailbox for apartment 54. He didn't know exactly what this meant. Had Stephanie Welles kept the apartment here in Isola while living in Chicago? Or had it been sublet or otherwise rented to someone who'd simply neglected to change the name in the box?

He pressed the bell-button under the box. Nothing. He pressed it again, ready to reach for the inner-lobby door when the buzz sounded. Nothing came. At the end of the row of mail-boxes, he found the super's box, and pressed the button under it. He waited several moments and was about to press it again when an answering buzz came. Leaping for the handle on the lobby door, he opened the door and stepped into a larger space that was dry with contained heat. Against the wall on his left, a pair of radiators hissed and whistled. A single elevator with a pair of spray-painted brass doors was on the rear wall. On the right of the lobby, taped to the wall there, Carella saw a piece of cardboard with the word *Super* hand-lettered onto it, a black arrow under it. He followed the arrow and knocked on the door to apartment 10. A man's voice said, "Yeah, who is it?"

"Police," Carella said.

"Who?"

"Police."

"Shit," the man said.

Carella waited. Behind the door he could hear shuffling and muttering, those famous vaudeville performers. At last the door opened. The superintendent was a white man in his late sixties, Carella guessed, wearing rumpled blue trousers, a tank-top white undershirt, and badly scuffed red velveteen house slippers. He looked grizzled and bleary-eyed. Through the open door to the room beyond the kitchen, Carella could see the edge of the bed with the covers thrown back. He suspected he'd wakened the superintendent, and further suspected he would not be overly receptive to questions about Stephanie Welles. The super's tone immediately confirmed all suspicions.

"Well, what is it?" he said.

"Sorry to bother you this time of night," Carella said.

"Yeah, well you already bothered me, so what is it?"

"I'm investigating a homicide, and I'd—"

"Somebody in this building?"

"No, sir."

"Then what do you want from me?"

"I'm trying to locate a woman named Stephanie Welles. I thought she might have—"

"She ain't home," the super said.

Carella looked at him.

"Where is she?" he asked.

"Working. She works nights."

"You mean she still lives here?" Carella asked.

"Of *course* she lives here. Why are you here looking for her if she don't live here?"

"She doesn't live in Chicago?"

"Do *I* live in Chicago? Do *you* live in Chicago?"

"I thought she'd moved to Chicago."

"No, she ain't moved to Chicago."

"Where does she work, can you tell me that?"

"You planning to bust her?"

"What for?"

"It's legal what she does."

"What does she do?"

"I won't tell you where she works if you're planning to go there and bust her."

"I want to ask her some questions about the woman who was killed."

"What woman?"

"Her name is Hester Mathieson, would you know her?"

"No."

"Would you know anyone named Jimmy Harris?"

"No."

"Or Isabel Harris?"

"No."

"Ever hear Miss Welles mention any of those people?"

"I don't know her that good," the super said. "I only know she works nights, and I know that what she does is legal. So if you're going to go running down there tryin' to bust her—"

"Running down where?"

"Where she works."

"Where's that?"

"I ain't tellin' you," the super said, and started to close the door. Carella put his foot into the wedge. "Get your foot out of there," the super said.

"I can find out where she works," Carella said. "But that'll mean more trouble for me."

"So?"

"So then I'll come back about your garbage cans."

"My garbage cans are fine."

"Or the pipes in your basement. Or the electrical wiring. Mister, I'll find something, believe me. I'm very good at finding something."

"I'll bet," the super said. "But you ain't gonna find Stephanie Welles by threatening me."

"Where does she work?" Carella said. "And stop pushing that damn door against my foot."

"You going to bust her?"

"I'm going to question her about a homicide victim."

"She didn't kill nobody."

"I thought you didn't know her too well."

"I know her well enough to know she didn't kill nobody."

"Where does she work?"

"Place called The Tahitian Gardens."

"What is it, a massage parlor?"

"It's a health club."

"Sure," Carella said.

"It's legal," the super said.

Carella took his foot out of the door, and the super slammed it shut.

10

The Tahitian Gardens was crosstown and slightly uptown on Talbot Avenue, four blocks from the Calm's Point Bridge. As short a time as ten years back, one might have said that The Tahitian Gardens was "in the shadow of the el." But there no longer *was* an elevated train running above Talbot Avenue, and so the turn of phrase, however fresh, did not now apply. Then again, ten years ago there was no such thing as a massage parlor in the city for which Carella worked, and so The Tahitian Gardens could not possibly have been there in the shadow of the el, or even in the shadow of the Law. Or, more correctly, if The Tahitian Gardens *had* existed on Talbot Avenue ten years ago, it *would* have been in the shadow of the el and also in the shadow of the Law. Today, it was neither. All clear, Harold? Try to concentrate, Harold.

The facade of the massage parlor was decorated with real bamboo poles and straw matting. The name was scorch-lettered into a wooden sign nailed to a pair of bamboo poles that formed an "X" across the door. A shorter piece of bamboo served as a handle. Carella opened the door and stepped into a room similarly decorated with bamboo and matting, but softer looking than the outside facade, in that it was lighted with subdued reds and greens emanating from bulbs hidden behind valances or tucked into niches. Some four feet from the door was a desk. A girl sat behind the desk, her back to the wall. She glanced up as Carella came in. Judging from her looks, she was either Chinese or Japanese, maybe Polynesian, certainly Oriental. She was wearing a Madame-Gin-Sling costume, the material looking like brocade, the collar coming an inch or so up on her neck, the sleeves short, her naked arms wreathed in jade bracelets. She smiled as the door whispered shut behind Carella.

He smiled back. He had not yet decided quite how to play this. If he identified himself as a cop, they might not even let him inside without a warrant. On the other hand, if he *did* manage to get inside, he'd have to identify himself to Stephanie Welles if he expected to get any information about the dead woman. He was still debating his approach when the girl behind the desk said, "Yes, sir, may I help you?"

He decided on a scam, hell with it.

"That depends on what you're offering," Carella said.

"Well, sir, why don't you have a seat, and I'll explain it to you."

"I wish you would," Carella said.

He took a chair beside the desk. The girl swiveled her own chair out toward him. The gown she wore was long and slitted to the thigh. A fringe of black underwear lace showed in the slit. She was wearing black satin shoes with extremely high heels and ankle straps. The telephone on her desk had a multitude of buttons on it, none of them lighted at the moment. The wall bearing the door had a fish tank set into it. The tank swirled with tropical fish and iridescent bubbles. To the right of where Carella sat, there was another door. It opened suddenly, and a girl wearing what appeared to be a bikini bathing suit came out, glanced at him briefly, walked directly to the desk, said "Benny," and put a pink slip of paper on the desk.

The Oriental girl repeated, "Benny," and took the slip and wrote something on it. The other girl turned, glanced at Carella again, opened the door, and went into the other room. The door closed slowly behind her.

"That was Stacey, one of our girls," the receptionist said.

"How many girls are there?" Carella asked.

"Six," the receptionist said.

"What's *your* name?"

"Well, why do you want to know that?"

"I'm just curious."

"My name is Jasmine."

"Ah, Jasmine."

"Yes. I was about to explain that this is a private health club, and that for a small renewable initiation fee, we offer the use of our facilities—including the shower, the sauna, and the whirlpool—plus unlimited bar service, and of course a massage by one of our girls, or by two of them, if you prefer."

"Two of them, I see," Carella said.

"We offer a half-hour session for twenty dollars and an hour session for thirty dollars. You understand, don't you, that an hour would normally cost forty dollars if we were doubling the price for a half hour, but instead—"

"Yes, it's quite a bargain," Carella said.

"It is."

"And for that I get a massage and…"

"Use of the facilities."

"And free drinks."

"Yes."

"What would *two* girls cost me?"

"Double what one girl would cost you."

"Oh. No bargains on that."

"No, I'm sorry," Jasmine said, and smiled. "I should explain to you that the girls work exclusively on tips. Whatever arrangements you make with them is private and personal."

"I see," Carella said.

"So what would you prefer?" Jasmine asked, and picked up a pencil and moved into place a pink pad upon which there was printing Carella could not decipher in the dimness of the room. "One girl or two? Half hour or hour?"

"Is an hour the longest I can have?"

"You can have two hours for sixty dollars."

"Can I take a half hour and then change my mind and decide on an hour if I need more time?"

"Well…We've never done it that way before."

"I see," Carella said. "Well, let me see if I understand this, okay?"

"Take your time," Jasmine said, and smiled again.

"This is a health club, and what you offer for your initiation fee is the facilities of the club and a girl to provide a massage. Whatever *other* arrangements I make with any of the girls is strictly private and personal and works on a gratuity basis."

"That's exactly right."

"You said a *renewable* initiation fee…"

"Yes."

"What does that mean?"

"It means you must renew it each time."

"I see. I pay each time."

"Yes."

Translated from the English, all of this meant that The Tahitian Club was renting Carella the use of a space for twenty dollars a half hour or thirty dollars an hour, and providing him access to one or two prostitutes who would perform sexual services for mutually agreed-upon additional fees. The club, if charged with violation of PL 230.25, Promoting Prostitution 2nd Degree, would undoubtedly claim as its defense that a person was advancing prostitution *only* when knowingly causing or aiding someone to commit or engage in prostitution (here at The Tahitian Club, all arrangements made between client and girl were strictly personal and private) or—

Providing persons or premises for prostitution (the club was a health club providing only massage, free drinks, showers, sauna, and whirlpool) or—

Operating or assisting in the operation of a house of prostitution or a prostitution enterprise (for the hundredth time, this was a *health* club!) or—

Engaging in any other conduct designed to institute, aid, or facilitate an act or enterprise of prostitution (sauna and whirlpools and massages and free drinks did not constitute an aid to the act of prostitution, and a single swallow did not a summer make).

"I'll take just one girl for a half hour," Carella said.

"All right, sir, what's your name, please? Just your first name, please."

"Andy," Carella said.

"All right, Andy, how did you hear about us?"

"What do you mean?"

"Did someone hand you literature on the street, or did you read one of our ads?"

"No, a friend told me about it."

"All right, Andy, would you like to pay me now, please? That'll be twenty dollars."

"Yes, sure," Carella said, and took a twenty-dollar bill from his wallet and wondered if the police department would reimburse him for the outlay. He could just see himself walking into the clerical office and handing Miscolo a chit for a visit to a whorehouse.

"Thank you," Jasmine said, taking the bill and putting it into a metal cashbox in the top drawer of her desk. There were a great many bills in that box.

"If you'll take this pink slip now," Jasmine said, ripping the top sheet from the pad, "and step into the lounge, one of our girls will take care of you. I know Stacey's free if you—"

"I had a particular girl in mind," Carella said.

"Oh," Jasmine said, and raised her eyebrows. "Then you've been here before?"

"No, my friend told me to ask for her."

"Who?" Jasmine said.

"Stephanie," he said, and cut himself short before he gave the last name.

"Stephanie?"

"Yes."

"We have no Stephanie."

"That's her *real* name," Carella said, and decided to go whole hog. "Stephanie Welles."

"Mm," Jasmine said. "But you see, *all* the girls here use their real names. They'd have no reason to *hide* their real names."

"I know," Carella said. "That's probably why she told my friend her real name, don't you think? Because all the girls use their real names and she had nothing to hide, right?"

"Mm," Jasmine said.

"So could I have her?" Carella asked.

"Well, as I told you—"

"I know she works here."

"Well, why don't you just go inside now and see if you can find anyone named Stephanie? Whatever transpires between you and any of the girls—"

"Yes, is personal and private."

"Right."

"Thank you. Can you tell me what Stephanie looks like?"

"I don't know anybody here named Stephanie," Jasmine said, and smiled.

"Okay thanks," Carella said and rose and opened the door on his right.

The room beyond was decorated just as the reception room was, with bamboo and straw. On the wall to the left of the door was a bar that ran its entire length. On the bar top there were half-gallon bottles of scotch, vodka, gin, and rye, as well as quart bottles of club soda and quinine water. A bucket of ice rested beside a pitcher of water and a dish of sliced lemons and limes. Plastic glasses were stacked along the wall behind the ice bucket. The wall opposite the bar was semicircular in design, lined with high-backed wicker chairs painted white and cushioned with pillows in brightly colored fabrics. Sitting in two of those chairs were a blonde and a brunette, each wearing the same bikini sort of costume the girl Stacey had been wearing. Both looked at Carella and smiled as he came into the room.

"Hi," the blonde said. "I'm Bobbie."

"Hi, Bobbie."

"I'm Lauren," the brunette said.

"Hello, Lauren."

"What's *your* name?"

"Andy."

"Would you like a drink, Andy?"

"Not right now, thank you. I'm looking for Stephanie."

"She's got somebody with her just now," Bobbie said.

"Think she'll be free soon?"

"I guess," Lauren said. "Why don't you have a drink meanwhile?"

"Scotch and a little water, please," Carella said.

"Could I have your pink slip, please?" Bobbie said, and got out of the wicker chair and walked across the room.

The costume, Carella now saw, was similar to what a stripper wore, the bra top clasping in the front, the G-string bottom covered with what appeared to be a scarf of the same material and color as the bra, tied diagonally across it. Bobbie was wearing high-heeled ankle-strapped pumps that gave her legs a singularly long look even though she was no taller than five six or seven. In the other chair, Lauren was looking at Carella. The bra top she wore seemed skimpier, perhaps because she was fuller in the bust. Neither of the girls looked older than twenty-five. Neither was beautiful, but both were attractive. Moreover, they looked clean-scrubbed, fresh, and wholesome.

"Here you go, Andy," Bobbie said, and smiled. "Scotch and water."

"Thank you," Carella said, and carried the drink to one of the wicker chairs.

"You've been here before, I take it," Bobbie said.

"No, I've never been here before. Or *any* massage parlor, for that matter."

"Then how do you know Steff?"

"A friend recommended the place to me."

"Oh, and he liked Steff, huh?"

"Yes."

"She must've liked him, too."

"What do you mean?"

"Well…She's Shana, you know."

"Here, you mean."

"Yeah. Shana. That's her name here. That's a nice name, I think. Shana."

"Bobbie's nice, too."

"Well, it's not bad," Bobbie said, "but Shana's better. If I had it to do over again, I think I'd call myself something like Shana. Maybe Sherry. Something like that."

"Mm."

"Though there's a lot of Sherrys around."

"There's a lot of Bobbies around, too," Lauren said.

"But not a lot of Shanas. That's my point. Steff picked a good one. I wonder where she got it from."

"There was once a Shana, Queen of the Jungle," Lauren said.

"No, that was Sheena."

The door to the reception room opened and a short fat man smoking a cigar came into the lounge. He was wearing a heavy brown overcoat that seemed to weigh him down. His shoulders were slumped, his face was windblown, his hair was disarrayed. He came puffing into the room, and the first thing he said was, "I need a drink. Fix me a drink, Blondie."

"It's Bobbie," Bobbie said.

"Great, it's Bobbie," the fat man said. "Fix me a bourbon and water."

"We don't have any bourbon."

"Great," the fat man said.

"We ran out just a little while ago," Lauren said. "We had a lot of bourbon-drinkers today."

"Great," the fat man said again, and puffed violently on his cigar. He looked distraught to the point of tears. It almost seemed he had come in here for the bourbon rather than the pleasure of the company.

"How about some rye?" Bobbie said. "That's like bourbon."

"Okay, rye," he said. "Rye and water."

"Could I have your pink slip, please?" Bobbie said, and the fat man handed it to her.

Carella hadn't yet figured out the accounting system. Bobbie had written nothing on either of the pink slips; she had merely placed them on the bar, under an ashtray. Sitting in the wicker chair, sipping at his drink, he studied first the louvered doors on his right and then the bamboo-covered door just beyond the far end of the bar.

Lauren was still watching him. "Drink all right?" she asked.

"Yes, fine."

"Colder'n a witch's tit out there," the fat man said.

"One more guy says that today," Lauren said, and rolled her eyes. "You sure you want to wait for Shana?" she asked Carella.

"Yes," Carella said.

"I mean, it's only your friend's hearsay, am I right?"

"That's right, but I promised him I'd look her up."

"Because I'm getting nice vibes from you," Lauren said. "I think we could get along nicely, you and I."

"We probably could," Carella said. "But really, I promised my friend. Maybe some other time."

"Maybe," Lauren said, and turned her attention to the fat man, who accepted the drink from Bobbie and swallowed it almost in one gulp.

"What a day I had today," he said.

"Yeah," Bobbie said, and nodded. "Saturday's always a rough day."

"Let me have another one of these, okay?" the fat man said. "What a day."

The bamboo-covered door at the far end of the bar opened and a girl walked into the room. Her eyes were a gray the color of smoke, heavily fringed with thick lashes, the lids lightly touched with blue liner. Her blonde hair was cut in something resembling a Dutch-boy bob, bangs on the forehead, a shingle effect at the back of her head. High cheekbones, a sweeping profile that curved delicately into her neck and shoulders. She was tall and slender and was wearing the same abbreviated costume the other girls wore. She said hi to everyone and to no one in particular, and then walked through the other door and out into the reception room.

"That was Shana," Lauren said.

In a moment she came back into the room, looked around, smiled at Carella, smiled at the fat man, and then said, "Everybody happy here?"

"Shana," Carella said, "a friend of mine suggested that I ask for you when I—"

"*I'm* taking the big blonde," the fat man said.

Carella turned to him.

"Yeah, you heard me, pal."

"There's plenty of everybody to go around," Lauren said. "Let's not argue about it, okay, fellas?"

"There's no argument," the fat man said. "I had a hard day. You want the big blonde, you can have her later. Right now I'm ready for my session."

"Here's your drink," Bobbie said.

"Thanks," the fat man said.

"What's your name?" Shana asked him.

"Arthur."

"Let me have Arthur's slip," Shana said.

"It's under the ashtray."

"How long did you plan on being here?" Carella asked pleasantly.

"What's it to you?" Arthur said, and puffed on his cigar and then took a swallow of the fresh drink.

"You said I could have Shana later, I just wanted to know how *much* later."

“That’s none of your business,” Arthur said, and puffed on the cigar again.

“What does it say on the pink slip, Shana?” Carella said.

“It says two hours on the pink slip,” Arthur said. “That’s what it says on the pink slip.”

“I can’t wait that long.”

“That’s tough noogies.”

“I’d like to talk to you a minute.”

“What about?”

“Something personal and private. Is there someplace we can talk personally and privately?”

“Try the toilet,” Lauren said.

“Where’s the toilet?”

“Through the louvered doors.”

“I’m not going in no toilet with you,” Arthur said. “I’m going for my session with Shana.”

“Arthur,” Carella said pleasantly, “this will only take a minute.”

“I haven’t got a minute.”

“And *I* haven’t got two hours,” Carella said, and smiled. “Come on, Arthur, let’s talk this over. I’m sure the girls here don’t want any trouble, I’m sure *you* don’t want any trouble. Let’s just talk this over like gentlemen, okay, Arthur?”

“I’ll give you a minute,” Arthur said, and pushed through the louvered doors.

Carella followed him. There were three curtained shower stalls at the far end of the room beyond. A pair of urinals on the wall bearing the louvered doors. A dozen lockers on the wall opposite the door. Sinks. A black man stood near the sinks. He was wearing a red jacket and string bow tie. He smiled as the men came in.

“We want to talk privately,” Carella said. “Would you mind stepping outside a minute?”

"Got to watch the lockers," the black man said.

"I'll watch them for you," Carella said.

"No, no, it's my job."

Carella took out his wallet, handed the man a five-dollar bill, smiled, and said, "We'll only be a minute."

"Well, okay," the black man said dubiously, but he took the five-dollar bill and went out through the louvered doors.

"So talk," Arthur said.

"Arthur," Carella said, "look." He reached into his pocket, pulled out the leather case to which his detective's shield was pinned, and opened it. "Shhh," he said, and put his finger to his lips.

"Great," Arthur said.

"I'm not making a bust," Carella said.

"Then what *are* you doing?" Arthur asked, looking even more distraught than when he had learned they were out of bourbon.

Carella noticed for the first time that he was wearing a gold wedding band on his left hand. "Arthur," he said, "you only have to worry about one thing. You only have to worry about not telling anybody outside that I'm a cop. You understand that?"

"This ain't my day," Arthur said mournfully.

"This is your day, Arthur," Carella said. "Believe me, it's still your day. We're going out there now, and you're going to tell Shana you've changed your mind about a session with her."

"If you're going to bust this place, tell me, okay? 'Cause I'll head straight for the door, okay? I can't afford to be caught in a place like this, I mean it. So do me that favor, okay?"

"This isn't a bust," Carella said. "Let's go, Arthur."

"We might as well shower first," Arthur said. "They ask you to shower here before you go in for your session."

"It figures," Carella said.

The shower had nothing to do with cleanliness; it had only to do with a legal defense known as entrapment. If Carella entered a room naked or wearing a towel, and a girl came into that room to give him a massage and to discuss fees for sexual services, it could be presumed that Carella had by his own conduct trapped the girl into offering herself to him. Considering this, and remembering that prostitution itself was the lesser of all the offenses in Article 230, a mere violation as opposed to the misdemeanors or felonies in the other sections of the article, it was hardly worth the trouble making an arrest. A violation was punishable by no more than fifteen days in jail and a fine of no more than $250. In cases where a policeman was dumb enough or eager enough to arrest a hooker, the girl was usually out on the street an hour after her pimp paid a $50 fine. There had been no recent massage parlor busts in the city for which Carella worked; the legal defenses were too plentiful. If you couldn't get the people operating the joint, and you couldn't get the girls performing the services, who was left? Guys like fat Arthur here, who was trembling inside his heavy overcoat at the thought of his wife finding out he'd been in Tahiti this Saturday night?

Carella went outside to tell Shana he was ready for his session.

He had showered, and dried himself, and wrapped an orange towel around his waist. The black man in the red jacket had given him a plastic bag into which he had put his holstered service revolver, his wallet, his leather shield-case, his keys, his cash, and his watch. The black man saw the Detective's Special, but said nothing; five bucks can sometimes go a long, long way. Carella wrapped the plastic bag inside a second towel, and then pushed through the louvered doors into the lounge. Shana was there waiting for him. Arthur was nowhere in sight. Neither were the girls who had been there earlier. Carella wondered which of them Arthur had chosen.

"Will you want to take a drink in with you?" Shana asked.

"No, that's fine," Carella said.

"What's in the towel?" Shana asked.

"Family jewels," Carella said.

"I meant the one in your *hand*," Shana said, and laughed. "Come on," she said, and opened the door near the end of the bar.

Carella followed her into a narrow corridor that had bamboo on the walls and straw mats on the ceilings and floors. She opened a louvered door onto a room some six feet wide and eight feet long. A bed was snugly recessed into the niche formed by one entire wall and parts of two others. Covering the bed was a form-fitting print in swirling reds, yellows, and blues. The three walls enclosing the bed were mirrored. The narrow floor space between the bed and the fourth wall was covered with straw mats. Bottles of colored lotions that looked like all the oils of Araby rested on the floor, against the wall. There was a slip bolt on the louvered door. Shana threw the bolt, turned from the door, smiled at Carella, and walked to the bed. Sitting on it, she took off her shoes.

"So," she said, and smiled again. "This is your first time in a massage parlor, huh?"

"Yes," Carella said.

"Let me explain how it works. I give you a body rub for the twenty dollars you paid outside—you booked for a half-hour session, didn't you?"

"Yes, a half hour."

"Okay. If there's anything you want in addition to the body rub, that's extra."

"How much is extra?"

"It's usually twenty-five for a hand job, forty for a blow job, and sixty for sexual intercourse. But Lauren tells me you know a friend of mine, so maybe we can make a special—"

"No, I don't know any friend of yours," Carella said.

"You don't? Lauren told me—"

"I was lying."

Shana looked at him.

"That's right," he said.

"Why?"

"I wanted to talk to you."

"You had to lie so you could *talk* to me?"

"I'd already asked for you by your real name. I had to go along with it."

"How'd you know my name?"

"It was in someone's address book."

"Whose?"

"Your aunt's. A woman named Hester Mathieson."

"I don't get this."

"I'm a cop," Carella said.

"Let me see the tin," she said.

"It's wrapped in the towel there. Believe me, I'm a cop."

"Is there a gun in there, too?"

"Yes."

"So what is this? A bust?"

"No."

"Then what are you doing here?"

"Your aunt—"

"Oh, Jesus, don't say it. Has something happened to her?"

"She's dead. Someone killed her."

"Oh, Jesus."

"I'm sorry."

"How?"

"Somebody cut her throat."

"Oh, Jesus!"

The room went silent. Down the hall Carella heard someone laugh. A door eased shut. He looked at the girl. She was staring down at the ankle-strapped shoes on the floor. The sloping tops of her breasts in the bra top were dusted with freckles. She sat with her hands in her lap, staring at the shoes. Her fingernails were long and manicured, the color a red as bright as blood. He wondered what he should call her. Until a moment ago she had been Shana, a girl who casually quoted prices for sex acts with a stranger. But the name in Hester Mathieson's book was Stephanie Welles, and mention of the murder seemed to have transported them both from this dimly lighted place of fantasy to a tenement hallway no less dimly lighted but only all too real.

"Miss Welles?" he said, and this seemed correct; she nodded briefly in response, still staring at her shoes. Against the wall the bottles of lotion shimmered with reflected light. "When did you see her last?"

"Before I started here."

"When was that?"

"About six months ago. May. Is that six months?

"You hadn't seen her since?"

"No."

"Were you particularly close?"

"I liked her a lot. I guess maybe I loved her."

"But you hadn't seen her since May."

"No."

"Had you *talked* to her?"

"You mean on the phone?"

"Yes."

"I tried to call her at least once a week. She was blind, you know. How could anybody…why would anybody…?" Stephanie shook her head.

"When did you talk to her last?"

"Last week."

"When last week?"

"Thursday night, I guess it was. I get Wednesdays and Thursdays off."

"What did you talk about?"

"Well, the usual."

"Which was?"

"Well, you see, I lied to her about the job here. I mean, that's why I stopped going to see her. Because if, you know, I had to sit there face to face and lie…She could sense things, you know. Blind people can sense things. And if I lied to her sitting right there in the *room* with her, well, she'd just *know* it, and I…I couldn't bear that. My mother's dead, you know, Aunt Hess was all I had, I didn't want to…to hurt her…or to…you know…by her finding out I'm working in a place like this."

"Where *did* you say you worked?"

"I told her I was a flight attendant. A stewardess. And I said I was based in Chicago and only got to the city here every now and then. I used to say I was calling from the airport. I told her I was trying to get my flight schedules changed so I could come see her again. I told her I was working on it. Meanwhile, I wrote to her a lot, and I called her whenever I could."

"How'd you manage writing to her?"

"What do you mean?"

"You told her you were living in Chicago."

"Oh. I have a girlfriend there, she used to work here at the Tahitian. She forwarded my aunt's letters to me, and then I'd send my answers back, you know, for her to mail from Chicago."

"Wouldn't it have been easier to just quit the job here, find some work your aunt—"

"Well, the money's good," Stephanie said, and shrugged.

"How'd you get started here?"

"Well, I don't want to talk about it. I needed a job, that's all."

"There are lots of jobs in this city."

"They don't pay as much as this one. The job here gave me plenty of money for myself, and enough to send Aunt Hess a little every now and then. Besides, I wanted a Benz."

"A what?"

"A Mercedes-Benz. I wanted one for the longest time. So I answered an ad in one of the fuck-papers, and took the job. I'm paying off the car now, I bought it on time. I make a lot of money here. And I'm really good at it," Stephanie said, and shrugged. "I give good blow jobs."

"How often did you send money to your aunt?"

"Every now and then."

"How much?"

"Fifty dollars, a hundred. It depended."

"Did anyone *know* she had this extra money coming in?"

"Why? Was she robbed? Did someone rob her?"

"No, it doesn't look that way. But sometimes people get envious and—"

"It wasn't that much money. I sent her whatever I could, but it wasn't a fortune. Anyway, my aunt never told her business to anybody. I'm sure she wouldn't have told anybody she was getting money from me."

Again there was laughter down the hall. A girl's laughter, high and genuine. Stephanie reached for a tissue in a box resting on the floor. She blew her nose, and tucked the tissue into the waistband of the skirted scarf covering the G-string. Then she looked at her watch.

"The last time you spoke to your aunt..." Carella said.

"Yeah," Stephanie said, and nodded. "But could you please hurry it up, cause you paid for a half hour, you know, and they like us to keep track of the time."

"Did she mention anything that was frightening her?"

"No."

"Any threatening letters or phone calls?"

"No."

"Anything that was worrying her, or troubling her…"

"Nothing," Stephanie said.

"Nothing," Carella repeated.

Driving back home to Riverhead, the faulty car heater clanking and rattling but doing little otherwise to defrost the windshield, he began adding up what he had. The tally came close to the nothing he had gotten from Stephanie Welles. He bunched his gloved fist, rubbed it against the rime forming on the glass, and cleared a spot about the size of a melon. He knew it would frost over again in no time at all, but meanwhile, he enjoyed the luxury of being able to see the road ahead. It was not yet 11:30, there wasn't much traffic going out of the city this early on a Saturday night.

The case had begun on Thursday with the murder of Jimmy Harris, had lurched into Friday morning with the subsequent murder of Jimmy's wife, and had zigged and zagged an essentially unrewarding path across the city and the state until it smashed into a dead-end brick wall with the murder of Hester Mathieson earlier tonight. Thursday, Friday, Saturday, three days, and the case was still as cold as a herring, red or otherwise.

Carella was tired and he was irritated and he was probably inconsolable, but he tried nonetheless to console himself with facts because he knew that in police work there *were* no mysteries; there were only crimes and the people who committed them. The people were sometimes professionals—as were armed robbers and burglars and some murderers. Or they were sometimes amateurs—as were *most* murderers. Or they were sometimes crazies—as were most pyros and some murderers and a mixed bag of other lawbreakers as unrelated as rapists or false-alarmists or muggers or parakeet-thieves or—

The facts, please.

Three blind people killed in as many days. Nothing stolen from any of them. Apartment of the first two victims turned inside out and upside down. Okay, the murderer was looking for something. What? Was it something Jimmy had buried? Dirt under his fingernails—soil, *soil.* So, yes, he had possibly buried something. Then why did the killer tear up the furniture and overturn the lamps and dump forks and knives all over the floor and generally behave badly? Because he didn't *know* beforehand that Jimmy had *buried* whatever it was he was looking for. All right, then, did he *find* whatever Jimmy had buried? Yes, he found it. How do you know? Because he didn't similarly ransack Hester Mathieson's apartment. If he'd already found what Jimmy had buried, there was no need to search for it elsewhere. Good. In fact, brilliant. Then why did he bother to *kill* Hester Mathieson? If she had nothing he wanted, why did he kill her?

Problems, problems. There were always problems in the murder business. Carella had called Meyer the moment he'd got home from Fort Mercer, hoping to learn if Meyer had found any evidence of recent digging in the Harris apartment or in the backyard. He had his speech all prepared; he'd worked on it during the latter part of the tedious downstate drive. When Meyer got on the phone, he was going to say, "Well, did you dig up anything?" He was chuckling even as he dialed the familiar number, but he'd got no reply. Meyer was undoubtedly still at the wedding; it was not every day of the week that someone like Irwin the Vermin got married. Carella thought back to the day Irwin got bar mitzvahed. If memory served—and it did—that was the same day Cotton Hawes got transferred to the Eight-Seven. He could remember their first meeting in the lieutenant's office, Hawes explaining that he'd been named after Cotton Mather the Puritan preacher, and immediately saying it could have been worse, he might have been named Increase. He'd taken him out into the squadroom and introduced him to Meyer, who was fretting about a liquor store murder that would surely cause him to miss Irwin's—

The facts, please. Stick to the facts.

Three blind people dead in as many days. Nobody can remember anybody who had anything against Jimmy or Isabel or Hester. Nice people. Nice *blind* people, in fact, than which there are no people nicer. Except that Jimmy's mother thought he was cooking up a crooked scheme like armed robbery or something with one of his old Army buddies, a likelihood Carella considered tantamount to discovering diamond mines on Mars—but who could tell? It's a wise child who knows his own father, and it's an even wiser mother who can spot a budding criminal in the little bugger she'd nursed and weaned. Hadn't Jimmy, after all, once belonged to a street gang named the Hawks? He had indeed. This did not bespeak a lad who'd followed the straight and righteous all his livelong days, oh no. This bespoke a lad who'd bashed a few skulls in his time, and stomped a few ribs, and generally misbehaved as badly as the killer who'd torn up his apartment looking for something that may or may not have been buried, whatever the hell *that* might have been.

If it was buried in the apartment, it had to be small; there were no fields or pastures in a city apartment. There were backyards, of course, and maybe Jimmy had gone down there to do his digging, *if* he'd done any digging at all, at all. This information would have to wait on the call to Meyer tonight or tomorrow morning. Tomorrow and tomorrow and tomorrow crept in this petty pace, but it never got to be Sunday. It was still twenty minutes to Sunday, and God knew how many weeks or months to Monday. Carella had the feeling Monday would never again come.

So here was this nice blind person named Jimmy Harris, whose mother thought he was cooking up a larcenous scheme involving guns, and here was his sweet and innocent blind wife, Isabel, who was painting the town red or at least living it up a bit in this or that motel with her employer, who was madly in love with her and who planned to marry her. A pair of nice blind people, one of whom was *maybe* planning something criminal, the other of whom was already *doing* something criminal, adultery being a crime in the city for which Carella worked—a Class B misdemeanor, no less, punishable by at least three months in jail or a fine of $500.

He should have mentioned that to old Janet upstate there at Fort Mercer. He should have said, "Janet, do you know that there is a section of the Criminal Law titled 'Adultery' and defined as 'engaging in sexual intercourse with another person at a time when one has a living spouse, or the other person has a living spouse'? Did you know that, Janet?" But then again, she hadn't invited him to break the law, she had only invited him to dinner at a great little restaurant she knew. And besides, why was he thinking of her once again while driving back home yet another time?

Hester Mathieson was another nice blind person who only happened to have a hooker for a niece. Which wasn't bad, of course, if you didn't mind the fact that the money your niece sent you was dirty money. Hester couldn't have minded because, first of all, she didn't know her niece was in the life, and secondly, she didn't know that the C-notes coming to her irregularly were earned in a profession that was presumably victimless but that supplied the boys in the mob with the cash for the pursuit of *other* victimless crimes like selling dope to teenagers. Arthur may not have realized it tonight, but the $60 he'd paid to old sloe-eyed Jasmine for his two hours of bliss with a prostitute went directly to the bad guys who were running the operation. And whereas Stephanie Welles, also known as Shana, hadn't told Carella much, he knew for certain that a goodly portion of every nickel she received for those very good blow jobs she knew how to perform *also* went to the boys in the mob. The boys were *not* nice people, and whereas Carella could see no connection as yet between Shana's occupation and the death of her aunt, he knew that where there was rat shit, you were bound and certain to find rats sooner or later.

So there they were, Jimmy and Isabel and Hester—three nice blinds, so to speak. Oh yes, they each and separately had a few skeletons hanging in the closet, but maybe this was meaningful and maybe it was not. And here was Carella, not knowing which way to turn next, knowing only that he had to handle this one the way he handled all the other ones. Dig for the facts, evaluate the facts—which he'd done already and which he had to admit left him exactly nowhere. And then dig for further facts, which you could then evaluate in the hope that they, too, would leave you exactly nowhere, in which case you could quit the force and become a street cleaner, or at least go home to sleep.

Carella yawned.

He bunched his fist again and wiped at the frosted windshield again, and then decided he would go to Diamondback in the morning to try to find out why Jimmy Harris's nightmares had persisted long after the good Major Lemarre had exposed and explored and explained the trauma that had presumably caused them.

11

Carella was hoping against hope that it wouldn't turn out to be the Eight-Three.

The Eight-Three was the precinct in which Fat Ollie Weeks worked.

Isola was divided into twenty-three precincts, and five of those were up in Diamondback. The Diamondback precincts were, for some reason known only to police commissioners past, numbered not in consecutive but in bi-consecutive order. First there was the Seven-Seven on the easternmost tip of the island, bordering Riverhead and taking in the area surrounding Devil's Break. The Seven-Seven was considered a lucky precinct, but only because of the twin sevens and the allusion to the game of craps; actually, it had the highest crime rate in the entire city, higher even than the notorious 101st in West Riverhead. The 101st was called Custer's Last Stand in honor of Detective-Lieutenant Martin Custer, who ran the squad up there. It was a curiosity of police jargon that the 87th, for example, was referred to as the "Eight-Seven," and the 93rd was referred to as the "Nine-Three," but the 101st was called the "Hundred and First" rather than the "One-oh-One." Go figure it.

Moving right along, folks, the precinct west of the Seven-Seven was the Seven-Nine, bordering the River Harb and affording a fine view of the Hamilton Bridge from its squadroom windows—if you peeked through the peaks and minarets of a thousand-some-odd tenements between the station house and the river. The Eight-One was on the other side of the Diamondback River and ran southward all the way to Hall Avenue, where North Diamondback officially became South Diamondback—try to pay attention, Harold. The Eight-Three and the Eight-Five sat like a pair of nuns, one facing the river, the other facing Hall Avenue, in that part of Diamondback bearing such religious names as St. Anthony's Avenue and Bishop's Road and Temple Boulevard and Tabernacle Way. The Eight-Seven, somewhat less sacrosanct except to those who worshipped it, bordered both on its eastern end. On the 87th's north was the river, on its south was Grover Park. End of geography lesson.

Fat Ollie Weeks was a detective in the Eight-Three. Carella did not like working with him. That was only because Ollie was a bigot. Carella did not like bigots. Ollie was a good cop and an excellent bigot. His bigotry extended to everyone and everything. He missed being a misanthrope by a hair. That was because there were some people he actually liked. One of those people was Steve Carella. Since the affection was somewhat less than mutual, Carella tried to avoid wandering into the Eight-Three except out of dire necessity. Carella even avoided *calling* the Eight-Three unless a hatchet murderer was last seen on the steps leading up to the station house there. His dislike of Fat Ollie bordered on ingratitude; the man had, after all, helped them crack at least two cases in recent memory.

Carella hoped it would not be the Eight-Three. On the telephone he asked Sophie Harris where she'd been living when her son Jimmy was eighteen, and then held his breath in anticipation of her answer. The telephone line crackled and spit. Sophie said she'd lived on Landis and Dinsley. Carella let out his breath and then thanked her more profusely than her simple answer seemed to have warranted. Landis and Dinsley was in the Eight-Five.

They went up there at 10:00 that Sunday morning. Meyer had a hangover, but he was able to report with some lucidity about what he'd discovered, or rather what he had *not* discovered, in the Harris apartment yesterday.

"The way I figure it," he said, "something was buried in that window box, and somebody later dug it up."

"Jimmy?"

"Maybe. Or maybe the killer, I packed a specimen of the dirt in an evidence—"

"Soil," Carella said.

"What?"

"It's soil, not dirt."

"Yeah—in an evidence bag and sent it over to the lab. This was before I went to Irwin's wedding, I want you to know. You had me very busy yesterday."

"Did you check out the backyard?"

"I went down there before I left the building. I didn't see any signs of digging."

"How'd the window box look?"

"What do you mean?"

"Was it dumped on the floor like the rest of the stuff in the apartment?"

"The dirt, you mean?"

"Yeah, the soil."

"No, it was in the box."

"Well, if the killer went throwing everything all over the place, why was he so neat with the window box?"

"Then maybe it wasn't the killer," Meyer said, and shrugged, and then winced. "My head hurts when I shrug," he said. "I shouldn't drink. I really shouldn't drink. I can hold my liquor, I don't get drunk, but I always have a terrible hangover the next day."

"What do you drink?" Carella asked.

"Scotch. Why? What does it matter what I drink?"

"Some drinks give you worse hangovers than other drinks. Gin gives you terrible hangovers. So does bourbon. Cognac is the worst."

"I drink scotch and I have a hangover," Meyer said. "That's because I'm Jewish."

"What's that got to do with it?"

"Indians and Jews get terrible hangovers from drinking scotch," Meyer said. "Jewish college girls get headaches from eating Chinese food, did you know that? It's from the monosodium glutamate in it. It's called the Jewish College Girl Syndrome."

"How do you happen to know that amazing fact?" Carella asked.

"I looked it up."

"Where?"

"In the library. Under 'Jewish College Girls.'"

"I've never in my life looked under a Jewish college girl," Carella said.

"The reason I looked it up, I was working on this case," Meyer said, "where an Indian—"

"Yeah, yeah," Carella said.

"God's truth. An Indian was lacing a Jewish college girl's Chinese food with scotch, and she was getting terrible headaches all the time. I finally arrested the Indian."

"Did the headaches go away?"

"No, but the Indian did. For six years."

"What did the girl do about the headaches?"

"She went to see a headache doctor. He told her she was wearing underwear a size too small."

"How did he know?"

"He looked it up."

"Under what?"

"Under*wear*," Meyer said, and both men burst out laughing.

They were still laughing when they showed their shields to the patrolman stationed outside the front steps of the 85th Precinct. The patrolman looked at the shields and then looked at the two men. He suspected they were imposters, but he let them go inside, anyway; hell with it, let the desk sergeant's mother worry. The building that housed the 85th looked very much like the one that housed the 87th—twin green globes flanking the entrance doors, wide steps leading up to those doors, muster room beyond, brass rail just before the muster desk, sergeant sitting behind the high wooden desk like a magistrate in a British court. They showed him their shields and said they wanted to talk to someone in the Detective Division.

"Anyone in particular?" the sergeant asked.

"Anyone who might be familiar with street-gang activity in the precinct."

"That'd be Jonesy, I guess," the sergeant said, and plugged a line into his switchboard. He waited, and then said, "Mike, is Jonesy up there? Put him on, will you?" He waited again. "Jonesy," he said, "I've got a pair of detectives down here, want to talk to somebody about street gangs. Can you help them?" He listened, and then said, "Where you guys from?"

"The Eight-Seven," Meyer said.

"The Eight-Seven," the sergeant repeated into the phone. "Okay, fine," he said, and pulled out the plug. "Go right upstairs," he said, "he's waiting for you. How's Dave Murchison? He's your desk sergeant there, ain't he?"

"Yes, he is," Carella said.

"Give him my regards. Tell him John Sweeney, from when we used to walk a beat together in Calm's Point."

"We'll do that," Meyer said.

"Ask him about the ham and eggs," Sweeney said, and laughed.

The detectives of the 85th had somehow managed to wheedle from petty cash, or someplace, the money for a printed sign. It read DETECTIVE DIVISION in bold black letters. Just below the words was a pointing carnival-barker hand that looked like what someone's great-grandmother might have seen. It gave the otherwise decrepit muster room a look of antiquity and shoddy dignity. Up the iron-runged steps they went, just as if they were home. Turn the corner, walk down the hall, there was the bull pen. No slatted-rail divider here. Instead, a bank of low filing cabinets that formed a sort of wall across the corridor. Just inside the battered metal barrier was a desk. A huge black man in shirtsleeves was standing behind the desk, a clearly anticipatory look on his face.

"I'm Jonesy," he said. "Come in, have a seat."

A plastic nameplate on his desk read *Det. Richard Jones.* The desktop was strewn with familiar DD report forms, departmental flyers and notices, hot car sheets, stop-sheets, all-state bulletins, B-sheets, mug shots, fingerprint cards—the usual clutter you'd find on the desk of any detective in the city. There were four men besides Jonesy in the squadroom. Two of them sat typing at their desks. One was leaning against the grilled detention cage, talking to a young black girl inside it. Another was at the water cooler, bending over to look at the spigot.

"Steve Carella," Carella said, and took a chair alongside Jonesy's desk. "This is my partner, Meyer Meyer."

"What can I do for you?" Jonesy asked.

At the water cooler, the detective straightened up and said to no one in particular, "What the fuck's wrong with this thing?" No one answered him. "I can't get any water out of it," he said.

"We're looking for a line on a street gang named the Hawks."

"Right," Jonesy said.

"You know them?"

"They're inactive. Used to be a bopping gang, oh, ten, fifteen years ago. Half of them got drafted, busted, or killed, the others went the drug route. Haven't heard a peep from them in years."

"How many members were there?"

"Maybe two dozen in the nucleus group, another fifty or so scattered throughout Diamondback. These gangs like to think of themselves as armies, you know what I mean? In fact, some of them *are*—four, five hundred members all over the city. Once the shit is on, it's important how many guys they can put on the street. We had a fight three weeks ago, I swear to Christ this one gang put a thousand guys in the park. Gang called the Voyagers, I love those grand-sounding names, don't you? Had it out with a Hispanic gang in Grover Park. The Eight-Nine put us onto it because the other gang is in their precinct. Gang named the Caballeros. What a bunch of bullshit," Jonesy said.

"About the Hawks," Carella said. "Would you be familiar with someone named Lloyd?"

"Lloyd what?"

"That's all we've got. He would have been president of the gang twelve years ago."

"My partner'd know more about that than me. He's the one started this detail. We were getting so much gang activity in this precinct we had to create a special detail, would you believe it?

Two men who should be taking care of people getting robbed or mugged, got to waste our time instead riding herd on a bunch of street hoodlums. Let's take a look at the cards, see what we got on this Lloyd. I'm not sure they go back that far, but let's see."

They went back that far.

Whoever Jonesy's partner was, he had done a fine job of compiling individual dossiers not only for members of the Hawks but for every other street-gang member in the precinct. The card on Lloyd Baxter was typical of a "leader's" card. He had been a truant throughout his elementary, junior high, and high school career, finally dropping out the moment he could do so legally, at the age of sixteen, and getting busted six months later for Burglary Three, defined as "knowingly entering or remaining unlawfully in a building with intent to commit a crime therein." The building was, naturally enough, a school. Lloyd Baxter smashed a window and went in there with the alleged intent to steal typewriters. He copped a plea for the lesser charge of Criminal Trespass Three, "knowingly entering or remaining unlawfully in or upon premises," a simple violation for which the punishment was three months and/or a fine of $250—just what a prostitute might have got. He was sentenced to three months in jail, and the sentence was suspended because he was a juvenile. Four months later, immediately after the probationary period ended, Lloyd Baxter was arrested for Assault Three. By that time he was sergeant at arms in the street gang known as the Hawks and the person he assaulted was a kid named Luis Sainz, who was president of a gang called Los Hermanos. Again Lloyd got off with a suspended sentence, probably because his victim was a punk like himself and the judge thought it foolish to pay for the care and feeding of hoodlums who might otherwise do away with each other if left to their own devices on their own turf. The week he beat the assault rap, Lloyd was elected president of the Hawks, a conquering hero returning home to ticker-tape parades and consequent droits du seigneur.

One of the prizes awarded to the newly elected leader was a girl named Roxanne Dumas, who sounded like either a stripper or a great-granddaughter of the late French novelist, neither of which she was. She was, instead, a fifteen-year-old girl whose parents had come from the lovely island of Jamaica, her forebears having been part English, part French, her nature amiable and benign until the city got hold of her.

It was some city, this city.

Roxanne was twelve when her parents moved from Jamaica into a section of the city inhabited almost exclusively by legal immigrants or illegal aliens from various Caribbean islands. And even though the mix was predominantly Jamaican, the neighborhood had been dubbed "Little Cruz Bay" by law-enforcement officers, later bastardized to "Little *Cruise* Bay" when it became a happy hunting ground for teenage prostitutes of island extraction—the white-collar white workers of this city being extremely tolerant when it came to a little *café au lait* on their lunch hours. Roxanne missed initiation into the oldest profession by a whisper; her parents moved from Little Cruise Bay to Diamondback when she was thirteen, into a neighborhood where tan was black and black was beautiful, *whatever* the nation of your origin. When Roxanne was fourteen, she began "going" with a boy of sixteen who was a member of the Hawks. She was fifteen when Lloyd Baxter assaulted the president of Los Hermanos to himself become president of the Hawks. Lloyd was seventeen at the time, an impudent age for a president; there were street-gang leaders who were in their late twenties, some of them married and with children of their own. Lloyd and Roxanne hit it off at once. Her former boyfriend, a kid named Henry, merely shined it on without a murmur; he was by then shooting twenty dollars' worth of heroin a day and was well on his way to a career as a raging junkie. Henry died of an overdose two years later, shortly before the supposed Christmas trauma Jimmy Harris related to Major Lemarre during his stay at Fort Mercer.

There was nothing in the police dossier about Roxanne Dumas having been raped by members of the gang and carried bleeding to a vacant lot. The dossier went much beyond the Christmas twelve years ago, detailing the disposition of each gang member—drafted, busted, hooked, burned, or snuffed. But there was nothing about the basement rape; nothing about a bleeding teenage girl being found in a vacant weed-filled lot on a street corner near the clubhouse; nothing about a hospital admitting Roxanne as an emergency patient, wherever she'd been found or wherever she'd dragged herself. Either the beat patrolmen had been derelict, Roxanne had crawled off unnoticed, the records kept by Jonesy's partner were incomplete—or the incident had never taken place at all.

The records seemed fastidious enough. According to his dossier, Lloyd had resigned as president of the Hawks at the ripe old age of twenty-three, four years *after* the alleged basement rape. He had been in and out of trouble with the law ever since, but his biggest fall occurred six years ago when he was busted for Robbery One and sentenced to ten at Castleview. He'd served three, and was currently out on parole and working in a car wash on Landis Avenue. He was now thirty-one years old.

Five years ago, when Lloyd was serving the first year of his sentence at Castleview, Roxanne married a dope pusher named Schoolhouse Hardy. That was his real name. She was twenty-four when she became Mrs. Hardy. She was twenty-eight when Schoolhouse got busted and sent away under the state's stringent dope laws. Schoolhouse would not be seeing his wife again for a long, long time—except on visiting days. He was now thirty-seven, she was twenty-nine. According to the follow-up on her, she had begun working as a beautician in a place called The Beauty Hut last August, shortly after Schoolhouse was sentenced to twenty-five at Castleview for unlawful possession of eight ounces of cocaine. There was no indication in the records that she had ever again seen Lloyd Baxter from the day he was sent away to the present.

They thanked Detective Richard Jones for his time, and went to look up the long-ago sweethearts at their separate last-known addresses.

834 North 89th was a four-story brownstone with wrought-iron railings flanking the front stoop. They found a mailbox listing for Lloyd Baxter in apartment 22, rang the bell, and got an answering buzz almost at once. The interior hallway was spotlessly clean; in fact, it smelled of disinfectant. The linoleum on the steps was worn and patched, but it, too, had been scrubbed to within an inch of its tired life. A gleaming window on the first floor let in frosty November sunlight. They continued climbing, Meyer puffing audibly and blaming it on his hangover, until they came to the second floor. There were only two doors on the landing, one opposite the other. They knocked on the door to apartment 22, and the door opened instantly.

The black man who looked out at them was perhaps six feet four inches tall, wearing only belted trousers and looking very much like a magazine ad extolling the merits of weight lifting. Bare-chested and barefooted, broad-shouldered and strikingly handsome, he looked out at the two detectives in clear surprise, eyebrows raising at first and then coming together into a frown.

"Yeah, what is it?" he said, obviously annoyed.

"Police," Carella said, and showed him the shield. "Are you Lloyd Baxter?"

"I'm Lloyd Baxter. What now?"

"All right for us to come in?"

"What's the beef? I'm gainfully employed, I go see my PO when I'm sposed to, and I ain't so much as spit on the sidewalk in months."

"No beef," Meyer said.

"Then what are you doing here?"

"We have some questions."

"About what?"

"About something that happened twelve years ago."

"I can hardly remember what happened twelve *minutes* ago."

"Is it okay for us to come in?"

"I'm expecting somebody," Baxter said. "I thought it was her at the door, matter of fact."

"We won't be long."

"I got to get dressed," he said, and looked at his watch.

"You can dress while we talk."

"Well," he said reluctantly, "come on in, then."

They stepped inside and he closed the door behind them and led them through the apartment into a bedroom on the street side. The room was simply furnished—bed, dresser, a pair of nightstands, a few lamps. Baxter took a clean white shirt from one of the dresser drawers and began unbuttoning it. "So what are the questions?" he said.

"Know anybody named Jimmy Harris?"

"Yeah. Man, this really *must* be twelve years ago. I haven't seen him since he got drafted."

"Christmastime twelve years ago," Carella said. "Does that ring a bell?"

"No. What kind of bell is it supposed to ring?"

"A girl named Roxanne Dumas."

"Yeah," Baxter said, and nodded, and put on the shirt. "What about her?"

"Was she your girlfriend?"

"Yeah. But, man, that's ancient history. She got married while I was upstate doing time. Guy named Schoolhouse Hardy."

"When's the last time you saw her?"

"Six, seven years ago," Baxter said. He was buttoning the shirt now, obviously pressed for time, glancing at his watch and then going back to the buttoning again.

"Do you remember what happened in the Hawks' clubhouse twelve years ago?"

"No, what happened?" Baxter asked, and tucked the shirt into his trousers. He zipped up his fly, tightened his belt, and then walked swiftly to the dresser and opened the top drawer. Searching there for a moment, he found a pair of blue socks a shade darker than the trousers he was wearing, sat on the bed, and began putting them on.

"You remember dancing with Roxanne?"

"I was *always* dancing with Roxanne. She was my woman. I don't understand this," Baxter said, looking up, one sock on, the other in his hands. "What's supposed to have happened, man?"

"Do you remember a record with drums on it?"

"Come on, man, every record I ever heard's got *drums* on it."

"You were dancing with Roxanne and there were five other boys in the room. You told them to quit watching you. You told them to go upstairs."

Baxter was pulling the other sock onto his foot now. He looked up again, clearly puzzled. "Yeah?" he said.

"Do you remember?"

"No."

"The boys said they were tired. The Hawks had been rumbling with another gang…"

"We were *always* rumbling with other gangs. Man, I still don't get what you're after."

"The boys grabbed you and held you against a basement post."

"The boys *grabbed* me?" Baxter said, and burst out laughing. "You talking about *me*?" he said, still laughing, and rose from the bed and walked toward the closet. "Take an *army* to grab me and hold me against no post. I been this big since I was fourteen, ain't nobody *ever* grabbed me but the mother-fuckin' cop who busted me, and *he* was holdin' a cannon in his fist. Ain't nobody on the Hawks ever grabbed Lloyd Baxter and messed with him. Be some busted legs, they even *thought* about it. Be some bodies strewn all over the sidewalk," Baxter said, shaking his head in utter disbelief, and opening the closet door and taking from the floor there a pair of black patent leather shoes. "Where'd you get this shit, man? Whoever told you anything like that?"

"Jimmy Harris."

"Told you some cats in the club jumped me?"

"Told his doctor."

"Why'd he tell a doctor no shit like that?"

"You're saying it didn't happen?"

"You bet your ass that's what I'm saying," Baxter said, plainly insulted by the very notion. He sat on the edge of the bed again and began putting on his shoes.

Carella looked at Meyer. Meyer shrugged. "We have reason to believe Roxanne Dumas was raped in that basement room twelve years ago," Carella said.

"What?" Baxter said, and burst out laughing again. "Man, these are *fairy* tales, you understand me? These are *pipe* dreams."

"She *didn't* get raped, is that what you're saying?"

"Who'd rape her, man, would you tell me? If you knew Roxanne was my woman, would *you* rape her, man? Would you even *wink* at her, man?" Baxter stood up again.

The detectives watched him as he went to the closet for a tie. They were both thinking they would not have winked at Baxter's girlfriend. Baxter made his selection, a simple blue-and-red-striped silk rep, lifted the collar of the shirt, slipped the tie around his neck, and began knotting it.

"So none of this happened, is that it?" Carella said.

"None of it, man."

"You're sure you're remembering correctly?"

"I'm sure."

"Then why would Jimmy have said it happened?"

"Man, I guess you got to go ask Jimmy."

There was no asking Jimmy, not anymore there wasn't.

But there still remained the lady in question, Roxanne Hardy née Dumas, who—if indeed she had been raped—could be considered an unimpeachable source of information on the subject. If she had not been raped, Carella didn't know what to think. Neither did Meyer. Of the two, Carella was perhaps more psychologically oriented than his partner, but both men were conditioned to believe—after having seen films like *The Three Faces of Eve* and *David and Lisa*, and *Spellbound* and *Marnie*, and any one of a thousand television dramas depicting mental patients who were severe catatonics standing in corners with their faces to the wall till some understanding psychiatrist unlocked the past for them and let the sunshine in on the trauma that was causing all their pain—after having seen mental rehabilitation happen dramatically and suddenly once the patient knew what was bugging him, Meyer and Carella were both ready to accept Lemarre's contention that Jimmy's nightmares were rooted in Roxanne's rape twelve years ago. Except that now Lloyd Baxter had told them there'd *been* no rape, *been* no such event that might have irritated a man Lloyd's size and caused him to break you in itty-bitty pieces.

Which left Roxanne.

They did not find her till a little after 3:00 that afternoon. They had tried her last-known address and were told by the landlady there that she'd moved out, oh, at least six months ago, she didn't know where. They had then checked the Isola telephone directory for a place called The Beauty Hut, and had found a listing for one on The Stem. They did not expect anyone to answer the phone there—this was Sunday—and no one did. But they drove over anyway, hoping to find something open in the immediate neighborhood—a delicatessen, a bar, a restaurant, a luncheonette, a movie theater—anything where there might be someone who knew the person who owned The Beauty Hut.

The stores immediately adjacent to it were a closed pawnshop on its left and a closed lingerie shop on its right. Two doors down was an open countertop store selling pizza by the slice. It was now past 2:00 in the afternoon, and neither of the men had yet had lunch. They each ordered two slices of pizza and an orange drink, and Carella asked the counterman if he knew who ran the beauty parlor down the street. The attendant told him it was a woman named Harriet Lesser. Carella asked if he knew where Harriet Lesser lived, and the counterman said, no, she only came in every now and then for a slice of pizza—why? Was Carella a cop? Carella said, yes, he was a cop, and then he finished his pizza and both he and Meyer paid their own separate tabs and went to the telephone at the back of the store where a directory was hanging on a chain.

The directory was frayed and frazzled, but it told them there were thirty-three Lessers (thirty-three, count 'em, thirty-three) in Isola, fourteen of which were clearly business establishments like Lesser Drafting Service, Inc., Lesser Marine and Lesser Volkswagen, which left nineteen Lessers to go, and none of them named Harriet. There were two H. Lessers in the directory.

They tried calling them first. One was a Helen and the other was a Hortense. It was not until almost 3:00 that they discovered a Harriet Lesser who was the wife of a Charles Lesser and who (hallelujah!) owned The Beauty Hut. They told her who they were and what they wanted, and she gave them Roxanne Hardy's new address. They got into Carella's car again, and drove downtown and crosstown, arriving at her apartment at twelve minutes past the hour.

The woman who opened the door was tall and lissome, with a smooth pecan-colored complexion and luminous brown eyes that looked puzzled now by the presence of two white men on her doorstep. She was wearing a striped caftan that flowed about her body like a huge sail in the wind, tight across her abundant breasts, flaring out below to end just above her ankles and her bare feet.

"Yes?" she said.

"Mrs. Hardy?" Carella said.

"Yes?"

"Police," he said, and showed her the shield.

She examined it without interest. The puzzlement left her eyes and a look of mild curiosity replaced it—a slight lifting of one eyebrow, a bemused expression about the mouth.

"May we come in?" Carella asked.

"For what purpose, Officer?" she said, and there was in her voice the lilt she'd brought with her from Jamaica seventeen years before, when she was still a girl of twelve unfamiliar with the ways of any city bigger than Kingston.

Carella didn't know quite how to put his question. Should he ask her flat-out if she'd been raped twelve years ago by four assorted members of the Hawks? He might have done just that, if Lloyd Baxter hadn't seemed quite so certain that nothing of the sort had happened. Instead, he said, "Mrs. Hardy, I understand you have some knowledge of a street gang called the Hawks," and realized at once that he was referring to *carnal* knowledge, and again wondered about the subterranean workings of his own mind, and by extension, Jimmy's. If Jimmy *hadn't* witnessed a rape, then what the hell *had* traumatized him: The recurring nightmares hadn't come out of thin air, they were rooted somewhere in his unconscious. All right—*where?*

"I used to know some members of the Hawks, yes," Roxanne said. "But that was a long time ago." Her voice was soft; it sounded almost nostalgic.

"May we come in, please?" Carella said. "We'd like to ask you some questions about the gang."

"Yes, all right," she said, and stepped aside to let them into the apartment.

The place was still with late-afternoon sunlight that streamed bleakly through the kitchen window and touched the hanging potted plants with silver. She led them into a modestly furnished living room, and beckoned gracefully to the two easy chairs that sat on either side of a color television set. She herself sat on the sofa opposite them, pulling her legs up under her Indian-fashion, the caftan tented over her knees.

"What is it you want to know?" she asked.

"We'd like you to tell us what happened just before Christmas twelve years ago," Carella said.

"Oh my," she said, and laughed suddenly. "We were all children then."

"I realize that," Carella said. "But can you remember anything important that happened around that time?"

"Important?" she said, and raised her shoulders expressively, rather like a dancer, her hands opening wide to further expand upon the theme of places and events too distant to recall.

It occurred to Carella that Lloyd Baxter and Roxanne Hardy were two of the most strikingly good-looking people he'd ever met. It seemed a pity they hadn't chosen to remain together—

The cop suddenly took over. *Why* hadn't they chosen to stay together? Was it because Lloyd had allowed the rape? Or was it because she'd invited it?

"It would have been something very important," Carella said, and felt suddenly as though he were playing Twenty Questions. Meyer caught his eyes. They both acknowledged silently and at once that the time had come to quit pussyfooting around. "Mrs. Hardy," Carella said, "were you raped shortly before Christmas twelve years ago?"

"What?" she said.

"Raped," he said.

"Yes, I heard you," she said. "My," she said. "Raped," she said. "No," she said. "Never. Not twelve years ago, and not ever." Her eyes met his. "*Should* I have been?"

"Jimmy Harris said you were."

"Ah, Jimmy Harris."

"Yes. He said four members of the Hawks strong-armed Lloyd Baxter and then forced themselves upon you."

"Lloyd? Have you met Lloyd? No one strong-arms Lloyd. No, sir. Not Lloyd."

"Mrs. Hardy, if this never happened...Where do you suppose Jimmy got the idea?"

"I don't know," she said, and smiled pleasantly, and Carella knew at once that she was lying. Until this moment, she'd been speaking the truth, but now the smile was false, the eyes above the smile were not smiling with it, she was lying. Meyer knew she was lying, too; the men glanced at each other, and separately wondered who was going to attack the lie first.

Meyer stepped in delicately. “Do you think Jimmy made the whole thing up?” he asked.

“I really don’t know,” Roxanne said.

“Your being raped, I mean.”

“Yes, I understand. I don’t know why Jimmy told you something like that.”

“He didn’t tell *us*.”

“He didn’t? You said—”

“He told his doctor.”

“Well…” Roxanne let the word trail. She shrugged. “I don’t know why he did that,” she said.

“Seems a pretty strange thing to invent, doesn’t it?”

“Yes, it certainly does. What kind of doctor was this? A shrink?”

“Yes.”

“A prison shrink?”

“No. An Army doctor.”

“Mm,” she said, and shrugged again.

“Mrs. Hardy,” Carella said, “how well did you know Jimmy Harris?”

“Same as the other boys,” she said.

“The other boys in the gang?”

“Yes. Well, the club. They called it a club. It *was* a club, I guess.”

“About two dozen boys altogether, is that right?”

“Well, there were others all over Diamondback.”

“But two dozen in the immediate gang.”

“Yes.”

“And you knew Jimmy about as well as you knew any of the others.”

“Yes.”

She was still lying. He knew she was lying, damn it. He looked at Meyer; Meyer knew it, too. They weren’t going to let go of this.

They were going to sit here and talk her blue in the face till they found out why she was lying.

"Would you say you were friendly with him?" Meyer asked.

"Jimmy? Oh yes. But I was Lloyd's girlfriend, you understand."

"Yes, we understand that."

"So I only knew the other boys casually, you see."

"Mm," Meyer said.

"The way your wife—are you married?"

"Yes."

"And you?"

"Yes," Carella said.

"Well, the way your wives would know other detectives you might work with, the same as that."

"That's the way you knew Jimmy Harris."

"Yes."

"You thought of yourself as Lloyd's wife, is that it?"

"Well, no not his *wife*," she said, and laughed. The laugh was phony; it had none of the genuine resonance of her earlier laughter. She was still lying, there was still something she was hiding. "But we *did* have an understanding with each other. We were *going* with each other, you see."

"What does that mean?" Carella asked. "No other girls in Lloyd's life…"

"That's right."

"And no other boys in yours?"

"Exactly."

"It seems strange, though, that Jimmy would come up with this story about the boys' having raped you."

"It certainly does," Roxanne said, and laughed again. This time the laugh ended almost before it escaped her throat.

"Did he ever…?" Carella said, and cut himself short. "No, forget it."

"What were you about to say?" Meyer said, playing the straight man.

"I just wondered...Mrs. Hardy, Jimmy never made a *pass* at you, did he?"

"No," she said. "No, never."

Another lie. Her eyes would not even meet his now.

"Never, huh?"

"No."

"Are you sure?"

"Yes, of course I'm sure. I was Lloyd's girlfriend, you understand."

"Yes, I understand that."

"I was faithful to Lloyd."

"Yes. But that doesn't necessarily mean *Jimmy* was faithful to him. Do you see what I mean, Mrs. Hardy? If Jimmy ever approached you—"

"No, he didn't."

"—sexually, then perhaps that might account for what he told his doctor."

"Why is this important to you?" she asked suddenly.

"Because Jimmy Harris is dead, and we don't know who killed him," Carella said.

She was silent for several moments. Then she said, "I'm sorry to hear that."

"Mrs. Hardy...If anything ever happened between you and Jimmy, or between you and any of the other boys on the Hawks, anything that might have prompted someone to start thinking of revenge or retribution—"

"No," she said, and shook her head.

"Nothing happened."

"Something *did* happen," she said. "But no one knew. Only Jimmy knew. And me."

"Could you tell us what it was, please?"

"It won't help you. No one knew."

She looked at them for a long time, not saying anything, debating silently whether or not she wished to reveal whatever secret she had carried for the past twelve years. She nodded then, and said in a voice almost a whisper, "It was raining. It was very cold outside, it seemed as if it should be snowing…"

Her voice, as she spoke, seemed to become more and more Jamaican, as though the closer she came to the memory of that day twelve years ago, the more she became the seventeen-year-old girl she then was. As they listened, the present dissolved into the past, only to become the present again—a *different* present, but an immediate one nonetheless; whatever had happened in that basement room so long ago seemed to be happening here and now, this instant.

It is raining.

She is surprised by the rain, she thinks it should be snowing at this time of year, it's so cold outside. But it's raining instead, there is thunder and lightning. The lightning flashes illuminate the painted basement windows high on the cinder-block walls. Thunder crashes everywhere around them. They are alone in the basement room. It is 4:00 in the afternoon on the Wednesday before Christmas.

They are alone here by chance. She has come looking for Lloyd, but there's only Jimmy standing by the record player with a stack of records in his hands. The cinder-block wall is painted a blue paler than the streaked midnight blue that covers the windows. Lightning flashes again, thunder sounds. Jimmy puts a record on the turntable. He tells her the other guys are right this minute in the Hermanos clubhouse, over in Spictown, negotiating a truce. He'd have gone with them, he says, but his mother cut her hand, he had to rush her to the hospital. Lightning again, the bellow of thunder. Cut herself decorating the Christmas tree, he says. The music is soft and slow and insinuating. The thunder booms its counterpoint.

"You want to dance?" he says.

She knows at once that she should refuse. She is Lloyd's woman. If Lloyd comes back unexpectedly and finds them dancing together, there will be serious trouble. She knows this. She knows they will hurt her, she knows she can expect no mercy from Lloyd, the code is the code, they will whip her till she bleeds. Last summer, when they caught one of the Auxils talking to a Hermanos on the street, they stripped her to the waist, tied her to the post, and the sergeant at arms gave her twenty lashes. She whimpered at first, and then began screaming each time the whip raised another welt on her back, the welts opening at last and beginning to bleed. They threw her out in the gutter, threw her blouse and brassiere out after her, told her to go to the Hermanos if she liked them so much.

That was last summer, but this is now, and this will be worse. This will be dancing with a brother when Lloyd isn't around. Be different if he was here, nothing would be said of it. But he is not here, she is alone with Jimmy, and she is frightened because she understands the danger. But it is exactly the danger that attracts her.

She laughs nervously and says, "Sure, why not?"

Jimmy takes her in his arms. The music is slow, they dance very close. He is excited, she can feel him through his trousers and through her skirt. They are dancing fish, he is socking it to her, grinding against her. There is more thunder. She is still frightened, but he is holding her very tight, and she is getting excited herself. She laughs again. Her panties are wet, she is dripping wet under her skirt. The record ends, the needle clicks and clicks and clicks in the retaining grooves. He releases her suddenly and walks to the record player, and lifts the arm from the record. There is silence, and then lightning streaks the painted windows again, and thunder crashes. He walks to the door.

She stands motionless in the center of the room near the post. She is afraid they will tie her to the post with her hands behind her back. This is a serious offense, she is afraid they will whip her across her naked breasts. She knows of a girl in another gang who was whipped that way for the offense of adultery. The offense is clearly lettered on the rules chart that hangs on the clubhouse wall. Adultery. She is about to make love to a brother, but she is Lloyd's woman, and that is adultery, and they will hurt her badly for it. They will hurt Jimmy, too. They will force him to run the gauntlet, hitting him with chains and pipes as he runs between his brothers lined up on either side of him.

And when it is all over and done with, when they've given her the fifty lashes, she's certain she'll receive in punishment, fifty or maybe a hundred because she's the president's woman, across her naked breasts, the sergeant at arms methodically and deliberately beating her with the seven-thonged whip; when they've forced Jimmy through the gauntlet and have left him bruised and bleeding and unconscious on the ground, why, then both of them will be thrown out of the club to fend for themselves. The club is their insurance in a hostile world of enemy camps that grow like toadstools in the surrounding streets. There is no help from the Law in these streets, there is no help from parents who are scrounging for the big white dollar out there, there is only aid and comfort from your brothers and sisters in the clubs.

If you don't belong to a club, you are anybody's.

If you're a boy, you're anybody's to beat up on, anybody's to rob, anybody's to cut or burn or snuff. If you're a girl, you're anybody's to hurt, anybody's to fuck, anybody's to do with what they want. This is the city. You need insurance here. Belonging to the

Hawks' auxiliary is her insurance, and she is about to have it canceled only because she is a stupid bitch. She knows she's being dumb, she knows that. But she wants Jimmy Harris, and she suspects she's maybe wanted him from the first time he began coming on six months back, and she began looking the other way and making believe it wasn't happening. It was happening, all right. It is happening right now. He is locking the basement door, double-locking it like he's expecting a raid from a hundred gangs, putting the chain on it in the bargain, and then coming back to where she's standing, and grabbing her tight, and kissing her hard on the mouth till she has to pull away to catch her breath.

His hands are all over her. He unbuttons her blouse, he touches her breasts, he slides his hands under her skirt and up over her thighs, he grabs her ass tight in nylon panties, she is getting dizzy standing there in the middle of the room. She falls limp against the post, and he does it to her standing there against the post. Rips her panties. Tears them in his hands, rips them away from where she's wet and waiting, unzips his fly and sticks it in her. He comes almost the minute he's inside her, and she screams and comes with him, the hell with the Hawks, the hell with Lloyd, the hell with the whole world. They grab each other like it's the weekend ending, they cling to each other there against the post in the middle of the basement, the lightning and thunder crashing around them. She begins crying. He begins crying, too, and then makes her promise she won't ever tell anybody in the world that he cried.

12

Monday morning came at last.

The telephone on Carella's desk was ringing. He picked up the receiver and said, "87th Squad, Carella."

"This is Maloney, Canine Unit."

"Yes, Maloney."

"You were supposed to call me," Maloney said.

"I just got here this minute," Carella said, and looked up at the clock. "It's only a quarter to nine, Maloney."

"I told you to call first thing in the morning."

"This *is* first thing in the morning," Carella said.

"I don't want to get in no argument about whether it's first thing in the morning," Maloney said. "I been here since eight o'clock, *that's* first thing in the morning, I don't want to get in no argument. All I want to know is what disposition is to be taken with this dog here."

"Yeah," Carella said.

"What does *that* mean, yeah?"

"It means, give me a minute, okay?"

"This dog is not a nice dog here," Maloney said. "He won't let nobody go near him. He won't eat nothin' we put in his dish, he's a fuckin' ungrateful mutt, you want to know."

"That's how he was trained," Carella said.

"To be ungrateful?"

"No, no. To take food only from his master. He's a seeing-eye dog."

"I know what he is. We don't need no seeing-eye dogs down here. Down here, we need dogs who sniff out dope, that's what we need down here. So what do you want me to do with him? You don't want him, he goes to the shelter. You know what they do at the shelter?"

"I know what they do."

"They keep the mutt three weeks, then they put him away. It's painless. They put him in a container, they draw all the air out of it. It's like going to sleep. What do you say, Coppola?"

"Carella."

"Yeah, what do you say?"

"I'll send someone down for him."

"When?"

"Right away."

"When is right away?"

"Right away is right away," Carella said.

"Sure," Maloney said. "The same way first thing in the morning is quarter to nine, right?"

"I'll have somebody there by ten o'clock."

"It's the Headquarters building, eighth floor. Tell him to ask for Detective Maloney. What do you guys do up there, work half a day?"

"Only when we're busy," Carella said, and hung up. Detective Richard Genero was at his desk, studying his dictionary. Carella walked over to him and said, "What's the good word, Genero?"

"What?" Genero said. "Oh," he said, "I get it. The good word."

He did not smile. He rarely smiled. Carella imagined he was constipated a lot. He wondered suddenly why no one on the squad called Genero "Richard" or "Richie" or "Dick" or anything but "Genero." Everyone else on the squad called everyone else by his first name. But Genero was Genero. Moreover, he wondered why *Genero* had never noticed this. Was it possible that people outside the squadroom also called him Genero? Was it possible that his *mother* called him Genero? Did she phone him on Fridays and say, "Genero, this is Mama. How come you never call?"

"How would you like to do me a favor?" Carella said.

"What favor?" Genero asked suspiciously.

"How would you like to go downtown to pick up a dog?"

"What dog?" Genero asked suspiciously.

"A seeing-eye dog."

"This is a gag, right?"

"No."

"Then what dog?"

"I told you. A seeing-eye dog down at Canine."

"This is a gag about when I got shot in the foot that time, right?"

"No, no."

"When I was on that stakeout in the park, right?"

"No, Genero, wrong."

"When I was making believe I was a blind man, and I got shot in the foot, am I right?"

"No. This is a real job. There's a black Labrador that has to be picked up at Canine."

"So why are you sending me?"

"I'm not *sending* you, Genero, I'm *asking* if you'd like to go."

"Send a patrolman," Genero said. "What the hell is this? Every time there's a shit job to be done on this squad, I'm the one who gets sent. Fuck that," Genero said.

"I thought you might like some air," Carella said.

"I've got cases to take care of here," Genero said. "You think I've got nothing to do here?"

"Forget it," Carella said.

"Send a goddamn patrolman."

"I'll send a patrolman," Carella said.

"Anyway, it's a gag, you think I don't know it?" Genero said. "You're making fun of that time I got shot in the park."

"I thought you got shot in the foot."

"In the foot in the park," Genero said unsmilingly. Carella went back to his own desk and dialed 24 for the muster room downstairs. When Sergeant Murchison picked up, he said, "Dave, this is Steve. Can you send a car to the Headquarters building for me? Eighth floor, ask for Detective Maloney, he'll turn over a black Labrador retriever."

"Is the dog vicious?" Murchison asked.

"No, he's a seeing-eye dog, he's not vicious."

"There are some seeing-eye dogs will bite you soon as look at you," Murchison said.

"In that case, tell your man to use a muzzle. They carry muzzles in the cars, don't they?"

"Yeah, but it's hard to get a muzzle on a vicious dog."

"This dog isn't vicious," Carella said. "And, Dave, could you send somebody right away? If the dog isn't picked up by ten, they'll send him to the shelter and they'll kill him in three weeks."

"So what's the hurry?" Murchison said, and hung up.

Carella blinked. He put the receiver back on the cradle and looked at it. He looked at it so hard that it rang, startling him. He picked up the receiver again.

"87th Squad, Carella," he said.

"Steve, this is Sam Grossman."

"Hello, Sam, how are you?"

"*Comme ci, comme ça,*" Grossman said. "Was it you who sent this soil sample to the lab? It's only marked '87th Squad.'"

"Meyer did. How does it look?"

"It matches what we got from under Harris's fingernails, if that's what you're looking for. But I've got to tell you, Steve, this is a fairly common composition. I wouldn't consider this a positive make unless you've got corroborating evidence."

"Corroborating supposition, let's say."

"Okay, then."

"Anything on the Harris apartment?"

"Nothing. No alien latents, footprints, hairs, or fibers. Nothing."

"Okay, thanks. I'll talk to you."

"So long," Grossman said, and hung up.

Carella put the receiver back on its cradle. An Army corporal was standing just outside the slatted-rail divider, looking tentatively into the squadroom. Carella got up and walked to the divider. "Help you?" he said.

"Sergeant downstairs told me to come up here," the corporal said. "I'm looking for somebody named Capella."

"Carella, that's me."

"This is from Captain McCormick," the corporal said, and handed Carella a manila envelope printed in the left-hand corner with the words *U.S. Army, Criminal Investigations Division.*

"You're here early," Carella said.

"Actually, we got the packet yesterday, but there was nobody in the office. Mailroom clocked it in at four-oh-seven P.M. Guys in St. Louis must've put it on a plane late Saturday night. That's pretty good time, don't you think?"

"That's very good," Carella said. "Thanks a lot."

"Don't mention it," the corporal said. "How do I get to Reuter Street? I've got to make a pickup on Reuter Street, the recruiting office there."

"That's all the way downtown," Carella said. "Are you driving?"

"Yeah."

"When you come out of the station house, make a right, and then another right at the next corner. That's a one-way street heading north, it'll take you straight to the River Highway. You want the westbound entrance. Take the highway downtown till you see the sign for Reuter."

"Thanks," the corporal said.

"Thank *you*," Carella said, and gestured with the manila envelope.

"Don't mention it," the corporal said again, and did a smart about-face and went down the corridor.

Carella carried the envelope back to his desk and opened it. The sheaf of papers was thin but unfamiliar. It took him a while to get used to the forms themselves, and then another while to digest the information they contained. He made notes as he went along, not knowing whether the Xeroxed papers were his to keep and not wanting to mark them. McCormick had seemed specific about protocol on the telephone Friday. He guessed he would have to return the papers to the captain when he was through with them.

James Randolph Harris had entered the Army on the seventeenth day of May, ten years ago. He was sent to Fort Gordon, Georgia, for his basic training, and from there, to Fort Jackson, South Carolina, for advanced infantry training. At the end of August he was sent overseas as a private first class in D Company, 2nd Battalion of the 27th Infantry, 2nd Brigade of the 25th Infantry Division. It did not say so in his field file, but Carella knew from the photograph they'd found in the Harris apartment that Jimmy had been in the 2nd Squad's Alpha Fire Team.

If Carella recalled his own Army days correctly, there were four platoons in a company, and four squads in a platoon, which meant that in D Company there were sixteen squads altogether. Each platoon had a 1st, 2nd, 3rd, and 4th Squad, Army squads being labeled numerically rather than alphabetically. Since there were four platoons, there had to be four 2nd Squads. But there was nothing in the folder that gave the number of Jimmy's platoon. Carella was assuming that if Jimmy had contacted an old Army buddy for assistance with a scheme, it would have been a man in his immediate combat team. But in order to zero in on Alpha, he had to know the number of the platoon.

The file dutifully reported that Jimmy had been wounded in action on the fourteenth day of December and then went on to describe the nature of the wound in strictly medical language. At the end of December he was transferred from the camp hospital to a hospital in Honolulu, and from there, to another hospital in San Francisco, and finally to the General Hospital at Fort Mercer. His DD Form-214 showed that he had been honorably discharged with full disability pension in March. That was all.

Carella needed more.

Sighing, he opened his personal telephone directory, and leafed through the LPs till he came to the listing for U.S. Army. Under that he found the number he had called at Fort Jefferson the other day, and below that, the number for the National Personnel Records Center in St. Louis. He looked up at the wall clock. It was twenty after 9:00, which meant that it was only twenty after 8:00 in St. Louis; there were sometimes drawbacks to living in a huge sprawling nation. He jotted the number onto a piece of scrap paper, and then took three DD report forms from his top desk drawer, separated them with two sheets of carbon, and began typing up his report on the interviews with Lloyd Baxter and Roxanne Hardy.

As he typed he wondered what Major Lemarre might have thought about Roxanne's revelation. The major had seemed so certain that Jimmy was telling the truth about that basement rape twelve years ago. Instead, it hadn't been a rape at all. Not a hundred-dollar gold-plated rape, nor even a two-bit tissue-paper rape. It had, instead, been a pair of teenage kids with the hots for each other, enjoying the pleasure of each other's company against a basement post—listen, there were worse ways. The thing Carella didn't understand was why Jimmy had lied. And why hadn't the major caught the lie? Surely a trained psychiatrist should have been able to see through the false memory. There was no question but that Roxanne had told the truth about what happened that day; her retelling of the story had been too intense. But then again, so had Jimmy's version—and it was Jimmy who'd been having the nightmares.

Carella was frankly puzzled. There hardly seemed anything of nightmare proportions in the sex Jimmy and Roxanne had shared that day, unless it was fear of punishment. Perhaps Jimmy was tortured by the idea of getting caught. Running the gauntlet was never any fun, even back in medieval times, and the modern street-gang version was no improvement on the original. Jimmy probably worried like hell about what had happened that day with Lloyd's woman. He must have been familiar with gauntlet runs, must have visualized himself in the victim's position—lead pipes crashing on his skull, tire chains flailing his chest, booted feet stomping him into the ground.

Thoughts like that could give a man nightmares, sure enough. Must have walked the streets expecting Lloyd's hand to fall on his shoulder at any moment—*Hello, Jimmy, baby, I hear you done my woman.* Jimmy must've had his defense all prepared, must've concocted a rape story to rival that of the Sabine Sisters—*No, Lloyd, you got it all wrong, man. I didn't do her, it was the* other *guys. I'm the one tried to stop them, in fact.* It wasn't the truth he'd spilled out to Major Lemarre, it was his *defense.* He must've thought he was caught at last, the way Lemarre kept circling that nightmare, coming back to it over and over again, getting closer and closer to that rainy day in the basement. So he'd dragged out the rape. *This is what* really *happened, Doc. This is what* really *happened, Lloyd. Let the other guys run the gauntlet. I'm the good guy, I tried to stop them.*

Well, maybe, Carella thought, and looked at the clock again. It was time to call St. Louis. He dialed the area code and then the number and listened to the phone ringing on the other end. He wondered what St. Louis was like. He had never been to St. Louis. He visualized cowboys running cattle through the streets. He visualized tough guys drinking rotgut in saloons or dancing with girls wearing net stockings and red garters.

"National Personnel," a woman's voice said.

"This is Detective Carella, 87th Squad, Isola," he said. "I have a packet here from Captain McCormick at Fort Jefferson..."

"Yes, Mr. Carella?"

"And I need some further information."

"Just one moment, sir, I'll put you through to Mr. O'Neill."

"Thank you," Carella said.

He waited.

"O'Neill," a man's voice said.

"Mr. O'Neill, this is Detective Carella, 87th Squad, Isola. I have a packet here from Captain McCormick at Fort Jefferson, and I need some further information."

"What sort of information?" O'Neill asked.

"I'm investigating a homicide in which the victim was a man named James Harris, served with the Army ten years ago, D Company, Second Battalion..."

"Let me take this down," O'Neill said. "D Company, Second Battalion..."

"Twenty-seventh Infantry," Carella said. "Second Brigade of the Twenty-fifth Infantry Division. I don't have a platoon number. He was in Alpha Fire Team of the Second Squad."

"Rank?"

"Pfc."

"Service number?"

"Just a second," Carella said, and consulted Jimmy's file. He found the number and read off the eight digits slowly. O'Neill would later be feeding this into a computer, and Carella didn't want any errors.

"Discharged or deceased?" O'Neill asked.

"Both," Carella said.

"How's that possible?"

"He was discharged ten years ago and killed last Thursday night."

"Oh. Oh, I see. I meant...What I meant, we have the records here for anyone who was either discharged or killed in action. The Department of the Army would have the records on anyone retired from the service, or with the reserve. This man was discharged, you said?"

"Yes."

"Honorable discharge?"

"Yes. Full disability pension."

"He was wounded?"

"Yes."

"When?"

"December fourteenth, ten years ago next month."

"Okay," O'Neill said, "what is it you want to know?"

"The names of the other men in his fire team."

"On the date you just gave me?"

"Yes."

"That might be possible," O'Neill said. "Depends on who filed the action report."

"Who normally files it?"

"The OIC. Or sometimes the—"

"Would that be the officer in command?"

"Yes, or sometimes the noncommissioned officer in command. There's usually a second lieutenant in charge of a platoon, and an E-Seven assisting him. If neither of those two witnessed the particular action that day, then the squad leader may have filed the action report, or even the E-Five leading the fire team. Do you understand how this is broken down?"

"Not exactly," Carella said. "In my day the squad was the basic unit."

"Well, it still is, but now the squad's broken down into two fire teams, Alpha and Bravo. You've got five men in each team, with an E-Six leading the full squad, for a total of eleven men. The way each fire team breaks down, there are two automatic riflemen who are Spec Fours or E-Threes, a grenadier who's usually an E-Four, two riflemen who are E-Threes, and an E-Five leading them."

"I don't know what all those numbers mean," Carella said. "Spec Fours, E-Threes..."

"Those are designations of rank. An E-Three is a Pfc, a Spec Four is a specialist fourth class, a corporal. An E-Five is a three-striper, and so on."

"Mm-huh," Carella said.

"What I'm suggesting is that the action report may possibly list the men who were in Harris's fire team."

"Would that be in his personal file?"

"Yes," O'Neill said.

"Well, I've got his file right here, and the action report doesn't mention any other men in the fire team."

"Who signed the report?"

"Just a minute," Carella said, and dug through the sheaf of papers again. "A man named Lieutenant John Francis Tataglia."

"That would've been his platoon commander," O'Neill said. "That's his Field 201-File you've got there, huh?"

"Yes."

"And the action report doesn't name the men in his fire team, huh?"

"No."

"Would there be what we call a Special Order in his file?"

"What's that?"

"It's an order assigning a man to such and such a squad, and sometimes it'll list the other men in the squad by name, rank and service number."

"No, I didn't run across anything like that"

"Well then, I guess we'll have to cross-check with Organizational Records. That may take a little while," O'Neill said. "May I have your number, please?"

"Frederick 7-8024."

"That's in Isola, right?"

"Yes, the area code here—"

"I have it. What was your name again, please?"

"Detective Second/Grade Stephen Louis Carella."

"You're with a local law-enforcement agency, am I right?"

"Yes."

"I'll get back to you," O'Neill said, and hung up.

He did not get back till close to 11:00 A.M. Carella had gone down the hall to Clerical for a cup of coffee, and was just returning to his desk when the telephone rang. He put down the paper carton and picked up the receiver.

"87th Squad, Carella," he said.

"Harry O'Neill here in St. Louis. I'm sorry, but I didn't get a chance to run this through the computer till a few minutes ago. I've got the company roster here—that's a long sheet that lists all the men in a company and breaks the company down into four platoons, listing the men alphabetically and by rank. James Harris was in D Company's Third Platoon. Now…Depending on the morning reports of each platoon, you'll sometimes get a breakdown of the squads and fire teams in those squads. The clerks in the Third Platoon kept very nice records. I've got those names you wanted."

"Good," Carella said, "let me have them, please."

"Got a pencil?"

"Shoot."

"Rudy Tanner, Pfc, automatic rifleman. That's T-a-n-n-e-r."

"Got it."

"Karl Fiersen, E-Four, grenadier."

"Carl with a C?"

"With a K."

"Would you spell the last name for me, please?"

"F-i-e-r-s-e-n."

"Go on."

"James Harris and Russell Poole, both Pfc's, riflemen. That's Russell with two esses and two els, and Poole with an e."

"Okay."

"The sergeant leading the team was an E-Five named Robert Hopewell, just the way it sounds."

"Right," Carella said.

"Did you want the names of the platoon commander and his assistant?"

"If you've got them."

"Commander was a man named Lieutenant Roger Blake, later killed in action. The next one's a tough one, I'd better spell it. Sergeant John Tataglia, that's T-a-t-a-g-l-i-a."

“Are you sure about that?”

“About what?”

“Tataglia’s rank. Isn’t he the lieutenant who signed the action report? Just a second,” Carella said, and spread the sheaf of papers on his desk. “Yes, here it is, Lieutenant John Francis Tataglia.”

“Well, he’s listed as a sergeant on this.”

“On what?”

“The platoon’s morning report.”

“Any date on it.”

“December third.”

“The action report is dated December fifteenth.”

“Well, one or the other must be wrong,” O’Neill said. “Unless he was promoted in the interim.”

“Is that likely?”

“It’s possible.”

“Can I get some addresses for these people?”

“I thought you’d never ask,” O’Neill said.

The list of last-known addresses for the four men in Jimmy’s fire team, as well as the man who’d once been his platoon sergeant, broke down this way:

John Francis Tataglia
Fort Lee
Petersburg, Virginia

Rudy Tanner
1147 Marathon Drive
Los Angeles, California

Karl Fiersen
324 Barter Street
Los Angeles, California

Robert Hopewell
163 Oleander Crescent
Sarasota, Florida

Russell Poole, the last man on the list, was also the only man from Alpha who lived in the city. Or, at least, he *had* lived in the city when he was discharged from the army. His address was listed as 3167 Avenue L, in Majesta.

A series of phone calls to Directory Assistance came up with address confirmations for Robert Hopewell in Sarasota and Russell Poole here in the city. There were no telephone listings for Rudy Tanner or Karl Fiersen in Los Angeles; Carella could only assume both men had since moved. There was nothing else he could do to locate them, unless they'd been in trouble with the Law since their discharge. He called the Los Angeles Police Department and asked for a records search in their Identification Section. The detective-sergeant to whom he spoke—in Los Angeles, they were rather more paramilitary concerning rank than were the police in this city—promised Carella he'd get back to him by the end of the day.

Carella then called Fort Lee, Virginia, and learned that John Francis Tataglia, the erstwhile platoon sergeant who'd presumably been promoted to second lieutenant, was now *Major* Tataglia and had been transferred to Fort Kirby this past September. Fort Kirby was in the adjoining state, some eighty miles over the Hamilton Bridge. Carella called the major there at once, and told him he'd be out to see him that afternoon. The major did not remember Pfc. James Harris until Carella explained that he was the man who'd been blinded in action. Cotton Hawes was just coming through the slatted-rail divider as Carella hung up the phone. He signaled to him, and Hawes walked over to his desk; his red hair had been tangled by the wind outside, his face was raw, he looked fierce and mean.

"Are you busy?" Carella asked.

"Why?"

"I need someone to call Sarasota for me, do a telephone interview. I've got to go out to Fort Kirby right away."

"Sarasota? Where's that, upstate?"

"No, Florida."

"Florida, huh? Why don't I just fly on down there?" Hawes said, and grinned.

"Because I also want you to go see a man in Majesta. What do you say?"

"What am I supposed to do with the three burglaries I'm working?"

"This is a homicide, Cotton."

"*I've* got a homicide too," Hawes said. "Somewhere on my desk, I'm sure I've got a homicide."

"Can you help me?"

"Fill me in," Hawes said, and sighed.

13

In order to get to Fort Kirby in the bordering state, one drove over the Hamilton Bridge and through a community called Baylorville, which in the good old days used to be the pig-farming center of the state. Nowadays there was nary an oink to be heard in the vicinity, but the place stank nonetheless, and Meyer put his handkerchief to his nose the moment they began driving through it. He was beginning to discover that he had a very sensitive olfactory mechanism, a quality he had not recognized in himself earlier. He wondered how he could put this to good use in the crime-detection business. Meanwhile, he looked out dismally at the rows of factories and refineries, incinerators and mills that lined the parkway. The weather had turned bleak and forbidding. Even without the benefit of the smokestacks belching their filth and stench into the air, the sky would have been the color of gunmetal.

Both men sat huddled inside their overcoats. It was 12:30 by the car clock, and Fort Kirby was still forty miles away. The parkway tollbooths were spaced exactly five miles apart; Carella kept rolling down the window on the driver's side and handing quarters to toll collectors. Meyer kept track of the quarters they spent. They would later turn in a chit to Clerical, hoping they'd one day be reimbursed. In the police department, chits were questioned closely, the operative theory being that people in law enforcement were all too often crooks themselves, educated as they were in the ways of thieves. After all, who was to say that the 50¢ spent for a bridge toll had not instead been spent for a hamburger, medium rare? Carella asked for receipts at all of the tollbooths. He handed these to Meyer, who clipped them to the inside cover of his notebook.

It was twenty minutes past 1:00 when they reached Fort Kirby. Carella identified himself to the sentry at the gate in the cyclone fence surrounding the base. A huge sign, black lettered on white, advised that no one but authorized personnel would be admitted to the area. The sentry examined Carella's shield and ID card, checked a sheaf of slips attached to a clipboard, and then said, "The major's expecting you, sir. You can park just this side of the canteen, that's the redbrick building there on your right. The major's in A-4."

"Thank you," Carella said.

Major John Francis Tataglia was a man in his early thirties, with close-cropped blond hair and a blond mustache that hung under his nose like an afterthought. He was slight of build, perhaps five feet nine inches tall, with alert blue eyes and an air of total efficiency about him. You could visualize this man on a parade ground standing at attention in the hot sun, never wilting, never even perspiring. He rose from behind his desk the moment the sergeant ushered Carella and Meyer into his office. He extended his hand.

"Major Tataglia," he said. "Pleased to meet you."

Both detectives shook hands with him, and then took seats opposite his desk. The sergeant backed out of the room like an indentured servant. The door whispered shut behind him. From somewhere out on the drill field, they could hear a sergeant bellowing marching orders, "Hut, tuh, trih, fuh," the repetitive chant oddly and overwhelmingly evocative. For Carella, it recalled his own basic training so many years before. For Meyer, inexplicably, it brought back with an almost painful rush the days when he played football for his high school team. Beyond the major's wide window, November sprawled leadenly. It was a good month for memories, November.

"As I told you on the phone," Carella said, "we're investigating a series of homicides—"

"More than one?" Tataglia said. "When you told me you were looking for information about Harris, I assumed—"

"There've been three murders so far," Carella said. "We're not sure they're all related. The first two most certainly are."

"I see. Who were the other victims?"

"Harris's wife, Isabel, and a woman named Hester Mathieson."

"How can I help you?" Tataglia asked.

The top of his desk was clear of papers and even pencils. A brass plaque read *Maj. J. F. Tataglia.* A folding triptych picture frame showed photographs of a dark-haired woman and two little girls, one with dark hair, the other with hair as blonde as the major's. He touched the tips of his fingers together and held them just under his chin, as though in prayer.

Meyer kept watching him. With his extrasensory olfactory awareness, he detected the scent of cologne emanating from behind the major's desk. He had never liked men who wore cologne, even if they were athletes being paid to advertise it on television. He did not like Tataglia altogether. There was something prissy about the man, something too starchily precise. He kept watching him. Tataglia had apparently decided Carella was the spokesman here; Meyer watched Tataglia, and Tataglia watched Carella.

"We have reason to believe Harris may have contacted an old Army buddy regarding a scheme of his," Carella said.

"What sort of scheme?"

"An illegal one, possibly."

"You say possibly..."

"Because we don't really know," Carella said. "You were in command of the 3rd Platoon, is that correct?"

"Yes."

"Were you present when Harris was blinded?"

"Yes. I later filed the action report."

"And signed it as commanding officer."

"Yes."

"That was on December fifteenth. He was blinded on December fourteenth—is that correct?—and you filed the report on December fifteenth."

"Yes, those are the dates," Tataglia said.

"Had you been recently promoted?"

"Yes."

"Before the action in which Harris..."

"Yes, a week or ten days earlier. We'd begun Operation Ala Moana at the beginning of December. Lieutenant Blake was killed shortly after the choppers dropped us in. I was promoted in the field. For the rest of the operation, I was acting OIC."

"You were promoted to lieutenant?"

"Yes, second lieutenant in charge of the entire platoon. This was no simple vill sweep, you understand. This was a vast encircling maneuver involving a full battalion—mechanized units, artillery, air support, the works. The day before Harris got blinded, our recon patrol found an enemy base camp a mile to the southwest. We were marching toward it through the jungle when we got hit."

"What happened?"

"An L-shaped ambush. The first fire team was fully contained in the short side of the L. Bravo was just entering the long side. There was nothing we could do. They'd closed the trail and lined it with rifles and machine guns, and we were caught in the crossfire. We hit the bushes, hoping they hadn't been lined with punji stakes, and we just lay there returning fire and hoping Bravo would get to us before we all were killed. Bravo came in with the 3rd Squad right behind them, a machine-gun squad. It was a pretty hairy ten minutes, though. I was amazed we got through it with only Harris getting hurt. A grenade got him, almost tore his head off."

"No other casualties?"

"Not in Alpha. Two men in Bravo were killed, and the 3rd Squad suffered some wounded. But that was it. We were really lucky. They had us cold."

"Would you remember which of the men Harris was closest to?"

"What do you mean? In the action? When he was hit?"

"No, no. Who were his friends? Was there anyone he was particularly close to?"

"I really couldn't say. I'm not sure if you understand how this works. There are forty-four men in a platoon, plus the commanding officer and the platoon sergeant. The lieutenant will usually set up his command post where he can best direct the action. I was with that particular fire team on that particular day because they were first in the line of march."

"Then you didn't know the men in Alpha too well."

"Not as individuals."

"Even though the operation had started at the beginning of the month?"

"I knew them by name, I knew their faces. All I'm saying is that I had very little personal contact with them. I was an officer, they were—"

"Yes, but you'd only recently been promoted."

"That's true," Tataglia said, and smiled. "But there's not much love lost between top sergeants and the men under them. I was an E-Seven before Lieutenant Blake got killed."

"How did he get killed?" Meyer asked.

"Mortar fire," Tataglia said.

"And this was?"

"Beginning of the month sometime. Two or three days after the drop, I'm not certain of the date."

"Would you know if Harris kept in touch with any of the men after his discharge?"

"I have no idea."

"Have *you* been in contact with any of them?"

"The men in Alpha, do you mean?"

"Yes."

"No. I correspond regularly with the man who commanded D Company's First Platoon, but that's about it. He's a career soldier like myself, stationed in Germany just now, got sent over shortly after the reunion."

"What reunion is that, Major?"

"D Company had a big reunion in August. Tenth anniversary of the company's arrival overseas."

"Where'd the reunion take place?"

"Fort Monmouth. In New Jersey."

"Did you attend the reunion?"

"No, I did not."

"Did your friend?"

"Yes, he did. He mentioned it in one of his letters to me. Actually, I'm sorry I missed it."

"Well," Carella said, and looked at Meyer. "Anything else you can think of?" he asked.

"Nothing," Meyer said.

"Thank you very much," Carella said, rising and extending his hand.

"I'm sorry I couldn't be more helpful," Tataglia said.

The DD report was on Carella's desk when they got back to the squadroom. Meyer asked him if he wanted a cup of coffee, and then went down the corridor to Clerical. The clock on the wall read 3:37. The shadows were lengthening; Carella switched on his desk lamp and picked up the report. A handwritten note was fastened to it with a paper clip:

Steve—
Here's the report on the telephone interview with Hopewell. Doesn't add up to much, but that's it. I called the Majesta number you gave me for Russell Poole, got his mother, and later called him where he works. He gets home at three, I made an appointment to see him then. If I'm finished late, I'll call you from home.
Cotton

Carella took the paper clip from the report, crumpled Hawes's note, and threw it in the wastebasket. Hawes was a better typist than most of the men on the squad. The report looked relatively neat:

DETECTIVE DIVISION SUPPLEMENTARY REPORT	SQUAD	PRECINCT	PRECINCT REPORT NUMBER	DETECTIVE DIVISION REPORT NUMBER	PAGE NUMBER
	87	87	87-1029	RL-3871	1

NAME AND ADDRESS OF PERSON REPORTING

Surname	Given Name	Initials	Number	Street	Village	DATE OF ORIGINAL REPORT
HOPEWELL	ROBERT	163 Oleander Crescent, Sarasota, Florida				11/19

DETAILS

TELEPHONE INTERVIEW - Called Hopewell at home listing, referred by wife Mary Louise to business. Hopewell is in lawn and garden furniture business, located Southgate Shopping Center, Route 61, Sarasota. Told me he has lived in Sarasota all his life, was married when he got drafted into the Army. Same address as then. He remembered James Harris and also the action when Harris got blinded. Described it as an L-shaped ambush. Alpha Fire Team caught by surprise, rescued by Bravo and a machine-gun squad. Harris was hit by a fragmentation grenade, carried by medics to field hospital, later evacuated by chopper to base hospital. THIS WAS LAST HOPEWELL EVER SAW OF HARRIS. Hopewell was E-5 and squad leader. Time of action, platoon commanding officer was with them. Lieutenant John Tataglia. HOPEWELL HAS NOT SEEN ANY OF FIRE TEAM SINCE HIS DISCHARGE FROM ARMY. He himself was later wounded in battle March following year.

He seemed sorry he missed recent reunion of D Company, but could not afford fare to Forth Monmouth, New Jersey where reunion held. Tenth anniversary Company's arrival overseas. Correspondence with other man in Alpha – Karl Fiersen, grenadier, now residing Amsterdam, Holland – indicated party was huge success. When asked if James Harris had xxxxx attended, said he did not know. He expressed sorrow when told that James Harris had been killed.

DATE OF THIS REPORT 11/22

RANK	SURNAME	INITIALS	SHIELD NUMBER	COMMAND	SIGNATURE OF COMMANDING OFFICER
Det 3rd/Gr	HAWES, Cotton		31-784-32	87th	

Majesta, of course, had been named when the British owned America. It had been named after His Majesty King George. Lots of things were named after King George in those days. Georgetown was named after King George. In those days, when the British were dancing quadrilles and even common soldiers sounded like noblemen, Majesta was hilly and elegant. "Oh, yes, Majesta," the British would say. "Quite elegant." Majesta nowadays was still hilly, but it was not elegant. It was, in fact, inelegant. In fact, it was what you might call crappy.

There were some people in Majesta who lived all the way out on the tongue of land that jutted into the Atlantic, within the city limits but far from the city proper and also the madding crowd. These people felt that Washington and the Continental Congress had been misguided zealots. These people were of the opinion that Majesta would have fared better as a British colony. A case in point was neighboring Sand's Spit, which even today seemed very *much* like a British colony. That was because the people out there drank Pimms Cups during the summer months and talked through their noses a lot. The people on Sand's Spit were enormously rich, most of them. Some of them were only terribly rich. The people in Majesta were miserably poor, most of them. Some of them were only dreadfully poor. Russell Poole was pretty goddamn poor.

He lived with his mother in a row of houses that resembled those one might have found in England along Victoria Street or Gladstone Road—the apple does not fall far from the tree. Russell Poole was black. He had never been to England, but often dreamt of going there. He did not know that England had its own problems with people of a darker hue—the tree does not grow far from the fallen apple. Poole only knew that he was poor and living in a dump. He did not like the looks of Cotton Hawes. Cotton Hawes looked like a mean mother-fucking cop. Poole told his mother to go in the other room.

Hawes didn't much like the looks of Russell Poole, either.

Actually, the men looked a lot alike, except that one was white and the other was black. Maybe that made all the difference. Poole was about Hawes's height and weight, a good six feet two inches tall and 190 pounds. Both men were broad-shouldered and narrow-waisted. Poole did not have red hair like Hawes—but then again, who did? Poole closed the door on the bedroom his mother had just entered, and then said, "Okay, what's this about?"

"I told you on the phone," Hawes said. "James Harris was murdered."

"So?"

"You were in his squad overseas, weren't you?"

"Yes. I say again—so?"

"When's the last time you saw him?"

"In August."

"This past August?"

"Yes."

"Where was that?"

"The company reunion in New Jersey."

"What'd you talk about?"

"Old times."

"How about *new* times?"

"What do you mean?"

"Did he mention any plans he might have had?"

"Plans for what?"

"Plans involving Alpha."

"What kind of plans?"

"You tell me," Hawes said.

"I don't know what you're talking about."

"Did he mention needing Alpha's help with anything?"

"Nothing."

"Some kind of business deal, maybe?"

"I told you. Nothing."

"Who else was there? From Alpha, I mean."

"Just four of us."

"Who?"

"Me and Jimmy, and Karl Fiersen who was on his way to Amsterdam, and Rudy Tanner who flew in from California."

"Do you know where we can reach these other men?"

"I've got Tanner's address. Fiersen said to just write him care of American Express in Amsterdam."

"You exchanged addresses?"

"Yeah, we all did."

"Jimmy, too?"

"Jimmy, too."

"You gave him your address?"

"We all gave each other our addresses."

"Did Jimmy write to you?"

"No."

"Would you know if he wrote to any of the other men?"

"How would I know?"

"Was Lieutenant Tataglia at the reunion?"

"No. We were surprised about that because he was stationed at Fort Lee in Virginia, and that's not such a long haul to New Jersey. Tanner came all the way from California."

"How'd you know where he was stationed?"

"Tataglia? Well, there was a captain there at the reunion, he used to be in command of the First Platoon, some of the guys got talking to him. He told us Tataglia was a major now, and stationed at Fort Lee."

"Who'd he tell?"

"I forget who was standing around there. I think it was me and Jimmy and another guy from the squad, but not from Alpha."

"Who would that have been?"

"A guy from Bravo. There wasn't much left of Bravo. Two of them were killed in action the day Jimmy got wounded, and another guy was killed just after Christmas."

"The one who was at the reunion—do you know his name?"

"Of course I know his name. Danny Cortez, he lives in Philadelphia."

"Have you got *his* address, too?"

"Yeah, I took it down."

"Did Jimmy get his address?"

"I don't know. I didn't follow Jimmy around seeing whose address he took or whose address he didn't."

"But you know for sure that Jimmy took the addresses of the men who were in Alpha."

"Yeah, because we were all standing around bullshitting, and we used the same pencil to write the addresses."

"What were you bullshitting about?"

"I told you. Old times. We went through a lot together over there."

"What did you go through?"

"A lot of action. In the boonies and in the whorehouses, too."

"What do you mean by boonies?"

"The boondocks. You know, out in the jungles there. The boonies."

"What kind of action did you see?"

"Vill sweeps mostly. We'd surround a village in the night, and then attack at first light, before they left their women and their rice bowls to go off in the jungle again. We'd destroy whatever we found—AT mines, sugar, pickled fish, small-arms rounds, whatever the fuck."

"Were you on a vill sweep when Jimmy got wounded?"

"No, that was Ala Moana. That was a big operation. That was the whole battalion."

"How bad was it?"

"It wasn't good. We lost a lot more people over there than the newspapers made out. All the body counts were the *enemy*, you dig? Nobody bothered to count *us*."

“Did Jimmy get along with everybody in Alpha?”

“Yeah.”

“Everybody in the squad?”

“Yeah.”

“Can you think of anybody who might have wanted him dead?”

“Nope.”

“And that’s the last time you saw him, right? In August.”

“That’s the last time I saw him.”

“You want to let me have those addresses now?” Hawes said.

The telephone again.

The telephone was as vital a tool to policemen as was a tension bar to a burglar. They now had addresses for Rudy Tanner and a man named Danny Cortez, who’d been in Bravo Fire Team of the 2nd Squad. They also knew that Karl Fiersen could be reached care of American Express in Amsterdam, but that didn’t help them much because the city would never spring for a transatlantic call even if by some miracle they could get a phone number for Fiersen. They dialed Directory Assistance for Los Angeles and for Philadelphia, and came up with listings for both Tanner and Cortez. Carella talked to Tanner first. He asked almost the same questions about the action that December day, and got almost the same answers. Nothing that didn’t jibe. He kept reaching.

“When did you see him last?”

“August. At the reunion.”

“Did he mention any plans to you?”

“Plans? What do you mean?”

“Plans for himself and somebody in Alpha.”

“In Alpha? I don’t get you.”

“He didn’t ask for your help in some plan he had?”

“No. No, he didn’t.”

"Did he write to you after the reunion?"

"No."

"But you gave him your address, isn't that so?"

"Yes."

"And he gave you his address, right?"

"Yes."

"When's the last time you were here in this city?"

"August. On the way to the reunion."

"Haven't been back since?"

"No."

"Okay, thanks."

Hang up the phone, look at your notes, compare what you just got from Tanner with what you already have from Tataglia and Hopewell and Poole. Think about it. Wonder about it. Wonder especially about Jimmy's nightmares, which his doctor said were rooted in a basement rape that never took place. Make a note to call the police psychiatrist—what the hell was his name? Consider the possibility that the murders were motiveless.

There used to be a time when most murders started as family quarrels resolved with a hatchet or a gun. Find a lady dead on the bathroom floor, go look for her husband. Find a man with both legs broken and a knife in his heart besides, go look for his girlfriend's husband, and try to get there fast before the husband threw *her* off the roof in the bargain. Those were the good old days. Hardly ever would you get a murder where everything had been figured out in advance—woman wanted to get rid of her husband, she worked out a complicated plot involving poison extracted from the glands of a green South American snake, started lacing his cognac with it every night, poor man went into convulsions and died six months later while the woman was on the Riviera living it up with a gigolo from Copenhagen. Nothing like that. In the good old days your average real-life murder was a woman coming into the apartment and finding her husband drunk again, and shaking him, and then saying the hell with it, and going out to the kitchen for an ice pick and sticking him sixteen times in the chest and the throat. That was real life, baby. You wanted bullshit, you went to mystery novels written by ladies who lived in Sussex. Thrillers. About as thrilling as Aunt Lucy's tatted nightcap.

In the good old days you wrapped a thing up in three, four hours sometimes—between lunch and cocktails, so to speak. And usually it wasn't the butler who did it, nor even the foul fiend flibbertigibbet, but instead your own brother or your brother's wife or your Uncle Tim from Nome, Alaska. Nowadays it was different. One-third of all the homicides committed in this city involved a victim and a murderer who didn't even *know* each other when the crime was committed. Perfect strangers, total and utter, locked in the ultimate intimate obscenity for the mere seconds it took to squeeze a trigger or plunge a blade. So why not believe that Jimmy and Isabel and Hester were victims of someone totally unknown to any of them, some bedbug who had a hang-up about blind people?

Why not? Knew them only from their respective neighborhoods, saw them around all the time, shuffling along, their very presence disgusted him. Decided to do away with them. Why not?

Maybe.

Carella sighed, dialed the area code 215 for Philadelphia, and then dialed Danny Cortez's number. It was almost 5:30 on the squadroom clock, he hoped the man would be home from work already. The phone rang three times, and then a woman picked up.

"Hello?" she said. In that single word he thought he detected a Spanish accent, but that may have been because he knew Danny's surname was Cortez.

"I'd like to talk to Danny Cortez, please," he said.

"Who's this?" the woman asked, the accent unmistakable now.

"Detective Carella, 87th Squad in Isola."

"*Who*?" the woman said.

"Police department," he said.

"Police? *Que desea usted*?"

"I'd like to talk to Danny Cortez. Who's this, please?"

"His wife. *Qual es su nombre*?"

"Carella. Detective Carella."

"He knows you, my husband?"

"No. I'm calling long distance."

"Ah, long distance," she said. "One minute, *por favor*."

Carella waited. He could hear voices in the background, talking softly in Spanish. Silence. Someone picked up the phone.

"Hello?" a man's voice said.

"Mr. Cortez?"

"Yes?"

"This is Detective Carella of the 87th Squad in Isola. I'm calling in reference to a murder we're investigating."

"A murder?"

"Yes. A man named James Harris. He was in the Army with you, would you happen to remember him?"

"Yes, sure. He was murdered, you say?"

"Yes. I was wondering if you'd answer some questions for me."

"Sure, go ahead."

"When's the last time you saw him, Mr. Cortez?"

"Jimmy? In August. We had a reunion of the company. I went there to New Jersey. That was when I saw him."

"Did you talk to him then?"

"Oh, sure."

"What about?"

"Oh, many things. We were in the same squad, you know. He was Alpha Fire Team, I was Bravo. We were the ones got them out the day he was wounded. They were trapped there, we got them out."

"Were you very friendly with him?"

"Well, only so-so. We were in the same hootch, Alpha and Bravo, but—"

"The same *what*?"

"Hootch."

"What's that?"

"A hootch? You know what a hootch is."

"No, I don't."

"It's what we lived in. On the base. There were eight of us in a hootch, the noncoms had their own Playboy pad."

"Was it like a Quonset hut or something?"

"Well, it was more like a tent, you know, with wooden frames and the top half screened. Our hootch had a metal roof, but not all of them did."

"And eight of you lived in this hootch, is that right?"

"Yeah, four of us from Alpha and four from Bravo. The sergeants—the two team leaders and the squad leader—had their own hootch. But what I'm saying is the guys in Alpha were closer to each other than they were to the guys in Bravo, even though we were all in the same squad. That's because a fire team, you know, is a very tight-knit unit. You depend for your life on the guys in your own fire team, you understand me? You go through a lot together. Like Bravo went through a lot together, and Alpha went through a lot together, but on their *own*, you understand? Even though we were all in the same squad."

"Mm-huh," Carella said. "What did Alpha go through on its own?"

"Oh, lots of things. I mean, in combat and also off the base, you understand me?" His voice lowered. "In the bars, you know? And with whores, you know?"

"What did they go through in combat together?" Carella asked.

"Well, vill sweeps, you know. And on Ala Moana—that was a big operation—they were there when the lieutenant got killed."

"Lieutenant Blake, would that be?"

"Yeah, Lieutenant Blake. The platoon commander."

"Alpha was there but Bravo wasn't, is that it?"

"Well, we were already going up the hill. There was a patrol out, and the RTO radioed back that they found half a dozen bunkers and a couple of tunnels up the hill. We were moving out to join them."

"Bravo was?"

"Yeah. Alpha was resting."

"Resting," Carella said.

"Yeah. We'd all been through heavy fighting that whole month. Alpha was down where the lieutenant had set up a command post near some bamboo at the bottom of the hill."

"A command post," Carella said.

"Yeah. Well, not really a post. I mean, not buildings or tents or whatever. A command post is wherever the officer in command *is*. From where he directs the action, you understand me?"

"Mm-huh," Carella said. "And that's where the lieutenant was when he got killed? Down there with Alpha?"

"Yeah. Well, no, not exactly. This is what happened. Alpha was down there with the platoon sergeant—"

"Tataglia?"

"Yeah. Johnny Tataglia. Bravo was going up the hill to where the enemy was dug in. The lieutenant went back down to see where the hell Alpha was. To get Alpha so they could bring up the rear, you understand me?"

"Yes."

"That's when the mortar attack started. Bastards had zeroed in on the bamboo and were pounding the shit out of it."

"And that's when the lieutenant got killed?"

"Yeah, in the mortar attack. Frag must've got him. It was a terrible thing. Alpha took cover when the attack started, and then they couldn't get to the lieutenant in time."

"What do you mean?"

"Well, in the war over there, you had to pick up your own dead and wounded because if you didn't they dragged them off and hacked them to pieces. The enemy, you understand me?"

"Is that what happened to Lieutenant Blake?"

"Yeah. He must've got hit while he was going down the hill. Alpha told us later they couldn't go after him because of the mortars. All they could do was watch while he was dragged in the jungle. They found him later in an open pit—cut to ribbons. The bastards used to cut the bodies up and leave them in open pits."

"Mm-huh," Carella said.

"With bayonets, they did it," Cortez said.

"Mm-huh."

"So what I'm saying, you go through these terrible things together, you naturally get close to the guys who are in your own fire team. You understand me?"

"Yes, I do," Carella said. "This happened on the third of December, is that right?"

"I don't know, I couldn't tell you that. We weren't even *there*, you understand me? We were on our way to where they'd found those bunkers. It turned out there was a big cache up there. What I'm saying, there are things that are important to a person in combat because he's *in* them. But if he isn't there to experience them, well, then it's just another day for him. So I couldn't tell you if the lieutenant was killed on the third or the fourth or whenever. To me, it was just another day. I was out there on a search-and-destroy, I was in no danger at all. The mortars didn't come anywhere near us. All we heard was the noise. You ever been in a mortar attack? It makes a lot of noise, even from a distance."

"Mm-huh. Mr. Cortez, when you were at that reunion in New Jersey, did Jimmy talk to you about a plan he was considering?"

"A plan? No. We talked about what it was like overseas. What do you mean, a plan?"

"For making money."

"I wish he *would've* talked to me about it," Cortez said, and laughed. "I could *use* some money."

"You wouldn't know whether he'd approached any of the other men about such a plan?"

"No, I wouldn't know. I'll tell you, *none* of us are doing too hot, you understand me? In New Jersey we were all bitching about what a lousy deal we got. As veterans, I mean. If Jimmy had some plan to make money...Hey, I got to tell you, we'd have gone in with him in a minute." Cortez laughed again. "Long as it didn't cost us nothing."

"But you didn't know about any such plan?"

"No."

"Did you give Jimmy your address?"

"Yeah."

"Did he write to you after the reunion?"

"No."

"Did he telephone you, or try to contact you in any other way?"

"No."

"Mm," Carella said. "Well," he said, and sighed. "Thanks a lot, Mr. Cortez, I appreciate the time you gave me."

"I wish you luck," Cortez said, and hung up.

Sergeant Dave Murchison looked toward the iron-runged steps as Carella came down them into the muster room. In the swing room, two patrolmen had taken off their tunics and were sitting in their suspendered trousers and long-sleeved underwear, drinking coffee. One of them had just told a joke, and both men were laughing.

Carella glanced briefly through the open door to the room, and then walked to the muster desk. "I'm heading home," he said.

"What about the dog?" Murchison asked.

"What? Oh, Jesus, I forgot all about him. Did somebody pick him up?"

"He's downstairs in one of the holding cells. What do you plan to do with him?"

"I don't know," Carella said. "I guess I'll turn him over to Harris's mother."

"When?" Murchison said. "Steve, it's against regulations to keep animals here at the station house."

"Miscolo has a cat in the clerical office," Carella said.

"That's different. That's not in a holding cell downstairs."

"Shall I take the dog up to Clerical?"

"He'd eat Miscolo's cat. He's a very big dog, Steve. Have you seen this dog?"

"He's not so big. He's an average-sized Labrador."

"An average-sized Labrador is a very big dog. I'd say he weighs ninety pounds, that's what I'd say. Also, he won't eat."

"Well, I'll take him over to Harris's mother in the morning. I have to talk to her, anyway."

"You better hope Captain Frick doesn't decide to take a stroll down to the holding cells. He finds a dog down there, he'll take a fit."

"Tell him it's a master of disguise."

"What?" Murchison said.

"Tell him it's a criminal wearing a dog suit."

"Ha-ha," Murchison said mirthlessly.

"I'll get him out of here first thing in the morning," Carella said. "Dave, I'm tired. I want to go home."

"What the hell time is it, anyway?" Murchison said, and looked up at the clock. "I got a call from Charlie Maynard an hour ago, he said he'd be a little late. He's supposed to relieve me at a quarter to four, he calls at a quarter to five, tells me he'll be a little late. Now it's a quarter to six, and he *still* ain't here. When he called, I told him to get on Tarzan and ride over here as quick as he could."

"Get on Tarzan? What do you mean?"

"Tarzan was Ken Maynard's horse," Murchison said.

"No, Tarzan was Tom Mix's horse."

"*Tony* was Tom Mix's horse."

"Then who was Trigger?" Carella asked.

"I don't know who Trigger was. Buck Jones's horse, maybe."

"Anyway, Charlie Maynard isn't Ken Maynard."

"What difference does it make?" Murchison said. "He's two hours late either way, ain't he?"

Carella blinked. "Good night, Dave," he said, and walked across the room to the entrance doors, and through them to the steps outside. A fierce wind was blowing in the street.

The wind tore at the blind man's coat.

He clung to the harness of the German shepherd leading him, cursing the wind, cursing the fact that he had to go to the bathroom and he was still three blocks from his building. The trouble with running a newsstand was that you had to go in the cafeteria or the bookstore every time you had to pee. They were nice about it, they knew a man couldn't be out there on the corner all day long without going to the bathroom, but still he hated to bother them all the time.

He wondered what astronauts did. Did they pee inside their space suits? Was there a tube they had? He should have gone in the cafeteria before heading home. The bookstore was already closed, but the cafeteria was open twenty-four hours, and the manager said he didn't mind him coming in to use the men's room downstairs. Still, you couldn't go in there every ten minutes, take advantage of the man's hospitality that way. Tried to limit his necessity calls to lunchtime and then maybe once again mid-afternoon. Always took his lunch at the cafeteria so he could stay on friendly terms with the manager. He went in the bookstore only every now and then, when he felt embarrassed about going in the cafeteria. But it was different in the bookstore because he only bought from them every now and then, when he wanted to give a present to one of his sighted friends, and also they sold magazines same as he did, and he guessed they maybe thought he was in competition with them.

God, he had to pee!

The dog suddenly stopped dead in the middle of the sidewalk.

"What is it, Ralph?" he said.

The dog began growling.

"Ralph?" he said. "What's the matter, boy?"

He smelled something sickeningly sweet in that instant, cloying, medicinal—chloroform, it was chloroform. The dog growled again, an attack growl deep in his throat, and suddenly the harness jerked out of his hand and someone yelled in pain. He heard the shuffle of feet on the sidewalk, heard harsh breathing, the dog's low growl again, and then footsteps running into the night, fading. The dog was barking. The dog would not stop barking.

"All right," he said, "all right," and groped for the harness and found it. He patted the dog's head. "Take me home, boy," he said. "Home now. Home, Ralph."

At home, there was a telephone.

He called the police, not because he thought they'd do anything about it—police in this damn city never did *anything* about *anything*—but only because he felt outraged by the attack. The patrolman who arrived at his apartment immediately challenged him.

"How do you know it was an *attack*, Mr. Masler?"

The man's name was Eugene Maslen, with an "n." He had corrected the patrolman twice, but the patrolman kept saying Masler. Maybe he was hard of hearing. He tried again.

"It's Maslen," he said, "with an 'n,' and I know it was an attack because the dog wouldn't have begun growling that way if someone wasn't threatening us."

"Mm," the patrolman said. His name was McGrew, and he worked out of the Four-One downtown in the Financial District, near the Headquarters building. "And you say you smelled chloroform?"

"It smelled like chloroform, yes. From when I had my tonsils out."

"When was that, Mr. Masler?"

"When I was seven."

"And you remember what the chloroform smelled like, huh?"

"Yes, I remember."

"So what is it you're saying, Mr. Masler? Are you saying this person was trying to chloroform the dog?"

"I don't know what he was trying to do. I'm telling you he approached us with chloroform and the dog attacked him and bit him."

"Oh, the dog bit him. How do you know?"

"Because I heard the man yell."

"How do you know it was a man?"

"It sounded like a man yelling."

"What did he yell?"

"He just yelled in pain, but I can tell the difference between a man yelling and a woman yelling. This was a man."

"Your dog ain't got rabies, has he?"

"No, he had his shots just last month. The date's on the tag there. On his collar."

McGrew thought he should look at the tag, but this was a dog who'd already bit one person and he didn't want to be the second person getting bit tonight.

"Where did this incident take place?" he asked.

"Three blocks from here. On Cherry Street. Near the Mercantile Bank on the corner."

"You knew where you were, huh?"

"Yes," Maslen said, "I knew *exactly* where I was. I may be blind, but I'm not stupid."

"Mm," McGrew said, managing to sound dubious. "Well," he said, "we'll look into this, Mr. Masler, let you know if we come up with anything."

"Thank you," Maslen said. He did not for a moment believe anybody would look into it or come up with anything.

A second patrolman was waiting downstairs in the radio motor patrol car. They had routinely answered the 10-24—Past Assault—and when they got to Maslen's building, had decided it wasn't necessary for both of them to go all the way up to the fourth floor. McGrew's partner, whose name was Kelly, was asleep in the car when McGrew came down to the street again. McGrew rapped on the window, and Kelly came awake with a start, blinked first into the car and then through the window to where McGrew was bent over looking in. "Oh," Kelly said, and unlocked the door on the passenger side. McGrew got in.

"What was it?" Kelly asked.

"Who the hell knows?" McGrew said. "Whyn't you take a spin over to Cherry, near the Mercantile there."

"The bank there?"

"Yeah, the bank there." McGrew took the hand mike from the dashboard. He had called in a 10-88—Arrived At Scene—some five minutes ago, and now he radioed the dispatcher with a combined 10-80D and 10-98—Referred to Detectives and Resuming Patrol/Available. From the call box on Cherry and Laird, he telephoned the precinct and asked the desk sergeant to connect him with the squadroom upstairs. The detective who took the call was a man named Underhill. McGrew filled him in on the squeal, and then asked did Underhill want to come down there, or what?

"You at the scene now?" Underhill asked.

"Yeah, where it's supposed to have took place."

"Why don't you look around, give me a call back?"

"Look for what?"

"You said chloroform, didn't you?"

"Yeah."

"So look around, see if there's anything with chloroform on it. A rag, a piece of cotton, whatever. If you find anything, don't touch it, you hear me?"

"Okay," McGrew said.

"And look for bloodstains, too. You said the dog bit him, didn't you?"

"Well, that's what the blind guy told me."

"Okay, so look for bloodstains. If you find anything, call me right back. Did the blind guy get hurt?"

"No."

"Did his dog get hurt?"

"No."

"Is the dog rabid or anything?"

"No, he got his shots last month."

"So, okay, look around a little," Underhill said, and hung up.

McGrew went back to the car and opened the door.

"What are we supposed to do?" Kelly asked.

"Look around a little," McGrew said.

Kelly came out of the car with a long torchlight in his hand. He sprayed the beam over the sidewalk near the mailbox, and the call box, and the lamppost, and then began working his way back toward the wall of the bank.

"Look, there's some blood," he said.

"Yeah," McGrew said. "I think I better get back to Underhill."

Detective George Underhill did not want to leave the squadroom.

He was busy organizing the paperwork he'd assembled on a series of liquor store holdups just this side of Chinatown, and he was absorbed with the job, and besides, it was cold outside. Underhill had been born and raised in the state of California, where it was always warm and lovely, despite what songwriters had to say about its being cold and damp. Underhill did not like this city. Underhill liked San Diego. The reason Underhill was here in this city was that his wife's mother lived here in this city, and his wife wanted to be near her mother, whom Underhill hated almost as much as he hated this city. If Underhill had his druthers, which he didn't have, he'd have liked this city to break off and float away into the Atlantic, carrying his mother-in-law with it. That's how Underhill felt about this city and about his mother-in-law. But that goddamn McGrew had found blood on the sidewalk, and so Underhill guessed the dog had really bitten somebody. Whether the dog had bitten somebody about to *assault* the blind man was another question. Nobody had got hurt, not the blind man, and not the dog, either; Underhill figured this could not by any stretch of the imagination be categorized as an assault. He even wondered whether it could be categorized an *attempted* assault. In which case, why the hell was he contemplating going all the way over to Cherry and Laird on a night when they should be taking in the brass monkeys?

Underhill did not know that three blind people had been killed since Thursday night, two of them in the Eight-Seven and another in Midtown East. Carella's stop-sheet asking for information on unusual crimes and specifying attacks on blind people was at this moment on the desk of a Detective Ramon Jiminez, not six feet from Underbill's own desk in the detective squadroom of the 41st Precinct, but Underhill hadn't seen it. If he *had* seen it, he might have called Carella at once. But this wasn't a homicide Underhill was dealing with, this wasn't even an assault, this was *maybe* an attempted assault—or maybe it was just a grouchy old dog biting somebody just for the hell of it.

Being a conscientious man, however, he wired a stop to the commissioner of the Department of Hospitals at 432 Market, asking for information re patients seeking medical treatment for dog bites. He did not know where the man had been bitten, he guessed the leg, if anyplace, but he didn't specify this in his stop. It occurred to him belatedly that if any of the city hospitals came up with the name of a man they'd treated for dog bite, he would have no way of identifying a possible suspect unless he had a blood sample. That was why he called the police laboratory, and that was how it happened that a lab technician went to the scene at 8:15 that night and began taking blood samples from the sidewalk.

Carella knew nothing about any of this.

It was a big city.

14

Sophie Harris did not want the dog.

"I got no way of taking care of the dog," she said. "Chrissie's in school all day long, and I'm out workin'. What we goan do with a big dog like that in this small apartment? Who's goan take care of him?"

"I thought you might want him," Carella said.

"Ain't no dog goan bring back my Jimmy," she said "You better take him with you when you leave."

"Well," Carella said, and looked at the dog. Nobody seemed to want the dog. He'd be damned if *he* wanted the dog, either. The dog looked back at him balefully. Carella had removed the leather harness, but the dog still wore around his neck a studded leather collar hung with a collection of hardware. If he decided to keep the dog, he'd have to look at all those metal discs and whatever else was hanging there, find out what shots the dog had already had. He did not want a dog. He didn't even *like* dogs. Teddy would have a fit if he brought home a dog. "Are you sure you don't want the dog?" he asked Sophie.

"I'm sure," she said. They had put her son in the ground yesterday, she did not want any damn dog reminding her that he was gone forever. Buried him side by side with the daughter-in-law she'd loved, both of them gone now. Made Sophie want to bust out crying all over again, here in the presence of the policeman. She had to learn to control these sudden fits of weeping that came over her.

"Well," Carella said, "I'll have to find something to do with him." He looked at the dog again. The dog looked back. "Anyway," Carella said, "that isn't my only reason for coming here this morning. Mrs. Harris, do you remember telling me that Jimmy had contacted an old Army buddy..."

"Yes."

"For help with what you thought might have been an illegal scheme."

"Yes."

"And you said you didn't remember the man's name."

"That's right."

"If I gave you some names, would that help?"

"Maybe."

"How about Russell Poole? Did your son call him or write to him?"

"That doesn't sound familiar."

"Rudy Tanner?"

"No."

"John Tataglia?"

"I really don't remember. I'm very bad with names."

"Robert Hopewell?"

"I'm sorry, but—"

"Karl Fiersen?"

"All those names sound alike to me."

Carella thought about that. He guessed that Tanner *did* sound something like Tataglia and maybe Russell Poole and Robert Hopewell *could* be mistaken one for the other. But there was nothing Fiersen sounded like but itself. And as for Cortez…

"Cortez?" he said. "Danny Cortez?"

"I can't remember," Sophie said. "I'm sorry."

"Did your son *write* to this person, or did he *call* him?"

"He wrote to him."

"How do you know that?"

"He told me."

"Did you see the letter?"

"No."

"Do you know what it said?"

"No, he didn't tell me what was in it. Only that he'd written to this man who was going to help him and Isabel get rich."

"Did he say how much money was involved?"

"No."

"Mrs. Harris, what would Jimmy have considered rich?"

"I got no idea."

"What do *you* consider rich?"

"I'd be the richest woman in the world if I could have my Jimmy and his wife back," Sophie said, and began weeping.

The dog didn't say a word all the way downtown. Kept sitting on the backseat looking through the window, watching the traffic. Carella wondered if he should take him to an animal shelter. He thought of what Maloney from Canine had told him about gradually drawing all the air out of a container. Maloney said it was just like going to sleep. Carella doubted that gasping for air was very much like going to sleep. He didn't like dogs, and he didn't know this particular dog from an inchworm—but he didn't think he would take him to a shelter.

He parked the car on Dutchman's Row, near the old Harrison Life building. As he locked the door, the dog on the backseat looked out at him. Carella said, "That's okay," and walked away from the car. The streets here were clogged with automobiles and pedestrians. On the corner a traffic cop was chatting with a dark-haired girl in a miniskirt, a fake-fur jacket and black leather boots. The girl looked like a hooker. The traffic cop was talking to the girl who was maybe a hooker, smiling at her, puffing out his chest, while horns honked and tempers soared and traffic backed up clear to the harbor tunnel. Carella dodged a taxi that had begun weaving in and out of the stalled traffic. The taxi almost hit him. The driver rolled down his window and shouted, "You tired of living, mister?"

He found the address for Prestige Novelty on the other side of the street, some four buildings down from the corner. Someone had spilled water on the sidewalk in front of the entrance door and the water had frozen into a thin, dangerous glaze. Carella automatically looked up to the face of the building, to see whether there were any window washers on scaffolds up there. Nothing, and no one. He wondered where the spilled water had come from. Mysteries. All the time, mysteries. He skirted the patch of ice and pushed his way through the revolving doors. On the lobby directory he found a listing for PRESTIGE NOVELTY, room 501. He took the elevator up, and then searched out the office in the fifth-floor corridor. Frosted-glass upper panel on the door, PRESTIGE NOVELTY in gold-leaf lettering beneath, which were the numerals 501. So far, so good. With brilliant deductive work like this—finding an office after having consulted a lobby directory—Carella figured he'd make detective/1st within the month. He opened the door. This, too, indicated high intelligence and good small-motor control—grasping a doorknob in one's right hand, twisting it, pushing the door inward. He found himself in a smallish reception room done in various shades of green, all bilious. There was an opening on the wall facing the door, a pair of sliding glass panels. Behind the panels was a dark-haired woman in her early thirties. He guessed this was Jennie D'Amato, with whom he had talked last Friday night. He approached the partition; one of the panels slid open.

"Yes?"

"Detective Carella," he said. "I'd like to talk to Mr. Preston, please."

"Oh," she said.

"Are you Miss D'Amato?"

"Yes."

"Is Mr. Preston in?"

"I'll see," she said, and slid the panel shut, and picked up the telephone receiver, and stabbed at a button in the base of the phone. He could hear her voice through the glass panels. "Mr. Preston? There's a Detective Carella here to see you." She listened, said, "Yes, sir," and put the receiver back on its cradle. She slid open the panel again. "I'll buzz you in," she said to Carella, and indicated a door on her right. Carella went to the door, took the knob in his hand, waited for the buzz that unlocked it, and opened it into the office beyond. Desks, filing cabinets. At one of the desks, a horse-faced woman working over what appeared to be the company ledgers. He supposed this was Miss Houlihan. She did not look up from the books.

"It's the door right there," Jennie said. "Just go right in."

"Thank you," Carella said, and walked to the door and knocked on it.

"Come in," Preston said.

He was sitting behind a large wooden desk, the bookcases behind him lined with leather-bound books that looked dusty and old. He was wearing a dark pin-striped suit, a white shirt, and muted tie. The last time Carella saw him he'd been wearing a bathrobe. He looked rather more elegant now, somewhat like a barrister out of *Great Expectations*, fringe of white hair framing his massive head, blue eyes alert and expectant under the white shaggy brows. He rose immediately, shook hands with Carella, and immediately asked, "Any news?"

"No, nothing," Carella said. "I'd like to ask you a few more questions, if you don't mind."

"Not at all. This other woman who was killed—"

"You know about that?" Carella asked at once.

"Yes, it was in the papers. Is her death linked to Isabel's?"

"We don't know yet."

"Because if it is…" Preston shrugged. "Well then, you're obviously dealing with a lunatic, isn't that so?"

"Possibly," Carella said. "Mr. Preston, I'm assuming that the relationship between you and Isabel was the sort in which there was a free exchange of dialogue."

"That's right."

"Did you ever talk about your separate marriages?"

"Yes, we did."

"Mr. Preston, we have good reason to believe that Jimmy Harris wrote to someone he knew in the Army, proposing some sort of business deal—possibly something illegal. Did Isabel ever mention this to you?"

"No, she did not."

"Never mentioned Jimmy contacting one of his old Army buddies?"

"No."

"Did she mention Jimmy going to the reunion in August?"

"Yes. In fact…"

"Yes, Mr. Preston?"

"We…stole a few days together."

"You and Isabel went away together, is that what you're saying?"

"Yes."

"While Jimmy was at the reunion?"

"Yes."

"Did she later mention anything that happened at the reunion?"

"No."

"Did Jimmy ever tell her about a plan to get rich?"

"She never mentioned such a plan to me."

"Mr. Preston, when we went through the Harris apartment, we didn't find anything like a diary or a journal that Isabel might have kept..."

"She was blind," Preston said.

"Yes, I realize that, but blind people can write in Braille, and I'm sure there are at least *some* blind people who keep diaries. Did Isabel ever mention a diary or a journal?"

"No."

"Where did she work, Mr. Preston?"

"Here, do you mean?"

"Yes."

"In the mailroom."

"Where's that?"

"Why do you want to know?"

"Because maybe she kept such a diary here at the office, where her husband wouldn't come across it."

"No, I don't think she kept a diary."

"But you're not sure."

"Well, I can't be sure, of course, but...She never mentioned a diary to me. I'm sure she would have mentioned it."

"Mr. Preston, may I see her desk, please?"

"I...I don't see what—"

"What's the problem, Mr. Preston?"

"There's no problem. It's simply that you'd be wasting your time."

"Well, it's *my* time, isn't it?"

"Yes, but..."

"What is it, Mr. Preston?"

"Nothing."

"Would you show me the mailroom, please?"

Preston sighed and rose from behind his desk. "This way," he said, and walked across the office to the door, and opened it, and stepped into the outer office, Carella following him.

The door to the mailroom was set alongside the desk at which Miss Houlihan still worked on the ledgers. This time she glanced up as the two men went past. There seemed to be a faintly quizzical look on her face. Preston opened the door to the mailroom as though he were opening the door to a vault. A girl sat at a desk inside the windowless room. There were brochures stacked on the floor beside the desk. The girl kept reaching for the brochures and stuffing them into envelopes. She did this mindlessly—reaching, inserting, moistening the envelope flaps, sealing the envelopes.

"Would you leave us, please, Beth?" Preston asked, and the girl rose at once and walked out of the room. Preston closed the door behind her. Idly, because he was not here to look through advertising matter for ashtrays, salt and pepper shakers, coasters, swizzle sticks, or other assorted souvenir items, Carella picked up one of the brochures.

On the cover there was a line drawing of a man and a woman kissing. Above the woman's head, and moving across the cover from left to right in delicate script lettering, was the legend *Marital Aids for Lovers*. Below the word *Lovers*, in a white heart on the extreme right-hand side of the cover, was the name of Preston's firm, and below that its address on Dutchman's Row. In the lower left-hand corner of the cover, in very small print, Carella read the words SEXUALLY ORIENTED ADVERTISING FOR ADULTS. Beneath this was the warning *This catalogue contains advertisements which may be deemed sexually oriented under the new postal law. That law is concerned with seeing that sexually oriented advertisements are not thrust upon minors or persons not desiring such advertisements. Accordingly if you are less than 21 years of age, or if you do not desire to view a sexually oriented advertisement,* DO NOT OPEN THIS CATALOGUE. *Please be kind enough to request that we remove your name from our mailing list. We will then remove your name and make every effort to see that you do not receive any more sexually oriented advertisements from us.*

"That's explicit enough," Carella said.

"It's in accordance with the law," Preston said.

"I'm sure it is," Carella said, and since he was well over twenty-one years of age, and since he was also desirous of viewing a sexually oriented advertisement, he opened the brochure.

The items advertised within were many and varied.

Here was a cordless massager in a handsome grain finish in a choice of ivory or walnut colors. Here on the facing page was a set of double remote-controlled Ben Wa balls. Here now was a Ben Wa fringed tingle ball, and here a series of love potions ranging from stingers to energizers to vaginal teasers to penis sweeteners and to more exotically erotic efflorescences variously called Cunnilingus Powder, Erectos Capsules, Vipe Spice, and Jungle Love. Here was a life-sized doll complete with breasts and vaginal pocket, the blonde with no clothes selling for $32.50, the blonde with lingerie selling for $37.50, similarly naked or attired brunettes coming somewhat cheaper, with nary a redhead in evidence. Here was a vibrodongo marital aid and here a vibro-*double*-dongo marital aid. Here was something called a vaginal pal portable marital aid of durable construction with real-looking hair in a handsome gift box—only $17.25. Here, too, was something called an autosuck vagina, described as a male marital aid and guaranteed to operate from a car's cigarette lighter.

The list of products went on and on, page after page of prosthetic extensions, electrical devices designed to provide sensuous vibrations, action playing cards featuring male-female "sexation" or female-female love, eight-track recordings or cassettes boasting "live stag-action," a bath mat covered with foam rubber breasts, a wristwatch with sexual positions substituting for the numbers on the dial, a sensuous dictionary with full-color photographs, and lastly but not least inventively, a lipstick in the shape of a penis—described as "a tasteful gift for any woman."

Carella closed the brochure. "Is this what you had Isabel Harris mailing for you?" he said.

"If she couldn't see it," Preston said, "how could it hurt her?"

Carella suddenly had the feeling that he could hack his way through the dense undergrowth of this city forever and still not reach a clearing where there was sunlight. He looked at Preston for only an instant, and then began searching through the desk that had been Isabel's. He did not find a diary, he did not find a journal, he did not find a goddamned thing. When he left the office, he went down the corridor to the men's room and washed his hands.

So now they snowballed it.

It was ten minutes past 12:00 on the Tuesday before Thanksgiving, and they sat in Lieutenant Byrnes's office, drinking coffee brewed in Clerical and eating sandwiches Hawes had called down for a half hour earlier. There were four of them in the office: Carella, Meyer, Hawes, and the lieutenant.

Byrnes was a compact man whose clothes seemed too tight for him, vest open across the barrel chest, jacket pinched across wide shoulders, tie pulled down, and shirt collar open as though to allow breathing space for the thick neck that supported his head. His hair was a gray the color of the city snow; his eyes were a flinty blue. The men of the 87th called him "Loot" or "Pete" or "Boss." He *was* the boss, the man in command of the squad's sixteen detectives, answerable in the precinct only to Captain John Marshall Frick, who theoretically ran the whole shebang but who, in practice, gave Byrnes and the detective squad almost complete autonomy. Byrnes had read the reports filed by Carella, Meyer, and Hawes, and now he wanted to know what the hell was happening. There were four crimes that irritated him more than any of the others rampant in this city. At the top of the list was homicide. Beneath that, but comparatively rare, was arson. Then came rape. And then pushing dope. In Byrnes's view, slitting the throats of blind people was tantamount to strangling innocent babes in their cribs. He was not too happy about the squad's progress on this case; he was, in fact, a bit cranky and unpredictable this morning, and the men sensed this displeasure and tiptoed around it like burglars in an occupied apartment.

"So why are you wasting time with all this Army business?" Byrnes asked.

"Well," Carella said, "the man was having nightmares, Pete—"

"*I* have nightmares, too. So what?"

"And also he'd contacted one of his old Army buddies about this deal he had in mind, whatever it was."

"That's according to his mother," Byrnes said.

"She seems like a reliable witness," Carella said.

"Witness to *what*?" Byrnes said. "She didn't see this letter he's supposed to have sent."

"But he told her about it."

"He told her he'd sent a letter to one of his buddies?"

"He told her the name, too."

"But she can't remember the name."

"That's right."

"Then what the hell good is she?" Byrnes said, and picked up his coffee cup, and sipped at it, and then put it down on his desk immediately; goddamn coffee was cold. "He could've sent the letter to *anybody* in Alpha—he had all their addresses, isn't that what you said?"

"Yeah, he got them at the reunion."

"Anyway, what's this letter got to do with his *murder*? I get back to what I asked you before: Why are you wasting time with all this Army business?"

"Because of the nightmares," Carella said, and shrugged.

"What he figures," Meyer said, "is that—"

"Does he stutter?" Byrnes asked.

"What?"

"Does Detective Carella stutter?"

"No, sir, but—"

"Then let him tell me *himself* what he figures."

"I don't know what I figure," Carella said. "But it bothers me that Jimmy Harris remembered a rape that never happened."

"That's if you believe the girl."

"I believe the girl," Carella said.

"So do I," Meyer said.

"What's that got to do with the *murders*?" Byrnes insisted. "The man was murdered, his wife was murdered, another woman was murdered."

"I don't think all three murders are related," Carella said. "I think the first two are, but I can't see any connection—"

"He just picked another victim at random, is that what you're saying?"

"No, not at random," Carella said. "Well, it *could* have been anybody, yes, in that sense it was random. But the victim had to be blind. He deliberately chose another blind person."

Hawes had been silent until this moment. He said now, very softly because he was in this case only peripherally and didn't want to make waves when the lieutenant was making enough waves of his own, "It *could* be a smoke screen, Pete."

"Nobody's that dumb," Byrnes said.

"You don't have to be smart to kill people," Meyer said.

"No, but you have to be dumb to try covering your tracks by killing somebody else."

"Let's look at the only thing we've got," Carella said.

"What's that?"

"Jimmy wrote to an Army buddy concerning a get-rich-quick scheme."

"Okay, go ahead."

"His mother thinks Jimmy may have had something illegal in mind."

"Like what?"

"She was only guessing, but she figured he needed somebody who knew how to use a gun. Okay, let's say he wrote to this person *after* the August reunion."

"Why after the reunion."

"Because he wouldn't have known any addresses *before* the reunion."

"Why didn't he just *talk* to the man?"

"What do you mean?"

"At the reunion. Why didn't he just go up to him and say, 'Listen, I want to hold up a liquor store, are you interested?'"

"Maybe he didn't get the idea till after the reunion," Meyer said.

"Wrote to the man in September sometime," Hawes said.

"And let's say the man agreed to go in with Jimmy. Wrote back, or phoned him, or whatever, told him, 'Okay, I'm in, let's rob a bank.'"

"Okay," Byrnes said.

"Okay, so they hold up the bank or the liquor store or the gas station or whatever..."

"Yeah?"

"And Jimmy stashes the loot in his apartment."

"In the window box," Meyer said.

"And won't tell his partner where he put it," Hawes said.

"So his partner follows Jimmy on his way home Thursday night, and tries to get him to talk, but Jimmy won't."

"So the partner slits his throat, and then goes to the apartment figuring that's where the loot is..."

"Turns the place upside down..."

"*Finds* the money..."

"Kills Isabel..."

"And then kills Hester Mathieson the next night..."

"To make it look like some nut's running around killing blind people."

"How does that sound, Pete?" Carella asked.

"It stinks," Byrnes said.

The police psychologist was a man named Manfred Leider. His primary job was to help members of the department who were having problems that could not be solved by the use of marital aids such as those Prestige Novelty sold through the mails. Occasionally, though, a law-enforcement officer came to him for information about criminal behavior. He had dealt with detectives like Carella before; he found the man sincere but limited. All too often, even the brightest of working cops had only a peripheral knowledge of the intricacies of psychiatric techniques. This one wanted to know about dreams. Where should he begin? Basic Freud?

"What exactly do you want to know?" he asked.

They were sitting in Leider's office on the fortieth floor of the Headquarters building on High Street downtown. The island was narrow here; beyond the windows they could see both rivers that bounded the city. The day was cold and clear and sharp, they could see for miles into the next state.

"I'm investigating a homicide," Carella said, "and the victim was having nightmares."

"Mm," Leider said. He was a man in his fifties, and he sported a graying beard that he thought made him look like a psychiatrist. In this state a psychiatrist had to go through four years of college, four years of medical school, one year of internship, three years of residency and another two years of clinical practice before taking the written and oral examinations he had to pass for a license to practice. That was why psychiatrists charged $50 an hour for their services.

Leider was only a psychologist.

When Leider first began to practice, even a garage mechanic could hang out a shingle and offer his services as a "psychologist," whatever *that* might have been. Times had changed; there were now stringent licensing procedures. But many psychologists, Leider among them, still felt somewhat inferior in the presence of a psychiatrist or—God forbid—that most elite and august personage, a psychoanalyst. At a tea or a soiree in the presence of such learned men, Leider often talked of glove anesthesia and eulalia and waxy flexibility. This was to show that he knew his stuff. The funny part of it was that he really *did* know his stuff. Leider should have gone to see a psychiatrist. A psychiatrist might have helped him with his feelings of inferiority. Instead, he spent eight hours a day in an office at the Headquarters building downtown, where he talked to working policemen who made him feel superior.

"What sort of nightmares?" he asked.

"Well, the same nightmare each time," Carella said.

"A recurring nightmare, do you mean?"

"Yes," Carella said. Leider made him feel inferior. He knew that the word he'd been looking for was "recurring," but somehow it had eluded him. Leider was wearing bifocal glasses. His eyes looked huge behind them. A crumb was clinging to his beard; he had probably just had lunch.

"Can you tell me the content of these recurring dreams?" he asked.

"Yes," Carella said, and related the dream to him:

It is shortly before Christmas.

Jimmy's mother and father are decorating a Christmas tree. Jimmy and four other boys are sitting on the living room floor, watching. Jimmy's father tells the boys they must help him decorate the tree. The boys refuse. Jimmy's mother says they don't have to help if they're tired. Christmas ornaments begin falling from the tree, crashing to the floor, making loud noises that startle Jimmy's father. He loses his balance on the ladder and falls to the floor, landing on the shards of the broken Christmas tree ornaments and accidentally cutting himself. The carpet is green, his blood seeps into it. He bleeds to death on the carpet. Jimmy's mother is crying. She lifts her skirt to reveal a penis.

"Mm," Leider said.

"That's the dream," Carella said.

"Mm," Leider said again.

"The dream was analyzed by a Major Ralph Lemarre…"

"An Army doctor?" Leider asked.

"Yes, a psychiatrist."

"A psychiatrist, mm," Leider said.

"And he seemed to think it was related to a gang rape that had taken place some years back."

"Some years back from *when*?"

"From when he was treating the patient."

"When was he treating the patient?"

"Ten years ago."

"Ten years ago, mm. And the rape took place how many years before that?"

"Well, that's just it," Carella said. "The rape *didn't* take place. We talked to the girl who was supposed to have been the victim, and it never happened."

"Perhaps she was lying. Many rape victims—"

"No, she was telling the truth."

"How do you know?"

"Because she told us what *did* happen, and it was a sex experience, but not a rape."

"What is it that happened?" Leider asked.

Carella told him all about Roxanne and Jimmy being alone down there in the basement on a rainy day. The intercourse against the basement post. Thunder and lightning outside. The fear of discovery and punishment.

"What I'm asking," Carella said, "is whether it's possible… Look, I don't know much about how this works. I'm trying to find out whether their making love in the basement that day could've become something different in Jimmy's mind, could've become a whole big rape scene in his mind, and could've eventually caused nightmares. That's what I want to know."

"You say there was fear of punishment involved?"

"Yes. If the leader of the gang had found out, they both would've been punished."

"Mm," Leider said.

"What do you think?" Carella said.

"Well, there's certainly a great deal of sexual symbolism in the dream, no question about that," Leider said. "A tree is a dream symbol for male genitalia, and any sharp weapon is a dream symbol for the penis. The broken Christmas tree ornaments—commonly called Christmas *balls*—would seem another reference to male genitalia. And the dream figure cutting himself would seem to symbolize penetration of the body—sexual intercourse."

"Then the dream *could* have—"

"And the memory," Leider continued, "which is in itself a sort of dream, since you tell me it never really happened, substantiates the dream material by utilizing *different* sexual symbolism to restate essentially the same thing. Freud used as symbols of sexual intercourse such rhythmical activities as dancing, riding, and climbing. In the false memory, the gang leader is first depicted as dancing with his girlfriend, isn't that what you said?"

"Yes, that's right."

"And you said the girl is carried later to a weed-covered lot..."

"Yes..."

"Well, in dreams of both sexes, pubic hair is represented as woods or bushes, so I guess by extension we can include weeds. *In* the dream, as I recall, the weeds have become a green carpet. The father figure bleeds to death on a green carpet, doesn't he?"

"Yes, that's right."

"Again we can refer back to the broken Christmas tree ornaments. A vase, or a flowerpot, or any such vessel—which a round Christmas tree ornament somewhat resembles—is a symbol for the female genitals, and the breaking might symbolize virginity and the bleeding normally associated with first intercourse. Was the girl a virgin, would you know?"

"I don't know. I would doubt it," Carella said.

"Mm," Leider said, and took off his glasses and wiped at the lenses. His eyes were a pale blue behind them; he looked suddenly weary, and much, much older. He put the glasses on again. His magnified eyes leaped into the room. "And of course we've got the violence—violent experiences in dreams can usually be interpreted as representations of sexual intercourse."

"But I thought dreams were designed to *mask* something," Carella said. "To *disguise* it."

"To hide it from the censor of the conscious mind, yes," Leider said. "If your outlook is strictly Freudian, you're bound to believe, quote, 'that what instigates dreams are actively evil and extravagantly sexual wishes, which have made the censorship and distortion of dreams necessary,' unquote."

"Mm," Carella said.

"Mm," Leider said. "But of course, that's very early Freud, and we've come a long way in the interpretation of dreams since then. In this case, where the patient was having recurring nightmares, I would guess he was trying to master the original trauma…to desensitize it, if you will, by exploring it again and again. That's what the dream-work would seem to indicate to me."

"*What* trauma?" Carella asked.

"I don't *know what* trauma," Leider said. "You know his history, you tell me."

"He was blinded in the war," Carella said. "I guess that could—"

"That would most certainly be traumatic," Leider said.

"But…no," Carella said, "because…Now, wait a minute. When Jimmy was telling Lemarre about the *rape*, he said God had punished him instead of the other boys. He told Lemarre the rape had everything to do with his getting blinded."

"But there was no rape," Leider said. "There was the trauma instead."

"Right, and the trauma *couldn't* have been him getting blinded, because he later blamed the blindness on whatever it was happened."

"So what was it that happened?" Leider asked.

"I don't know," Carella said.

"When was he wounded?"

"December the fourteenth."

"Had he been in any action before then?"

"Yes, they'd been fighting since the beginning of the month..."

You'd been fighting with another gang all that month—

Heavy fighting, man.

And now you were resting.

Yeah, and Lloyd told us to go on up.

"What is it?" Leider asked.

"Is it possible that...?"

"Is what possible?"

"I don't know," Carella said. "Let me...let me just put this together, okay?"

"Take your time."

His mouth was suddenly dry. He wet his lips with his tongue, and nodded, and tried to remember everything he'd read in Lemarre's report up there at the hospital while he himself was repressing all sorts of sexual desire for Janet, tried to remember the report in detail, and tried to remember everything Danny Cortez had told him on the phone yesterday.

We'd all been through heavy fighting that whole month. Alpha was down where the lieutenant had set up a command post near some bamboo at the bottom of the hill...Bravo was going up the hill where the enemy was dug in. The lieutenant went back down to see where the hell Alpha was...That's when the mortar attack started. Bastards had zeroed in on the bamboo and were pounding the shit out of it.

That was Danny Cortez talking about the third day of December, ten years ago, when Lieutenant Roger Blake was killed by a mortar fragment.

It was a terrible thing. Alpha took cover when the attack started, and then they couldn't get to the lieutenant in time...In the war over there, you had to pick up your own dead and wounded because if you didn't they dragged them off and hacked them to pieces. The enemy, you understand me?...Alpha told us later they couldn't go after him because of the mortars. All they could do was watch while he was dragged in the jungle. They found him later in an open pit—cut to ribbons. The bastards used to cut the bodies up and leave them in open pits...With bayonets, they did it.

That was still Danny Cortez, elaborating on the theme of jungle warfare. This now was Jimmy Harris talking about a rape that had never taken place.

Lloyd told us to go on up...Upstairs...The boys told Lloyd to shove it up his ass. Then they all grabbed him, you know, pulled him away from Roxanne where they were standin' there in the middle of the floor. Record still goin', drums loud as anything. Guy banging the drums there.

("All we heard was the noise," Cortez said. "You ever been in a mortar attack? It makes a lot of noise, even from a distance.")

There's this post in the middle of the room, you know? Like, you know, a steel post holdin' up the ceiling beams. They push him up against the post. I got no idea what they fixin' to do with him, he the president, they askin' for trouble there. I tell them, "Hey, cool it, this man here's the president." But they...they...they don't listen to me, man. They just...They keep holdin' him up against the tree, and Roxanne's cryin' now, she's cryin', man...The post, I mean. Roxanne's cryin'. They grab her. She fightin' them now, she don't want this to happen, but they do it anyway, they stick it in her, one after the other, all of them...They carried her outside afterward, they picked her up and took her out...'Cause she bleeding. 'Cause they hurt her when they were doin' it.

("All they could do was watch while he was dragged in the jungle," Cortez said. "They found him later in an open pit—cut to ribbons. The bastards used to cut the bodies up and leave them in open pits. With bayonets, they did it.")

"What is it, Mr. Carella?" Leider asked again. "Have you hit upon something?"

The dog was in a small office on the ground floor of the police garage, where a uniformed cop had promised to watch him while Carella was upstairs. The cop wanted to know what was wrong with the dog; he'd tried feeding him and the dog wouldn't take nothing. Carella said he was a seeing-eye dog. The cop looked at the dog and said, "So what does that explain?"

"He's trained to accept food only from his master."

"So where's his master?" the cop asked.

"Dead," Carella said.

"Then the dog's gonna starve," the cop said philosophically, and picked up the magazine he'd been reading, dismissing with that single gesture the vast and complicated world of canine problems.

Carella put one hand into the dog's collar and led him back to where he'd parked the car. He did not want a dog, and he especially did not want a dog that would not eat. He could visualize the dog getting skinnier and skinnier and finally wasting away to a shadow of his former self. He wondered if the dog had really been given all the shots a dog needed, whatever those shots might be. He did not want a dog, nor did he want a dog wasting away, but most especially he did not want a *rabid* dog wasting away. He decided to look at the assorted hanging clutter of metal junk on the dog's collar.

There was a brass tag stamped with the words *Dog License*, and the name of the city, and the year, and the six-digit license number. There was a stainless-steel tag stamped with the name and address of a Dr. James Kopel, presumably a veterinarian, and beneath that the words *I Have Been Vaccinated Against Rabies*, and the year, and a four-digit number. There was another stainless-steel tag with the words *Guiding Eye School* stamped on it, and beneath that the Perry Street address of the school. There was yet another stainless-steel tag stamped with the words *I Belong to James R. Harris*, and beneath that, Harris's address on South Seventh and a telephone number.

There was also a stainless-steel key.

Carella could not imagine why a dog was wearing a key around his neck until he saw the word *Mosler* stamped on the head of the key just below the hole where a metal ring fastened it to the collar. There was dirt—or rather, soil—caked around the edges of the hole. The key was a safety deposit box key, and Carella was willing to bet his next year's salary that it had once been buried in the flower box on the Harris windowsill. He knew the name of Harris's bank because he'd seen it on the passbook he and Meyer found in the apartment—First Federal on Yates Avenue. He also knew he would need a court order to open that box, key in hand or not. It did not hurt that he was downtown at the Headquarters building; the municipal, state, and federal courthouses were all scattered here within a five-block radius. He took the key from the dog's collar, and then led the dog back to the cop in the office.

"What, *again*?" the cop said.

15

It was a little past 2:00 when Sam Grossman called Detective George Underhill at the Four-One.

"I've got a report on that blood sample," he said.

"What blood sample?" Underhill asked.

"From the sidewalk."

"Oh, yeah," Underhill said. He had completely forgotten his request until just this moment. He had, in fact, forgotten it almost the instant after he'd called the lab last night. Now here was Grossman with a report. He did not know what he would do with the report, since there'd been no word from any of the city's hospitals about anyone seeking treatment for a dog bite. He picked up a pencil, and said, "Okay, let me have it."

"First of all, yes, it's blood," Grossman said, "and secondly, yes, it's human blood."

"What group?" Underhill asked.

"You might be lucky. It's group B."

"How does that make me lucky?"

"You'd be luckier if it was group AB because only three to six percent of the population falls into that group. As it is, your sample falls into the ten-to-fifteen-percent grouping."

"That makes me lucky, huh?"

"It could've been O or A, which are the most common groups."

"Okay, thanks a lot," Underhill said.

"Anything else I can do for you?"

"Not unless you know somebody got bit by a dog."

"Was this a dog-bite victim?"

"Yeah."

"The dog wasn't rabid, was he?"

"No."

"How do you know?"

"Guy told the investigating patrolman."

"Because if he's rabid—"

"No, no, he's a seeing-eye dog, how could he be rabid?"

"Seeing-eye dogs can be rabid," Grossman said. "Same as any other dog."

"Yeah, but this one had his shots."

"Who'd he bite?"

"We don't know. Somebody who tried to assault his owner."

"What do you mean?" Grossman said.

"Somebody tried to assault the owner, and the dog bit him."

"A blind man?"

"Yeah, the dog's owner. He's a seeing-eye dog, isn't he? So naturally the owner's—"

"Is this something you're working with Carella?" Grossman asked.

"No," Underhill said. "Who's Carella?"

"Of the Eight-Seven."

"No, I don't know him."

"Because he's working some homicides involving blind victims."

"This isn't a homicide," Underhill said. "This isn't even an assault, you want to know. Guy tried to attack a blind man, and the dog bit him."

"Where?"

"Where'd he bite him? We don't know."

"I mean, where did the attack take place?"

"Cherry and Laird."

"All the way down there, huh?"

"Yeah. Well, I got work here, thanks a lot, huh?" Underhill said and hung up.

Grossman put the receiver back on the cradle, thought for a moment about the odds against Underbill's case being related to Carella's, and decided to call the Eight-Seven, anyway.

Genero answered the squadroom phone.

"Eighty-seventh Squad, Detective Genero," he said. He always made sure he gave his title. Every other detective on the squad merely gave a last name; Genero gave any caller the full treatment.

"This is Sam Grossman at the lab," Grossman said. "I'd like to talk to Carella."

"Not here," Genero said.

"Where is he?"

"Don't know," Genero said.

"Do you have any idea when he'll be back?"

"Nope," Genero said.

"Who's working the blind-man case with him, would you know?"

"Meyer, I think."

"Is he there?"

Genero looked around the squadroom. "No, I don't see him."

"Well, ask either one of them to call me back as soon as possible, would you?"

"Will do," Genero said.

"In fact, let me talk to the lieutenant."

"I'll have the desk sergeant transfer you," Genero said. He jiggled the receiver bar, and when Murchison came on the line, he said, "Dave, put this through to the lieutenant's office, will you?"

Grossman waited. For a moment he thought he'd been cut off.

"87th Squad, Byrnes."

"Pete, this is Sam Grossman at the lab."

"Yes, Sam, how are you?"

"Fine. I've just been talking to a detective named George Underhill at the Four-One, he's working a case with a blind victim."

"A homicide?"

"Attempted assault. I have no idea whether this is related to Steve's case or not, but it might be worth contacting Underhill."

"Right, I'll pass it along to Steve."

"The perpetrator was bitten by the victim's dog," Grossman said. "You might want to put a hospital-stop on it right away."

"Didn't Underhill do that?"

"I don't know."

"I'll put somebody on it," Byrnes said. "Thanks, Sam."

"Don't mention it," Grossman said, and hung up.

Byrnes put up the phone and went out into the squadroom. Genero was staring at a pair of pale-blue bikini panties on his desk. Byrnes said, "What are you doing with those panties, Genero?"

"They're evidence," Genero said.

"Of what?"

"Fornication," Genero said.

"I wouldn't be surprised," Byrnes said. "Call the Department of Hospitals, put a stop out for any dog-bite victims. Ask them to refer back to Carella of the Eight-Seven."

"Is that what Captain Grossman wanted?"

"Yes, that's what he wanted."

"Does that mean I don't have to tell Carella he called?" "Leave a note on Carella's desk."

"Meyer's, too?"

"Meyer's, too."

"Shall I call the Department of Hospitals first?"

"If you think you can handle three things in a row without forgetting any of them."

"Oh, sure," Genero said.

The Supreme Court magistrate read Carella's affidavit, and then said, "What is it you want in that safety deposit box, Detective Carella? It doesn't say what you want."

"That's because I don't know what's in it, Your Honor," Carella said.

"Then how can you expect me to sign an order commanding you to open it?"

"Your Honor," Carella said, "as you'll note in the affidavit, this is a homicide I'm investigating, and I have reason to believe that whatever the murderer was searching for in the apartment of two of the victims—"

"Yes, yes, that's all here."

"Might be in the box, Your Honor, and might constitute evidence of the crime of murder."

"But you don't know what you're looking for specifically," the magistrate said.

"No, Your Honor, I do not."

"Do you have any personal knowledge of the existence of such evidence?"

"Only knowledge based on the fact that the murderer thoroughly searched the apartment for something, Your Honor, as stated in the affidavit."

"This is not personal knowledge of evidence in the box," the magistrate said.

"Your Honor, I don't think this would constitute an illegal search, any more than going through a victim's dresser drawers would constitute an illegal search at the scene of the murder."

"This is not the scene of a murder."

"I realize that, Your Honor. But I've had a court order, for example, to open a safety deposit box when all I was investigating was a numbers operation, a policy operation, Your Honor, and this is a homicide."

"In this other case, did you have personal knowledge of what you would find in the box when it was opened?"

"I had information from an informer."

"That constitutes personal knowledge," the magistrate said.

"Your Honor, I really would like to open that box. Three people have been killed already, all of them blind, and I think there may be something in there that can help me. There's probable cause to believe there's something in there, Your Honor."

"If I issued this warrant, it might do you more harm than good," the magistrate said. "Your application might later be controverted on a motion to suppress the evidence seized under it."

"I'd like to take that chance, Your Honor," Carella said. "Your Honor, there's no one who can be hurt here but the killer. We're not violating the victim's rights by opening that box, Your Honor."

"I'll grant the warrant," the magistrate said.

On the way uptown Carella wondered why the judge had given him such a hard time. He guessed the hard time was worth it. He guessed that protecting the rights of *one* person was the same as protecting the rights of *all* persons. It was almost 2:30 when he got back to the squadroom. He intended stopping by only to tell Byrnes where he was going and what he was about to do. It was good to give progress reports when the lieutenant was complaining about lack of progress. Genero was sitting at his desk, looking at a pair of pale-blue bikini panties.

"I put a note on your typewriter," Genero said.

"Thanks," Carella said, and pulled the note from the roller. It told him that Grossman had called. Grossman was spelled "Grosman." Carella was about to call him back when Byrnes came out of his office and told him about Underhill, and the attempted assault, and the dog bite. Carella said, "Okay, good," and filled him in on the safety deposit box and the court order, and then turned his name plaque to the wall on the Duty Chart, and went downstairs again to where the dog was dripping spit all over the backseat. He tried to remember the dog's name, but couldn't. Nobody's perfect.

The manager of the First Federal on Yates Avenue was a black man named Samuel Hobbs. He welcomed Carella into his office, shook hands with him, and then studied the court order with a solemnity befitting a command for a royal beheading. Carella extended the Mosler key to him. Hobbs pressed a button on the base of his phone. A black girl in her early twenties came into the office, and Hobbs asked her to locate the box number of James Randolph Harris and then escort Detective Carella to the vault and open the box for him. Carella followed her. She had long slender legs and a twitchy behind. She found the number of the box in a card file, and then led him into the vault. She smiled at him a lot; he was beginning to think he was devastating.

She opened the box drawer and pulled out the box. She asked him if he wanted a room. He said he wanted a room, and she carried the box to a cubicle with a louvered door, which he locked behind him. There was a pair of scissors on the wall-hung desktop, for the convenience of those customers clipping coupons. He lifted the lid of the box. There was only one thing in the box, a carbon copy of a typewritten letter. He looked at the letter. It was addressed to Major John Francis Tataglia at Fort Lee, Virginia. The letter was dated November sixth. It read:

November 6th

Hello, Major Tataglia:

I have decided that I want some money for my eyes. I was at the reunion of D Company in August, and I learned there that every one of the grunts is as pisspoor as me, so there's no sense asking them for any help. I talked to Captain Anderson who used to command the 1st Platoon, and he told me you're a major now stationed at Port Lee, which is where I'm writing to you. Major, I want some money from you. I want some money for my eyes. I want one thousand dollars a month from you, for the rest of my life, or I am going to write to the Army and tell them what happened to Lieutenant Blake. I am going to tell them you and the others killed Lieutenant Blake. I don't give a shit about you or any of them. The others can't help me cause they're as broke as I am, but you are a career officer and you can send me money, Major. I want the money right away, Major. I am going to give you till the end of the month, and if the first check for one thousand dollars isn't here by then, I will call the United States Army and tell them what happened during Ala Moana. You may think I can't prove nothing, Major, but that doesn't matter. I am a blind veteran with a full disability pension, and, Major, I don't have to tell you what kind of heavy shit can come down on you if an army investigation starts about what happened that day. You were the one stuck the first bayonet in him, Major, and if they call the other men they are going to have to say you did it all by yourself, or else they are going to have to admit they were all a part of it. None of them is in the Army no more, only you. You are in trouble, Major, if you don't send me the money. There is a copy of this letter, so if anything happens to me my wife will know about it, and you will be in even more serious trouble than you already are. So send me a check for one thousand dollars by the first of December, and keep sending me checks on the first day of each month or your ass will be in a sling. Send the checks made payable to James R. Harris, and send them to me at 3415 South 7th Street, Isola.

I will not wait past December 1.

Your old Army buddy,
James R. Harris.

This time Carella's warrant was a bit more specific. It read:

1. I am a detective of the Police Department assigned to the 87th Detective Squad.
2. I have information based upon my personal knowledge and belief and facts disclosed to me by the medical examiner that three murders have been committed, and that all of the victims were blind.
3. I have further information based upon my personal knowledge and belief and facts disclosed to me by Detective-Lieutenant Peter Byrnes, commanding officer of the 87th Detective Squad, that an assault was attempted against a blind man on the night of November 22, and that during the attempted assault the perpetrator was bitten by the victim's dog.
4. I have further information based upon my personal knowledge and belief that the attempted assault upon the blind man falls into that category of crimes known as "Unusual Crimes," and there is probable cause to believe that it is linked with the three homicides, each similarly falling into the "Unusual Crimes" category, and each occurring within a brief time span, starting with the first murder on Thursday night, November 18, and culminating with the attempted assault on Monday night, November 22.

5. I have further information based upon my personal knowledge and belief that one of the victims, James R. Harris, wrote an extortion letter to his former commanding officer, John Francis Tataglia, and that this letter was written on November 6, and that it demanded monthly payments of one thousand dollars for the remainder of the life of James R. Harris to keep him from divulging the information that Tataglia in concert with others killed Lieutenant Roger Blake on the third day of December ten years ago during an army operation called Ala Moana.
6. Based upon the foregoing reliable information and upon my personal knowledge, there is probable cause to believe that a dog bite on the person of John Francis Tataglia would constitute evidence in the crime of attempted assault and possibly in the crime of murder.

   Wherefore, I respectfully request that the court issue a warrant in the form annexed hereto, authorizing a search of the person of Major John Francis Tataglia for a dog-bite wound.

   No previous application in this matter has been made in this or any other court or to any other judge, justice, or magistrate.

Stephen Louis Carella	714-5632	Det/2nd	87th Squad
Police Officer	**Shield**	**Rank**	**Command**

The magistrate to whom Carella presented his application was the same one he'd asked for permission to open the Harris safety deposit box. He read the application carefully, and then signed the search warrant attached to it.

The sentry at the main gate would not let Carella through.

Carella showed him the warrant, and the sentry said he would have to check it with the provost marshal. He dialed a number and told somebody there was a detective here with a search warrant, and then he handed the phone to Carella and said, "The colonel wants to talk to you."

Carella took the phone. "Hello," he said.

"Yes, this is Colonel Humphries, what's the problem?"

"No problem, sir," Carella said. "I've got a court order here, and your man won't let me through the gate."

"What kind of court order?"

"To search the person of Major John Francis Tataglia."

"What for?"

"A dog bite, sir."

"Why?"

"He's a murder suspect," Carella said.

"Put the sentry on," the colonel said. Carella handed the phone through the car window to the sentry. The sentry took it, said, "Yes, sir?" and then listened. "Yes, sir," he said. "Yes, sir," he said again, and put the receiver back on its wall hook. "Third building on your right," he said to Carella. "It's marked Military Police."

"Thank you," Carella said, and drove through the gate. He parked the car in the gravel oval in front of a redbrick building, and then went inside to where a corporal was sitting behind a desk. He asked for Colonel Humphries, and the corporal asked him who should he say was here, and Carella told him who he was, and the corporal buzzed the colonel and announced Carella, and then told him it was the door just ahead, please go right in.

Colonel Humphries was a man in his early fifties, tall and suntanned, with a firm handclasp and a voice that sounded whiskey-seared. He explained to Carella that he had just spoken to the post commander, who had authorized the body search, provided an Army legal officer and an Army physician were present when the order was executed. Carella understood this completely. The Army was protecting the rights of one of its own.

The five of them assembled in the post dispensary—a lieutenant colonel, who was the appointed legal officer; a major, who was the Army physician; Colonel Humphries, who was the senior military police officer on post; Carella, who was beginning to feel a bit intimidated by all this brass; and Major John Francis Tataglia, who read the court order and then shrugged and said, "I don't understand."

"It gives him the authority to search for a dog bite," the legal officer said. "General Kihlborg's already approved the search."

"Would you mind stripping down?" Carella said.

"This is ridiculous," Tataglia said, but he began disrobing. There were no wounds on either of his arms, but there was a bandage on his left leg, just above the ankle.

"What's that?" Carella asked.

Standing in his khaki undershorts and tank-top undershirt, Tataglia said, "I cut myself."

"Would you take off the bandage, please?" Carella said.

"I'm afraid it'll start bleeding again," Tataglia said.

"We've got a doctor here," Carella said. "He'll remove the bandage, if you prefer."

"I'll do it myself," Tataglia said, and slowly unwound the bandage.

"That's not a cut," Carella said.

"It's a cut," Tataglia said.

"Then what are those perforations?"

"I don't know what you mean."

"Those are teeth marks."

"Are you a doctor?" Tataglia asked.

"No, but anyone can see those are teeth marks." He turned to the medical officer. "Major," he said, "are those teeth marks?"

"They could be teeth marks," the major said. "I would have to examine them more closely."

"Would you do that, please?" Carella asked.

The major went to a stainless-steel cabinet, opened the top drawer of it, and took out a magnifying glass. "Would you get up on the table here?" he asked. Tataglia climbed onto the table. The doctor adjusted an overhead light so that it illuminated the wound on Tataglia's leg. He peered through the magnifying glass. "Well," he said, "the wound *could* have been caused by the action of canine teeth and cutting molars. I can't say for sure."

Carella turned to the legal officer. "Colonel," he said, "I'd like to take this man into custody for further examination by the medical examiner and for questioning regarding three homicides and an attempted assault."

"Well, we're not sure that's a dog bite," the legal officer said.

"It's *some* kind of an animal bite, that's for sure," Carella said.

"That doesn't make it a *dog* bite. Your court order specifically authorizes search for a *dog* bite. Now, if this isn't a *dog* bite—"

"Your medical officer said the wound might have been caused—"

"No, I said I couldn't be sure," the medical officer said.

"All right, what the hell's going on here?" Carella asked.

"You want me to release this man from military jurisdiction," the legal officer said, "and I'm just not—"

"Only pending the outcome of our investigation."

"Yes, well, I'm not sure I can do that."

"Do I have to get a district attorney out here?" Carella said. "Okay, I'll call the city and get one out here. Where's the phone?"

"Take it easy," Colonel Humphries said.

"Take it easy, *shit*!" Carella said. "I've got a man here who maybe killed three people, and you're telling me to take it *easy*? I'm going to arrest this man if I've got to get the president on the phone, now how about that? He's commander in chief of the—"

"Just take it easy," Humphries said again.

"What's it going to be?" Carella said.

"Let me talk to the general," Humphries said.

"Go ahead, talk to him."

"I'll be back," Humphries said, and went into the next room.

Carella could hear the sound of a telephone being dialed. He began pacing. The Army officers looked through the window to the quadrangle beyond, avoiding his eyes. Tataglia had re-bandaged his leg and was putting on his clothes again when Humphries came back into the room.

"The general says it's okay," he said.

It wasn't that easy.

The legal officer went along with Tataglia to protect his rights, as was usual in this country—and which wasn't so bad when you got right down to it. Because supposing Tataglia *wasn't* the man who'd killed Jimmy and Isabel Harris, not to mention Hester Mathieson, huh? Suppose he *wasn't* the man who'd attacked old Eugene Maslen and been bitten by his dog Ralph? Suppose he'd been bitten instead by his wife or his pussycat, huh? That was why it was necessary to have Lieutenant-Colonel Anthony Loomis there to make certain the cops of the 87th did not work Tataglia over with rubber hoses—which cops nowadays didn't do, but which Loomis didn't know.

When Carella asked that a sample of Tataglia's blood be taken to compare with the blood that had been found on the sidewalk outside the Mercantile Bank on Cherry and Laird, Lieutenant-Colonel Loomis said he felt this was a violation of Tataglia's rights. An assistant district attorney named Andrew Stewart was up at the squadroom by then because this looked like real meat and they didn't want a multiple murderer to get away with murder even if his counsel *was* a hard-nosed career Army officer who also objected to a medical examiner taking a look at the wound to determine whether or not it was a dog bite. Stewart was a hard-nosed career man who hoped one day to become governor of the state. He had served with the United States Army during one of his nation's many wars, and he did not like officers and he especially did not like lieutenant-colonels.

"Colonel," he said, because that's what lieutenant-colonels were called in the United States Army, "I think I ought to let you in on a few secrets here before you find yourself behind enemy lines without support." He smiled like a chipmunk when he said this because he thought it was a pretty good metaphor, which in fact it was. "I am going to tell you all about Miranda-Escobedo and the rights of a prisoner. Or rather, since everybody nowadays talks about the rights of prisoners, I am going to tell you about the rights of law-enforcement officers. So pay attention, Colonel—"

"I don't like your condescending air," Loomis said.

"Be that as it may," Stewart said, and smiled his chipmunk smile again. "Let me inform you that a police officer may properly ask a prisoner to submit to a blood or Breathalyzer test, to take his fingerprints or to photograph him, to examine his body, to put him in a lineup, to ask him to put on a hat or a coat, or to pick up coins, or put his finger to his nose, or anything of the sort *without* warning him first of his privilege against self-incrimination or the right to counsel."

"That is *your* interpretation," Loomis said.

"No, that is the interpretation of the Supreme Court of this land, Colonel. The difference between any of these actions and a statement in response to interrogation is simply the difference between non-testimonial and testimonial responses on the part of the prisoner. The first need *not* be preceded by the warnings; the second must *always* be. So, Colonel, whether you like it or not, we're going to take a sample of Major Tataglia's blood, and we're also going to have an assistant ME look at that wound in an attempt to determine whether or not it was inflicted by a dog. Now that's it, Colonel, and we're well within our rights, and you can object till hell freezes over, but we're *still* going to do it. Is that clear?"

"I *am* objecting," Loomis said.

"Fine. And *I'm* calling the Medical Examiner's Office to arrange for a man to get here right away."

The assistant ME arrived some forty minutes later. It was now close to 9:00 P.M. He looked at the wound and said it appeared to be a dog bite. He then asked if the dog was rabid.

"Yes," Carella said.

The lie came to his lips suddenly and brilliantly. There was nothing in the rules that said you could not lie to an assistant medical examiner, so he instantly embroidered the lie. "The Canine Unit cut off the dog's head and tested the brain," he said. "The dog had rabies."

"Then this man had better be treated right away," the ME said, and then did an a cappella chorus on this dread disease, explaining that the incubation period might be anywhere from two to twenty-two weeks, after which the major could expect severe pains in the area of the healed wound, followed by headaches, loss of appetite, vomiting, restlessness, apprehension, difficulty swallowing, and eventual convulsion, delirium, coma—and death. He said the word "death" with a finality altogether fitting.

Tataglia remained unperturbed. He had no reason to believe that any of this was prearranged, which indeed it wasn't. Carella wasn't the one who'd called the Medical Examiner's Office, nor had he said a single word to the ME before the man asked if the dog was rabid. The question seemed a natural one, the answer seemed entirely truthful, and the ME's concern seemed only professional, that of a physician giving medical advice to a man in possible danger. But Tataglia didn't even blink.

Carella took Stewart aside, and the men held a brief whispered consultation.

"What do you think?" Carella asked.

"I think he's a cocky little bastard and we can break him."

"What about the colonel?"

"Loomis doesn't know his ass from his elbow when it comes to criminal law."

"Do *you* want to handle the Q and A?"

"No, you take it. You know more about the case than I do."

"Shall I show him the letter?"

"Advise him of his rights first."

"He may decide to clam up."

"No. When they're this fuckin' smart," Stewart said, "they're only dumb."

Both men walked back to where the others were clustered about Genero's desk. Genero had gone home long ago, but the blue bikini panties were still resting near his telephone.

"Major Tataglia," Carella said, "in keeping with the Supreme Court decision in *Miranda versus Arizona*, we are not permitted to ask you any questions until you are warned of your right to counsel and your privilege against self-incrimination."

"What is this?" Loomis asked suspiciously.

"This is known as warning your client of his rights," Stewart said, and smiled.

"First," Carella said, "you have the right to remain silent if you so choose. Do you understand that?"

"Yes, of course I do," Tataglia said.

"Good. Second, you do not have to answer any questions if you don't want to. Do you understand that?"

"Yes," Tataglia said wearily. "I understand it."

"Third, if you *do* decide to answer any questions, the answers may be used against you, do you understand that?"

"Yes, yes," Tataglia said, and actually yawned.

Carella thought, *We are going to get you, you little prick.*

"You also have the right to consult with an attorney before or during police questioning—"

"My attorney is Colonel Loomis."

"And to terminate the questioning at any time. Is all of that clear?"

"Yes, it is all perfectly clear," Tataglia said.

"Good," Carella said, and reached into his inside jacket pocket and took from it the letter he had found in the Harris safety deposit box. "Have you ever seen this before?" he asked.

"What is it?"

"I should really ask whether you've ever seen the *original* of this. This is a carbon copy. Have you ever seen the *original* of this?"

Tataglia took the letter and studied it. "No," he said at last.

"It's addressed to you," Carella said.

"At Fort Lee, Virginia. I was transferred from there in September. This letter is dated November sixth."

"Ah," Carella said.

"May I see the letter, please?" Loomis said.

"Certainly," Carella said, and handed it to him. "You never received this letter, is that right, Major?" he said.

"That's right," Tataglia said. "The Army isn't always very good at forwarding mail," he said, and smiled.

"What do you make of its contents?" Carella asked.

"Its contents?"

"Yes. You're seeing it for the first time now..."

"I haven't even read it," Tataglia said.

"Oh, I thought you'd read it. Colonel Loomis, would you give him the letter, please?"

"I wouldn't answer any further questions, if I were you," Loomis said. "Mr. Carella, Mr. Stewart, I would like to suggest—"

"Don't be ridiculous," Tataglia said, and took the letter from Loomis. "I have nothing to hide."

Good, Carella thought. *You're just what we think you are, and we're going to nail you to the wall.* He watched as Tataglia slowly and carefully read the letter. Finally, Tataglia looked up.

"Have you read it now?" Carella asked.

"Yes."

"For the first time, right?"

"That's right."

"What do you think of it?"

"I have no idea what it means."

"You don't know what it means?" Carella said.

"That's right."

"It seems to me that Jimmy Harris is suggesting that you stuck a bayonet in Lieutenant Blake."

"That's nonsense."

"Lieutenant Blake *was* killed, wasn't he?"

"Of course he was."

"But this isn't *how* he was killed. He wasn't killed the way Jimmy Harris suggests."

"He was killed when a mortar shell exploded near him."

"Ah," Carella said.

"I told you that when you came to see me yesterday."

"Yes, but Jimmy seems to have thought you stuck a bayonet in the lieutenant."

"I have no idea what Jimmy thought or didn't think. Jimmy is dead."

"So he is. He seems to have thought the others *also* stuck bayonets in the lieutenant."

"I repeat—"

"Because in his letter he says you and the others killed the lieutenant."

"I don't know what others you mean."

"I would guess the men in Alpha Fire Team, wouldn't you?"

"I don't know what the letter means. I can only think Jimmy was crazy when he wrote it."

"Ah?" Carella said. "You think he just invented all this, is that it?"

"I don't know what he invented or didn't invent. I only know that this is an obvious attempt at blackmail."

"Then you didn't stab Lieutenant Blake?"

"Of *course* I didn't!"

"Excuse me," Loomis said, "but I really feel the major should not answer any further questions. Major Tataglia, as your legal advisor—"

"I have nothing to hide," Tataglia said again.

"What happened that day?" Carella asked.

"What day?"

"The day Lieutenant Blake got killed."

"There was a mortar attack," Tataglia said, and shrugged. "He was killed by an exploding mortar shell."

"Was this before or after he ordered Alpha up the hill?"

"What hill?"

"Up the hill to attack the mortar emplacement."

"I recall no such order."

You'd been fighting with another gang all that month—

Heavy fighting, man.

And now you were resting.

Yeah, and Lloyd told us to go on up.

What did he mean by that?

I told you. Upstairs.

"The lieutenant didn't order Alpha up the hill?" Carella asked.

"I don't know what hill you mean."

"Where was the lieutenant's command post?"

"I don't remember."

"Wasn't it on the low ground? Near some bamboo?"

"I don't remember."

"This was the day you were promoted in the field, wasn't it?"

"Yes, but I don't remember where the command post was."

"Danny Cortez says it was near some bamboo at the bottom of a hill."

"I don't even know who Danny Cortez is."

"He was in Bravo. The lieutenant ordered Bravo up the hill, and then he came down to get Alpha. He ordered Alpha up the hill, too, didn't he?"

"No."

"But the men refused to go, didn't they?"

Damn straight, man. The boys told Lloyd to shove it up his ass. Then they all grabbed him, you know, pulled him away from Roxanne where they were standin' there in the middle of the floor. Record still goin', drums loud as anything. Guy banging the drums there.

"Isn't that what happened?" Carella asked. His scalp was beginning to tingle. He understood it completely now. It had taken him a long time to see it, but now it was crystal-clear. He didn't need Lemarre or Leider to explain what had happened that day. He *knew* what had happened. "Did you and the lieutenant struggle?"

"No, the lieutenant and I didn't struggle."

"Didn't you tell him the men didn't have to go up that hill if they didn't want to? Didn't you tell him they were tired?"

"I told him nothing of the sort."

"But he was *there*, isn't that right?"

"Where? I don't know what you mean."

"At the command post. He wasn't killed *before* he got to the command post, was he?"

"I don't…I don't remember when he was killed. We…The mortar attack started when he was coming down the hill."

There's this post in the middle of the room, you know? Like you know, a steel post holdin' up the ceiling beams. They push him up against the post. I got no idea what they fixin' to do with him, he the president, they askin' for trouble there.

"What was the lieutenant's first name?" Carella asked.

"What?"

"Lieutenant Blake. What was his first name?"

"Roger."

Roxanne's cryin. They grab her. She fightin' them now, she don't want this to happen, but they do it anyway, they stick it in her, one after the other, all of them.

"Danny Cortez saw it," Carella said. He was lying again. He didn't give a damn. He wasn't going to let this son of a bitch off the hook. If the courts reversed it later, the hell with it. He wasn't going to let him get away now.

"I…I don't know who Danny Cortez is."

"Bravo Fire Team. I told you before. Bravo. He saw it while he was going up the hill. He looked down, and he saw you and the lieutenant struggling—"

"No," Tataglia said.

"Saw you unsheathe your bayonet—"

"No."

"And stab him."

"No!" Tataglia screamed, and suddenly he put his face in his hands and began sobbing. "Oh, Jesus," he said, "I didn't want to…I didn't do it for…I was trying to protect the men. They were tired, they…I was their sergeant, I was the one they trusted. He wanted them to…The enemy was up there with mortars, how could we possibly…Oh, Jesus. I told him they didn't have to go if they were tired. We…He swung at me and I grabbed him and…we…we held him against a tree and I…I pulled my bayonet out of…out of…I stabbed him with it. The mortars were going everywhere around us, we…we all stabbed him. All of us but Jimmy. We all stabbed him. And then we…dragged him in the jungle and…and cut him…cut him…cut him up in pieces so it would look like the…the enemy did it.

"When I…when I got Jimmy's letter, I…I tried to remember, it was so long ago, it was…Who could remember? I could hardly remember. But I knew he could ruin me…I knew he…I had to protect myself, I have a wife and family, I love them, I had to protect them. I knew if the Army started an investigation, it would all come out, somebody would crack. So I—he'd given me his return address, you know, on his letter, you know—so I…I found him and I…I killed him. And then I went to his apartment looking for the copy he said he had, the copy of the letter—I gave his wife a chance, I really did, I gave her a chance to give it to me, but she wouldn't, so I…so I slit her throat with the same bayonet. The others—the lady with the accordion and the man I tried to kill last night—they were just so you'd think it was someone crazy."

He looked up suddenly. Tears were streaming from his eyes, his face was distorted and pained and plaintive.

"Did the dog really have rabies?" he asked.

So that was it.

They took Tataglia down and booked him for three counts of Murder One, and they threw in the attempted assault only because they knew the smoke screen would most certainly become part of the case when it was tried, and they didn't want any loose ends kicking around. As for the rest of it, that was the Army's business and the Army's job. Lieutenant-Colonel Anthony Loomis promised them he would set the wheels of military justice in motion the moment he got back to Fort Kirby. A full investigation into the murder of Lieutenant Roger Blake would be forthcoming, he said, and he was confident that *all* perpetrators would be brought before a convened court-martial. Carella thought it was interesting that he had used the word "perpetrators."

He left the squadroom at twenty minutes to 11:00. The night was blustery and cold. He walked with his head ducked against a fierce wind, clutching against his chest a wrapped hamburger he'd asked Miscolo to send out for while Tataglia was being booked. The dog was asleep on the backseat of the car. Carella had left the window on the curb side open a crack, figuring no one would try boosting an automobile belonging to a cop, the information clipped to the turned-down visor: POLICE DEPARTMENT. He unlocked the front door now, pulled up the lock-knob on the rear door, and then opened it and leaned into the car. He still couldn't remember the damn dog's name. He'd have to ask Sophie Harris what the dog's name was.

"Hey, boy," he said. "Wake up."

The dog blinked up at him.

"You want some hamburger?" Carella said, and opened the paper in which the hamburger was wrapped.

The dog blinked again.

"Miscolo sent out for it. It's cold, but it's very nice. Take a sniff."

He extended his hand to the dog, the hamburger on his open palm. The dog sniffed at it. Then he took a tentative nibble.

"Good," Carella said, and spread open the paper the hamburger was wrapped in, and put hamburger and paper on the seat beside the dog. By the time he came around to the driver's side of the car, the hamburger was gone and the dog was licking the paper. Carella sat behind the wheel a moment before starting the car, looking through the windshield at the green globes of the station house ahead, the numerals "87" painted on each in white. He wondered if there was anything he'd forgotten to do, decided there wasn't, and twisted the ignition key. It was his contention that when you finished your song and dance, the best thing to do was go home.

He went home.

ABOUT THE AUTHOR

Photograph © Dragica Hunter

Ed McBain was one of the many pen names of the successful and prolific crime fiction author Evan Hunter (1926–2005). Born Salvatore Lambino in New York, McBain served aboard a destroyer in the US Navy during World War II and then earned a degree from Hunter College in English and psychology. After a short stint teaching in a high school, McBain went to work for a literary agency in New York, working with authors such as Arthur C. Clarke and P.G. Wodehouse, all the while working on his own writing on nights and weekends. He had his first breakthrough in 1954 with the novel *The Blackboard Jungle*, which was published under his newly legal name Evan Hunter and based on his time teaching in the Bronx.

Perhaps his most popular work, the 87th Precinct series (released mainly under the name Ed McBain) is one of the longest running crime series ever published, debuting in 1956 with *Cop Hater* and featuring over fifty novels. The series is set in a fictional locale called Isola and features a wide cast of detectives including the prevalent Detective Steve Carella.

McBain was also known as a screenwriter. Most famously he adapted a short story from Daphne Du Maurier into the screenplay for Alfred Hitchcock's *The Birds* (1963). In addition to writing for the silver screen, he wrote for many television series, including *Columbo* and the NBC series *87th Precinct* (1961–1962), based on his popular novels.

McBain was awarded the Grand Master Award for lifetime achievement in 1986 by the Mystery Writers of America and was the first American to receive the Cartier Diamond Dagger award from the Crime Writers Association of Great Britain. He passed away in 2005 in his home in Connecticut after a battle with larynx cancer.

20238869R00179

Printed in Great Britain
by Amazon